MW01046817

Bouquet

Toss

Melissa Brown

For Bonnie -
Congrats on the contest!
Thanks for reading !!

Prologue

It has been three and a half years and the thought of him still makes me cry. Three and a half years and I still replay the scenes in my head; our first kiss, our first date and eventually our break up. I can't banish the days before he left me from my head; the days when I *knew* what was coming.

I will never forget the crying, the confusion, and my emails that were never answered. Our brief online chat while he was studying in France is still so fresh in my mind. Seeing him at our favorite bar just two days before graduation....and what happened after is something that will haunt me for the rest of my life. Is it possible that all of these things happened for a reason?

There must be a reason why I lie in bed at night and think about his voice, his smile, his beautiful laugh. It's been three and a half years and the simple thought of him evokes just as much emotion as it did when we were together. I wonder if I will ever see him again. I read books and see movies about lost loves who were simply too young when they met. They magically reunite later in their lives and live happily ever after. But, not us.

I try to imagine how he would contact me if he chose to do it. And then, reality sets in. He's not coming. He's not calling. And, he's not going to drive fifteen hours from South Carolina on the chance that I may be home on some random Saturday afternoon. Even if he wanted to, he doesn't have the courage to take a risk so big. That's not him. And, I have to deal with that. I just wish the memories would fade. I wish the songs wouldn't bring tears. And, I wish that his name would stop making my heart tremble. I want to forget. I need to forget. I deserve to forget. *I have to forget.*

Chapter 1
Bouquets

"Attention, all you single ladies…please make your way to the dance floor. It's time for the lovely bride to toss her bouquet," the DJ announces. I roll my eyes and turn towards Elise, my best friend in the world.

"Will you, at least, join me out there…*please*?" I beg. Elise shakes her head with a sympathetic grin.

"Daphne, my sweet, I'm getting married next weekend. I don't think I really qualify as a single woman, so come on, get out there and make me proud."

"Will this be lucky number seven, Daph?" Elise's fiancé, Henry, asks.

"*If* I catch it, yes," I scowl at Henry. He and all of my friends love to tease me about my "gift" or "curse" of always catching the bouquet at weddings. In fact, in the past two years, I have attended six weddings. And of these six weddings, I've caught all of the bouquets. Every.Single.One.

The first time it happened, I really was trying to catch it.

In fact, I almost elbowed the girl next to me because she started to get in my way. At that point, most of my friends were engaged. I really wanted to reach that stage in my life, so I dove for that sucker and caught it. I was thrilled. But, two weddings and two bouquets later, I was still single with no prospects in sight. So, I stopped making the effort.

It was when I quit trying to catch the damn flowers that things started to get interesting. No matter where I stood, those beautiful floral bunches found their way to me. At one reception, I purposely positioned myself in the far back, behind all the other single women. But, as one of the bridesmaids jumped to catch it, the bouquet bounced off of her left hand and landed right in mine. At another, I struck up a conversation with a bridesmaid to distract myself from the ball of roses coming at me. It was no use, though, as the bride gave it a perfect toss, right into my hands.

"I think it's kind of cool, Daph," Henry winks. He's such a sweetheart and a great match for Elise. I adore him.

"I do, too," my makeshift date, Rob, says. Elise and Henry have set us up for this event so that I wouldn't be dateless (again). He's not my type at all, but at least I don't have to feel like everyone's "Pathetic Single Friend Daphne" tonight. It seems that since we all left college, everyone has coupled off, but the stars haven't aligned for me yet. I'm still waiting for my other half and I can't help but wonder how many bouquets I'll be forced to catch before he arrives.

I smile at Rob and begrudgingly make my way out to the dance floor. Holly, the bride, is waiting patiently for all of her single friends to gather before tossing the bouquet of roses. She looks a bit tipsy and positively giddy. A large group of young women congregates in the small space, and for a moment, I am hopeful that my curse may be coming to an end. Kristy, a striking brunette, finds me amongst the crowd of single ladies and stands uncomfortably close. Maybe I can pass it to her without anyone noticing and finally be free of this vexation.

The DJ starts the countdown and Holly tosses the bouquet behind her. Without warning, the red bundle of roses flies directly at my forehead before landing at my feet. I am mortified. The crowd gasps and the flower girls giggle as I lean down to pick up the bouquet from the parquet flooring below. In order to conceal my embarrassment, I raise the bouquet above my head and force a giant smile. Laughter and applause fill the room as I make my way back towards my table.

"Here's to lucky number seven!" Rob raises his glass into the air, mimicking my movement with the bouquet. When he finally stops laughing, he asks, "How do you do that, Daphne? It's really incredible." He marvels.

"Seriously, Daph," Kristy adds, "That thing came zooming through the air like nothing I've ever seen! It's like it was meant for you or something."

Resisting the urge to become defensive, I simply take a dramatic bow, waving my right hand as if looking for applause. My friends respond with clapping hands. It feels good to laugh at myself. I'd probably cry my eyes out if I didn't.

Elise senses the frustration masked behind my fake laughter and dramatic bow. She takes my hand gently and leads me towards the patio. "Come on, Daph. I need some fresh air. Come sit with me." I'm grateful to have a friend who can read me so well. I desperately need a change of scenery and Elise, as always, comes to my rescue.

Sitting at a vacant table, Elise and I remain silent for several minutes, both looking down at the golf course below the banquet hall. Giggling can be heard at a distance, and I notice a bright teal bridesmaid dress, peeking from behind two large bushes. Black shoes and pants are also visible, causing me to smile in amusement.

"Well, someone is having fun down there," Elise observes. "I wonder which bridesmaid that is…" her voice trails off as she cranes her neck to see the couple's obvious make-out session.

"Ah, let's leave them alone. They're having fun," I smile.

"Daphne, how do you do that?" Elise asks in wonder.

"What do you mean?" I respond, perplexed.

"Two minutes ago, I could tell that you were so upset and frustrated with your love life yet you still manage to be happy for everyone else." Elise cocks an eyebrow, tilting her head towards the couple. "Even frisky bridal party members making out in the bushes."

"I'm a hopeless romantic, I guess. I'm always thinking of Happily Ever Afters."

"But, you seem so resistant to finding it, Daph. You haven't given Rob much of a chance, you know."

"Oh, Elise, I think I've been set up on enough dates by now to know that a guy like Rob is not for me."

"What's so wrong with him? He's a really great guy. He has his own apartment, a great job, he's funny…" I raise an eyebrow at Elise. She giggles, "Okay, okay, maybe his sense of humor is a *little* bit cheesy."

"A little bit? Elise, *come on*. The guy has been telling me jokes that I haven't heard since middle school. I have to hold back so hard not to laugh at him."

"Well, maybe you're not really giving him a chance. That is sort of your "M.O.", ya know, ever since---"

"Ugh, please don't say his name, Elise. I can't bear it; not tonight."

"Don't you think you'll feel a little better if you acknowledge the emotional hold Mayson still has on you after all these years?"

"An emotional hold? When did you get your degree in Psychology?"

"Daphne, be real. You haven't seen the guy in five years and yet you compare every guy you meet to him…every last one."

"I can't help it. No one compares."

"He broke your heart, Daph," Elise says softly, "Why are

you comparing people to that anguish, that heartache?"

"I wish I knew. I haven't felt that way about anyone else...not yet anyway." I pause, taking a deep breath, allowing myself to remember Mayson; gorgeous, charismatic, green-eyed Mayson. "Honestly, I haven't thought of him in a long time. Ever since you told me to stop writing in my journal, I sort of blocked him out. But, I guess he's there, deep in my subconscious, shooing other men away, keeping me single and alone."

"Ah, the bitterness journal; how could I have forgotten about your journal? Do you still have it?" Elise asks leaning forward, unbridled curiosity in her voice.

"I think so. I don't think I had the heart to throw it away," I reply, a wave of melancholy rushes over me.

"Perhaps it's time, Daphne. Perhaps it is finally time to get rid of it once and for all. Maybe then, you can let go of him. I know he was your first love." I raise another eyebrow at her, "Okay," she concedes, "your only love. But, there are so many guys out there who would love the opportunity to date you."

"Morgan thinks I should try online dating." Morgan is my cousin and she, like Elise, wants me to let go of Mayson and seek out happiness for myself.

"That sounds like a great idea. Being a teacher, you don't really have the chance to meet a lot of single men in the workplace."

"That's the understatement of the year. The only men at my school have been married for decades. That's the curse of working in a middle school. I should apply to high schools where all the young, hot male teachers work." I laugh.

"So, why don't you set up a dating profile?" Elise pushes further.

"I don't know." I shrug, avoiding eye contact, "Morgan thinks I'm afraid."

"Maybe she's right, Daphne. If you keep clinging to the idea of Mayson, you're not going to be able to move on."

"I didn't know I was clinging, Elise." Elise gives me a skeptical look, "Seriously!" I say with a defensive chuckle. She knows me all too well and I wonder who I'm really trying to convince, Elise or myself.

Two hours later, I pull into the parking lot of my apartment building. It is a small two-flat on a quiet suburban street. As I approach the building, the smell of take-out curry invades my senses. I climb the wooden stairs to my back door and let myself into my two bedroom apartment.

The bookcase in the corner of my guest room beckons me and I find myself hovering on my knees, still in my satin dress, looking for something that I have not seen in over a year. My journal.

I tear off my stilettos and sit down next to the shelf, lined with several notebooks, teaching binders and contemporary romance novels. Hidden, all the way at the edge, tucked between two very large dictionaries, is my journal. It's a simple leather bound book; the spine is covered in dust. In a way, I'm proud of the dusty film that lines this book, for it shows just how long it's been since I've written about him, about us.

I page through the book, my heart thumping in my chest as I'm brought back to him, to Mayson Holt, the boy who stole my heart, broke it and disappeared from my life five years ago. The man who I do not allow myself to think about. The man who still owns a very large piece of my soul.

The final entry catches my attention as the pain of that moment rushes back to me. I remember sobbing in my apartment that night, three and a half years after we last saw one another. Tears spill from my eyes as I'm brought back to that moment, the moment I hit my breaking point. The moment I had to stop thinking about him.

"It's time to let go, Daphne. You have to let go," I say to myself, tears streaming down my cheeks. I pick up my journal, walk down to the dumpster behind my building and toss the journal in. It takes every single ounce of strength in me to walk back into my apartment without retrieving that book. But, somehow I manage to do it without looking back. Perhaps I am ready...for real this time.

Chapter 2
Toast

"Do I look alright?" Elise is shaking. Her eyes are glazed over and I see her palms sweating. Gently taking her hands in mine, I look her square in the eyes.

"You look absolutely stunning, Elise. Take a deep breath." Elise takes in her breath and lets out an enormous sigh. The color starts to come back to her cheeks. I take this as a good sign to continue.

"You are marrying the man of your dreams. Henry is wonderful and today he will become your husband. Today you get to begin your future together as man and wife. All of your planning, it all culminates *today*. You've worked so hard and now you get to enjoy it! Be sure to breathe and take it all in, okay?" I ask her calmly.

"Yes, I think I can do that. Thank you, Daphne. I couldn't do this without you. I mean that." Affectionately, I smile at my best friend.

"Brushing the veil from her shoulders, Elise's deep brown

hair flows down her back. Her blue eyes glisten as she fights back the tears that are battling to spring from her eyes. She is so beautiful, such a sight to behold. Giving me her signature smirk, she lifts up her bulky gown and looks ready to walk to the chapel.

"Let's do this thing!"

As I watch Elise glide down the aisle towards the man she loves, I'm amazed at how anyone can be so confident in making such a life-altering decision. It's not that I don't believe in true love but, how do you know when someone truly is "the one?" Can you ever really know? Perhaps the fact that such a decision seems to be so far in my future is making it really hard to conceive at this particular moment. Almost like a nine year old wondering when she'll ever have her first boyfriend or her first kiss. Sometimes when something seems so far off in the future, it's hard to imagine it will ever take place. But, it does eventually happen.

Henry stares at Elise with such appreciation as she walks gracefully down the aisle. I am captivated by his expression, his obvious adoration for his beloved. I glance at Elise once again, hoping that she's noticing her husband-to-be and his obvious adulation. The exact same expression is spread across her gorgeous face. This is what love should look like, feel like. I watch them in awe throughout the ceremony as they say their vows and appear positively exuberant as they are pronounced husband and wife.

Two hours later, after some quality time with the photographer and plenty of cocktails, the other members of the wedding party and I make our way to our seats at the head table. Sitting down, I quickly check my handbag to make sure I've packed the note cards with my Maid of Honor speech written on them. Damn! That was the one thing I'd forgotten to check before leaving my apartment. Luckily, as my hand reaches in the tiny purse, I feel the thick cardstock and instantly relax. Public speaking is not terribly difficult for me. After all, it's part of my job description as a teacher. But, my desire to make Elise proud is making my palms sweat. She has always been so good to me, and I am determined to honor our friendship.

As I listen to Michael, the best man, give his speech, I try really hard not to focus on the fact that I'm next. Instead, I search the room looking for a friendly face to focus on. Elise's mom is crying tears of joy as she clenches her husband's hand. How sweet. I can only hope that my wedding will someday have the same effect on my own mother. By the time I finish observing Elise's mom, Michael is handing the microphone to me as the room fills with the sound of applause. I smile awkwardly and take the microphone from a very relieved Michael. I take a deep breath, grab my index cards and try my best to stand tall.

"Good evening, Ladies and Gentlemen." I begin, my heart thumping, "I am honored to be here tonight to welcome Henry into my family. No, Elise is not my sister by blood. But, over the last twenty years she has become a sister to me deep within my heart." I pause briefly to smile at Elise. Her eyes are beginning to well up with tears. I'm growing more confident by the second.

Before I continue, I remember my public speaking professor in college. He always said that you must scan a room in order to really connect with your audience. So, I decided to do just that. I turn to face the left side of the banquet hall, smile confidently and continue, "After all, sometimes it's the family you choose who end up meaning the most to you, and I can truly say that about Elise. We first became friends when I was a frizzy haired redhead getting teased on the playground by a much older bully. All of a sudden, this scrappy little brunette came out of nowhere and defended me. She chased that boy off in an instant and we were inseparable every moment after that. We've seen each other through so many things: terrible teachers, awful break-ups and catty sorority girls who made our lives miserable. It would take me hours to explain just how much she means to me. She is a treasure, an absolute treasure of a woman." Elise is sobbing next to me and I lift my eyes from my index cards in order to follow the instructions of my professor.

As my eyes make their way to the center of the room, I find myself looking at the wedding guests. Some of them look distracted or bored out of their minds while others listen intently to my warm words. Some drink from their wine glasses, and one even answers his cell phone. "So, Henry, I want to congratulate you on being the luckiest guy in the room. You've been lucky enough to find an extremely beautiful treasure and I hope that you will be so--"

Oh my god. I cannot believe my eyes. How could I have not noticed this earlier? Mayson. He's here! He is sitting in the far right corner of the room, almost near the exit, staring at me with a coy smile as he runs his fingers through his hair. Suddenly, I realize that I'm still holding a microphone and that I still need to finish this speech with some amount of grace and dignity. I can't let everyone in the room know that my stomach is doing gigantic flip flops. Fumbling with my cards, I do my best to refocus my attention the very best I can.

"I hope that you will be so happy with the wonder that is my friend, Elise. And, Mayson—" Elise gasps at my side as I accidentally say the name of my ex-boyfriend. He has invaded my subconscious! My cheeks turn crimson and my heart races so fast I can hardly breathe. I look down at my cards, desperate for them to pull me out of this disaster of a speech. "I mean, um, *Henry*, I can see how happy you make my lovely friend. You light up her life and you represent her happily ever after. She will always be my sister and so, Henry, I want to welcome you to my family as my new brother. I know that the two of you will share nothing but happiness in the many years to come."

I manage to fake a large smile as Henry grins at me. I have to finish on a strong note. I refuse to let Elise down.

"Congratulations to the beautiful couple. And here's to your happily ever after. Cheers!" The crowd erupts in applause. Elise rises out of her seat to embrace me tenderly, wiping tears from her eyes with her silken handkerchief. I somehow manage to hold back the tears that are threatening to spill from my eyes as I hold my friend tightly, dreading the end of this meal.

The next twenty minutes go by in a complete blur. Somehow, I manage to force down a few bites of my dinner, although my stomach is in knots. Staring off into space, not knowing how to react to the fact that Mayson is across the room, I consider my next move. But, what about Mayson? How will he proceed? Will he leave the reception in order to avoid a confrontation with me? Will he ask me to dance? I can't bear to contemplate it any longer. I have to escape. So, as dinner is wrapping up, I excuse myself to the ladies room.

Walking across the ballroom, one of the groomsmen is walking towards me with a big smile. He is very attractive, tall and thin with dark chestnut hair and a sexy goatee that frames his face beautifully...but I can't possibly focus on him right now.

"Hi, Daphne. That was a great speech," he grins.

"Oh, thanks. It's Tanner, right?" The second I question his name, I regret it. Of course I know his name! How ridiculous of me. Mayson has me so frazzled that in this moment I feel like I am someone else entirely; someone who is unable to form a coherent thought or remember the name of a man who had caught my attention just yesterday at the rehearsal dinner.

"Yep, that's me," Tanner looks a little disappointed that I stumbled on his name, "listen, would you like to grab a drink? I was just headed to the bar and I'd love to get to know you better." God, he's cute. But, I have to flee.

"Can I get a rain check?" I ask as casually as I can muster, "I'm headed to the powder room."

"Oh, of course," Tanner smiles, "I'll look for you later."

"Thanks," I reply, heading quickly to the ladies room. When I step inside the elegant sitting room, Elise is waiting for me.

"Daphne, honey, what's the matter? Your speech was beautiful, but you froze and turned so pale; you looked like you had seen a ghost. And then you said *Mayson's* name. Where on earth did *that* come from?" Elise says, as she eases her bulky dress out of an olive green armchair to stand beside me. She has no idea how correct she actually is. The reemergence of Mayson has disturbed me to my core.

"Oh, Elise, please don't worry about it. Go! Enjoy your evening with Henry. You're married now!" I say with as much enthusiasm as I can possibly muster. But, the cynical look in Elise's eyes tells me she's not buying it.

"Now, you listen to me, Daphne Harper. You are my best friend. And, I can read you like a book. Something happened to you during that speech. You need to tell me what's going on. Why have you been like a zombie ever since you sat back down? Don't you trust me?" Elise looks distraught. I have to tell her.

"No, Elise. That's not it. Of course I trust you. I trust you more than anyone else in the world. But, this is your wedding day. And I don't want to spoil it."

"Tough. Now, tell me, Daphne. Please."

"Fine, but remember you asked for this." I warn her, giving her one final moment of pause, hoping she will change her mind and rejoin her party. She doesn't budge.

"Mayson is here. I saw him during my speech. That's why his name flew out of my mouth without warning. Elise, why didn't you tell me you invited him? At least, then, I could have been prepared. Is he a friend of Henry's or something? I know they met a few times, but I never expected him to be here."

"Mayson? You mean your boyfriend-from-college-Mayson? He's not here. That's impossible!"

"So, you didn't invite him?"

"Absolutely not! I would never do that to you, Daphne!"

"Well, he's here."

"Are you sure it isn't someone who just resembles him?"

"C'mon, Elise, give me a little credit. I know what the guy looks like," I respond, tilting my head and raising an eyebrow.

"Sorry, that was stupid of me," Elise pauses with a pensive stare, "Maybe he's someone's date. There are quite a few unnamed guests here tonight."

"Oh my God, I hadn't thought of that." He's here with someone. The bad somehow managed to get worse. I take a deep breath and look my friend square in the eye, "Elise, please, you have to go and enjoy your wedding reception. I'm going to stay here for a little while to pull myself together. But, I will never forgive myself if I keep you from enjoying this night! Please, go, ok?" My voice is bordering on desperate. She nods in understanding.

"Ok, but I promise I'll check in later. Remember, I'm here for you, Daphne. And, I'm so sorry this is happening. Are you sure I can't convince you to forget about Mayson and join me on the dance floor? I would never forgive myself if I allowed you to lock yourself in the washroom for my entire reception. We've been planning this evening together for the last fifteen months! I need my Maid of Honor with me! We need to do it up right!"

"Listen, I will get myself under control, I *promise*. I would never abandon you on your wedding day. I just need a couple of moments to myself in order to get my bearings. Now, get out there and find your husband, *please* Elise," I say with a forced smile. Elise kisses me quickly on my forehead, nods solemnly and walks out of the restroom.

The plush armchair in the resting area of the washroom envelops me as I sink deeper and deeper into its soft upholstery, my heart racing and my forehead starting to sweat. What the hell am I going to do? I am trapped; trapped by Mayson's presence, trapped by my own insecurities, and even trapped by my lovely best friend who has just gotten married. I can't leave the reception, and I sure as hell can't stay locked in the restroom like a coward. I quickly fix my make-up and hair, take a very deep breath and head for the door. I am walking towards the bar when I hear my name.

"Daphne." I'd know that voice anywhere; husky and deep, but with a hint of softness.

"Mayson?" I somehow rally, trying my best to sound surprised. "What are you doing here? Are you a friend of Henry's?"

"No." He shakes his head, "I do remember him from school, but I wasn't invited. I'm actually here with a friend."

"Oh," I pause, trying to dissect his tone. A *friend*? That could mean just about anything. And, I needed to know if my Mayson was now someone else's Mayson. It will impact the way that I approach this entire situation.

"Would you like to grab a drink?" he asks, smiling awkwardly, those gorgeous green eyes staring into mine.

"As a matter of fact, I was just headed to the bar." I say, my voice trembling. This is not good.

As we walk towards the bar, I see Tanner is standing with the other groomsmen. He raises his glass with an expectant smile and I remember my promise of a drink. Damn it. There is no way that I can balance Mayson and another incredibly cute guy right now. I'm confused enough as it is! Feeling awful, I turn away from his gaze. As I focus my eyes back on Mayson, I can see Tanner's smile diminish out of the corner of my eye. My heart sinks.

A few minutes later, I find myself sitting at a table near the dance floor. Mayson is seated beside me and I silently wonder where his date is. I was so shocked to see him during my speech that I didn't have time to notice her. All I can remember is the color blue from her dress. My eyes search the room for a young woman in blue, but to no avail. The only women wearing blue are those with silver hair and deep wrinkles. None of them could possibly have been his date, his "friend."

"Are you alright? You seem really preoccupied." Mayson says uneasily.

"Oh, I'm fine," I smile, my voice shaking a bit, "It's just a little surprising to see you here tonight."

"Yeah, it is weird, isn't it?" He stops and stares at the guests on the dance floor, a conflicted look upon his face. He glances towards me, smiles gently and asks, "By any chance, would you like to dance, Daphne?"

"Sure, that would be nice," I say with a tinge of hope. Were the gods trying to send me a message? Should I not have parted with my journal? Did I have to make the decision to forget him in order to fall in love with him all over again? As he reaches for my hand and leads me to the dance floor, my heart pounds frantically in my chest.

"I have a confession to make," Mayson says, looking sheepish, "I knew you'd be here tonight. That's part of the reason I agreed to come."

"Really?" I was genuinely shocked at this sudden admission. Could it be that Mayson had been thinking of me these past few years? Is it possible that I'm not alone in clinging to our past? The thought seems so impossible, yet here he is with me in his arms, slowly gliding me across the dance floor.

"Yes, of course. I know that you and Elise are best friends so I was certain that you'd be here. So, I took a gamble and came here with Daniela. You remember Daniela, right?"

"Daniela?" Of course, Daniela! She was a college classmate and was also in Mayson's architecture program. She had even studied in France with Mayson. Daniela was such a tomboy that I had never thought of her as someone whom Mayson would choose to date. I had completely forgotten that she was also a friend of Elise's from the dorms and that she would be invited to the wedding. Things finally made sense.

"Yeah, we actually got a job in the same firm. It was all

because of the year we spent in France. We presented our projects and were both hired. Small world, huh?"

"Sure," I say with a smile, still unsure if he was friends with Daniela or dating her, "So, are you two very close?"

"We're not dating…if that's what you're trying to ask me." He flirts, his bright green eyes sparkling under the giant chandelier above our heads.

"So, where is this architecture firm the two of you work for?" I'm pressing for more information, of course, but I'm trying my very best not to seem too obvious.

"Well, Daniela works for the division based out of Milwaukee. And, I'm in Denver."

"Wow, so you did it. You always wanted to move to Denver." I say, trying desperately to hide my disappointment. Denver was a thousand miles away.

"Yeah, I've been there since college and I've loved every minute. But, Daniela and I have been collaborating on a new library for our old campus. The firm selected each of us, naturally, because we are Illinois alumni. So, we've been meeting there every few weeks to work on the project."

"Wow. That is really exciting, Mayson. I'm happy for you."

"Thanks, Daphne. That means a lot to me," he pauses, looking deep into my eyes and continues, "Look, I'm sorry for the way things went down right before graduation. You must think I'm such an ass for sleeping with you and then never calling. Especially since that was the first time--"

"Don't worry, Mayson," I interrupt, "That wasn't my first time, if that's what you're worried about." The lie feels awful leaving my lips. Why did I feel the need to hide the truth from him?

"It wasn't?" he asks incredulously. He seems hurt, but why?

"No, so don't you worry," I say with a hint of sarcasm, "you haven't scarred me for life." Or had he?

"Well, I still felt like an ass for not calling. I was so busy getting acclimated in Denver and adjusting to life as an actual architect. And by the time I was really settled in, it seemed like too much time had passed. I figured you'd hang up on me or something if I tried to call."

"You could have tried, you know. I wouldn't have hung up." The words fall out of my mouth in a soft whisper. What am I doing? Am I trying to get crushed all over again? I gaze up at his beautiful forehead. His tousled hair is starting to sway into his eyes as we dance. Slowly, my fingers push the strands of hair from his long, silky eyelashes. He smiles sincerely and heaves a sigh.

"Well, that's good to know," He replies, leaning in closer to me, almost nuzzling into my neck. We continue to sway slowly on the dance floor. I glance around to find Elise. She's dancing with Henry and manages to give me an apprehensive smile. Mustering up the energy to look relaxed and calm, I perk up the corners of my mouth in return. I want so desperately to ease her concerns. If only I didn't have so many of my own.

After our dance has finished, Mayson surprises me with an early departure.

"Well, I'd better get back to Daniela. After all, she is my date." He stops, runs his fingers through his hair, takes a deep breath and continues, "It was really wonderful to see you. Are you still living with your parents?"

"No, I have an apartment a few towns over. It's closer to the school where I teach."

"Oh, yeah, I forgot that you wanted to be a teacher. That's awesome!"

How could he forget my chosen career path? Do I mean so little to him that he can't even be bothered to remember my life's passion? When we dated, all I could talk about were my teaching courses and how excited I was to be tutoring at the local high school. I was nothing if not a completely devoted teacher-in-training. It was such a large part of my identity, how could it have slipped his mind?

"Well, may I have your phone number then, Puddin'?" he winks at me and I feel like his conquest all over again. That was his nickname for me, at least whenever he had a bit too much to drink. I was always teasing him for his South Carolina accent. One night after too many bottles of beer, he started calling me Puddin', a nickname that made me melt into a big pile of mush. I never expected to hear it again after our last night together in college.

Hesitantly, I give him my phone number in the hopes that we may reconnect in the near future. Regretfully, I leave him on the dance floor and join the other bridesmaids, all of whom are wondering how I am dealing with the reemergence of the notorious Mayson. I shrug at their many questions, wishing I had an answer.

Later that evening, I catch Elise's beautiful bouquet. Was there ever any doubt? After my catch, I try my best not to make eye contact with him, but it proves to be impossible. His eyes bore into me and the air in my chest vanishes. What in the world have I gotten myself into?

Chapter 3
Sophomore Year (Spring Semester)

"Mayson, I was hoping that we could talk about us for a minute," I say, my blood is pumping furiously through my heart. Things have been different between us ever since returning to campus after Spring Break. Mayson is different; his calls are less frequent, and he hasn't slept over in more days than I can count. Something is wrong.

Elise has convinced me to talk to him and find out what's happening between us. But, I fear this conversation will only lead to bad things; that I may just give him the excuse he is looking for to walk away from me.

"Yeah, what do you want to talk about?" he asks looking down at his cafeteria tray.

"Well, we haven't really spent much time together lately. And, well, I've been sensing that you are pulling away. Have I done something to upset you?" My heart is racing, my fingers are trembling. I am terrified of where this conversation will lead; but I have to know what's going on. I have to know if I've lost him.

"Don't be silly. Of course not, I'm just really busy with classes. I didn't realize that the architecture program would be so time consuming. And, I really blew it off for a few months, so I'm trying to make up for all that wasted time."

All I can focus on is that word-- 'wasted.' Obviously all the time that Mayson and I have been a couple, he deems as wasted time. How awful. How can he say something so hurtful?

"Well, I didn't mean to waste your time, you know. I thought we were in love."

"Yeah, I know, but sometimes you have to make priorities, Daphne. I haven't been sticking to mine lately. I realized that while I was home." He pauses and takes a deep breath, staring at his mashed potatoes, "I realized a lot of things," he mumbles.

"Like what? Like about us?" I ask, desperately clinging to the hope that he will ease all of my fears. But, deep down, I know we are headed for a fall, a big one.

"Yes, Daphne, we spent so much time together that I lost a lot of time with my friends. And while I was home, I realized that friends come first. Friends will be there long after all the girls are gone." He won't look at me.

"Oh, so now I'm going somewhere?" My head is spinning and I am feeling a sudden urge to flee, from Mayson, from this conversation and from myself.

"Did you really think we *weren't* going to break up? I mean, everyone breaks-up eventually. It's inevitable. You can't say that you really thought this was going to be for the rest of our lives, can you?"

"Well, I'm certainly not going to say that now! God, Mayson, where is all this coming from? We don't have to plan our wedding or anything like that. We've been together for six months and it's been wonderful. I think I deserve to be a priority, just as much, if not more than your friends," I'm trying not to raise my voice too much, it feels like the walls are closing in on me. Two girls at the next table are already eavesdropping and I'm hoping not to draw the attention of any of the other students around us.

Suddenly, in the pit of my stomach, I wonder if this is about something else; the one source of tension that exists between us. My virginity. Mayson has been so patient with me, knowing that I haven't been ready, but deep down I've felt his frustration for months.

"Mayse, is this because we haven't...you know, slept together yet?"

"I don't know," Mayson replies, shrugging his shoulders with a nonchalance that runs chills up my spine. He shakes his head, staring at the table. "Maybe we need to take a break from one another. I have two years left at this University and I need to raise my GPA. I don't have time for all of this right now."

"Wow," I say, my heart breaking in two, "that's just fine. You focus on your work." And with that, I stand up, choking back the tears and walk out of the dining hall, leaving my tray on the table. Mayson doesn't say a word. He doesn't try to stop me. I've let him off the hook. What I feared the most is now my reality.

I hurry back to my dorm room and cry for three hours, clutching the stuffed dog that he gave me on our fourth date. As I look around my room, I'm overwhelmed by all of the memories surrounding me. Pictures of us together fill my bulletin board. CDs that we listened to while snuggling lay on the trunk next to my bed, old candles on my desk remind me of romantic nights spent talking about the future. Eventually, I cry myself to sleep, soaking my stuffed dog with tears.

Chapter 4
Profile (Present Day)

"I can't believe I let you talk me into this," I say to Morgan who is sitting on the floor of my bedroom. I'm stuck at my computer as Morgan forces me to do something I really don't want to do.

"I'm telling you, Daphne. Your profile sucks! You're never going to find the right guy because you're not really representing yourself accurately. You need to be real."

"I *am* being real, Morgan. My profile is brief, that's all. I don't feel the need to tell my life story on an online dating site."

"I know, Daphne. But, you need to give these guys a glimmer into how wonderful you are. Right now, all they know is that you're a teacher who lives in the suburbs. You've got to spice it up a little bit. Tell them that you make killer jell-o shots, stuff like that!"

"Oh, that's perfect. Then, I can attract a bunch of drunks!" The sarcasm drips from my voice.

"I think you're being a bit overdramatic, Cuz," she laughs,

paging through my new copy of Us Weekly, "I also think that if you put a little more effort into this, you might meet someone really cool. Besides, you need something to take your mind off of you-know-who." She's referring to Mayson. It's been three weeks since Elise's wedding and he still hasn't called. I am stewing in a very big way and Morgan knows it.

"I know you're just trying to help me. But, it's hard for me to put myself out there like that, on a computer screen no less. You know I'm not very internet savvy. Not like you. You're the Facebook queen of our generation," I tease.

Morgan doesn't have to find dates online. She has been seeing the same guy for a while and they are quite serious. His name is Matt and he seems to be perfect for my cousin. He has a sharp sense of humor and is laid-back and fun; the kind of guy who gets along with everyone he meets. I've seen Morgan go through many boyfriends and Matt is, by far, my favorite. He's kind of a workaholic, however, so it gives Morgan lots of time to spend with me, which I'm grateful for.

Morgan lives in the building next door on our little suburban street. It's nice having a friend so close by, especially one who's known me for my entire life. But, it also means that she can come over and hound me about my love life by making me update my silly dating profiles. I secretly love her for giving me the extra push I need. Without her, I probably would have avoided the whole thing.

"How about I page through my magazine, and you update my profile for me? How does that sound?" I ask, almost begging.

"But, then it won't be authentic. Besides, I want to read all the celebrity dirt."

"Hey, why don't we go for a walk and talk about this some more." I suggest, trying desperately to distract her. Standing up, I head straight for my keys.

"Not so fast, little missy. We have a job to do first. Now, scoot over. If you won't finish this, I will."

About an hour later, Morgan has created a beautiful

profile for me. Although I feel she was a bit too complimentary of my looks and personality, I secretly love how she presents me to available men. Maybe, just maybe, I will meet someone of substance; someone who will evict Mayson from my brain. After all these years, I never expected that he'd let me down again. But, maybe that is the problem. Maybe I should have expected it.

The following evening, I check the dating site to see if any guys have found my page interesting. Logging into my welcome page, I see that four guys have sent messages.

"Not bad," I say to myself with a grin, my confidence emerging.

As I sift through the emails from my potential suitors, I hear a "ding" from the website. Someone is trying to talk to me.

Cowboy85: Hey sexy.

Daphne307: Um…hello.

Cowboy85: I love your picture. Can't stop thinking about it. And lucky me, you logged on.

Daphne307: Well, thank you. What is your name?

Cowboy85: We'll get to that….

Daphne307: uh….ok.

(Right about now is when I should have blocked his ass)

Cowboy85: So, tell me, Miss Daphne. Do you like to take baths?

Daphne307: Where are you going with this, pal?
Cowboy85: Right now, I'm wondering if you'd like to take a bath with me.

Daphne307: That is a little forward, don't you think? Especially since I don't even know your name?

Cowboy85: Oh, you have no idea.

Daphne307: Dude, you're a little odd. Is this how you approach all of the women you are interested in?

Cowboy85: Sometimes. But, I'm really drawn to you. I'd like to bathe you in the finest strawberry jell-o….

What?!? Without wasting another second of my time, I quickly "x" out the conversation box and block the Jell-O Cowboy from my account. Blech! If this is online dating, I'm not so sure it's for me! My first conversation over the internet and it leads to bathing in gelatin products. This is going to be an agonizing process.

Uncomfortable laughter sweeps through me as I reach for the phone to call Morgan. Just before picking up the receiver, however, it rings. Hesitant to lift the phone from its cradle, I wonder if Morgan added my phone number to my profile. It'd better not be the Cowboy!

"Um, hello?" I answer, holding my breath and hoping for someone I know on the other end of the line. Then, an all-too-familiar voice speaks in a velvety tone. My pulse quickens and my lungs tighten within my chest.

"Daphne, hi, it's me. It's Mayson."

"Mayson, um… hi, how are you?" The words stumble clumsily out of my mouth. I never quite know what to say to this man.

"It's so good to hear your voice, Daphne." Something deep inside of me begins to tighten. I'd missed that voice more than I'd allowed myself to admit these past few weeks.

"It's been a while," I respond. "How is Denver?"

"Actually, I'm in Champaign, on campus. Remember that

project I told you about?" My heart skips a beat. He is less than two hours away.

"Yes, of course. That's very e-exciting." I stammer. What is he doing to me?

"Well, I was thinking that maybe we could get together. You're on summer break from teaching, right? My week is pretty slow. It'd be great to see you."

"What did you have in mind, Mayson?" My mind is racing.

"Well," he pauses. I try my best to slow my breathing as I wait for his reply, "I was thinking I could come and see your place. Take you to dinner?"

His voice almost sounds hopeful. Was Mayson actually nervous? We make plans for the following evening and a wave of excitement shoots through me. In less than twenty four hours, Mayson will be with me. As much as I hate to admit it, I'm ecstatic.

Chapter 5
Senior Year (fall semester)

I stumble into my apartment, throwing my keys on the floor, and walk with a determined drunken march to my bedroom. My computer is already on and I am no longer nervous. I am no longer afraid. I've had five beers tonight and they will help me to connect with him. I can only hope he'll be online.

Logging in to the University IM system is difficult since it takes me a while to type my password correctly. But, eventually it works and I see he's online.

"Let's do this," I say to myself, typing my instant message to the boy whom I miss so very much. It will be our first contact in months, ever since he told me he'd be studying in Paris for the semester.

DaffyGirl: Hey. What time is it in France?

Mayser: Hey, Stranger. It's 7:30 am. I'm getting ready for

class. You're up late.

DaffyGirl: I know. We just got back from the bar.

Mayser: Ah, I see. And you thought of me?

DaffyGirl: Of course. Was there any doubt?

Mayser: Not really ;)

DaffyGirl: Are you loving Paris?

Mayser: It's incredible, Daph. I'm amazed on a daily basis. I feel really lucky to be here.

DaffyGirl: I'm so happy for you. (Although, secretly I hate Paris)

Mayser: LOL. We went to an Irish Pub last night...in Paris. It was too funny. You would have loved it. I thought of you, actually. You would have fit in really well...your red hair, your freckles, drinking Guinness like an Irishman.

DaffyGirl: So, you thought of me, huh?

Mayser: I do from time to time...yes. And last night was one of those times.

DaffyGirl: Because I have red hair and I get drunk?

Mayser: Other reasons, too. I've been meaning to email you. Sorry about that. I've literally been in class for 10 hours per day, plus I spend additional time in the studio. I hardly ever see Daniela or any of the other people in the program outside of class.

DaffyGirl: So, you've been meaning to get in touch.

Mayser: Yeah...I've decided to stay through next semester. I'll be here for the entire school year.

Tears spring from my eyes as I read those words. Perhaps, I might never see him again. After all, this was our senior year. He'll go back to Charleston, and I'll move back home to the Chicago suburbs and that'll be it. It will be over. Somehow, I manage to type as my tears drip slowly onto my keyboard.

DaffyGirl: Wow, that's incredible.

Mayser: Yeah, I'm stoked. An entire school year in France — it's a dream come true for me.

DaffyGirl: So will you graduate with the class?

Mayser: Not sure yet. I may not be able to participate in convocation, but it's a small price to pay for this experience. I'll receive my degree regardless. I just might miss out on the pomp and circumstance.

DaffyGirl: True.

Mayser: Hey, are you ok?

DaffyGirl: Yep.

Mayser: Listen, I'm sorry to cut this short, but I don't want to be late for class. My professors here are incredibly strict regarding tardiness. Take care, ok?

DaffyGirl: Sure, of course. Goodbye, Mayson.

When will this boy stop making me cry? When will contact with him stop hurting so much? When am I going to learn that we are simply not meant to be? Still incredibly drunk from this evening's activities, I curl up in my bed and drift off into a drunken sleep.

Chapter 6
Dinner (Present Day)

"You look beautiful, stunning as ever." Mayson's tone is sexy and confident; not at all like the voice that I heard over the phone. But, then again, I have acquiesced. He is here now, sitting at a table of a local Italian restaurant with me, and I'm blushing like crazy, my cheeks burning with anticipation and curiosity. I feel like he's reading my mind, knowing how excited I am to be near him again.

"Thanks," I mutter, twirling my finger nervously in my hair.

"Why are you doing that?" Mayson smirks.

"What do you mean?" I'm puzzled. What *am* I doing?

"You're twirling your hair. I only remember you doing that before big exams or when you had a paper due. Are you nervous to be here with me, Daphne?" he's flirting with me, so confident. I want to punch him right in his smug face for being so damned arrogant.

"What kind of a question is that, Mayson? Of course I am.

I haven't seen you in five years and suddenly you're back in my life. I'm trying to figure out what you're doing here." I answer honestly, pausing before shrugging my shoulders. I've never been one to dance around an issue. It always feels better to work things out and move on because I need to know where I stand. But, it hasn't really given me much luck in the men department, especially with Mayson. Many times, I've felt that I've scared men away by being too direct. But Mayson, surprisingly, doesn't seem to shy away from my direct nature as he did in the past.

"Well, just relax. I'm really fortunate to be here with you. I just wanted to reconnect." Mayson takes a deep breath and continues, "I've missed you. That smile of yours has haunted me for years. Maybe you can unwind a bit and let me see it?" he grins, taking a sip of wine.

"Okay." I smile reluctantly. "So, I've haunted you, huh? Those are some big words to say after all this time, Mayson." I flirt, regaining my confidence. He knows exactly what I'm doing. Narrowing his eyes, he refills my wine glass with just enough wine to calm my nerves.

"Well, I don't want to start the evening with a lie." He says, leaning in close. His fingers lightly caress mine as they lay on the table in front of me. My first instinct is to pull away, but I can't do it. My hand feels as if it is glued to the table. I gently respond to his touch by moving my fingers back and forth under his.

Two hours later, the check is paid and the wine bottle is empty. Mayson calls a cab to take us back to my place. We sit close together in the car, his hands lightly caressing the small of my back as I stare out the window, my head on his shoulder. My brain is so fuzzy from the wine and my heart is trying desperately to understand what's happening. Longing for him to touch me further and terrified of what might (or might not) happen. My mind is conflicted; so turned on and yet so afraid of the morning light.

We arrive at my apartment and walk together towards the door. I turn to him and smile, "Well, this was--" and just like that, his mouth is on mine. His tongue twists greedily in my mouth, making me melt into the wooden deck below our feet. I turn to unlock my door as Mayson kisses the nape of my neck, pushing my hair aside, making me gasp. His hands run up and down my back, as I struggle with my lock. His breath is hot as he pulls me closer and closer to him at a feverish pace. Distracted by his frantic touch, I struggle to twist the key.

Quickly, Mayson reaches for the key and twists it until the door pops open. Slowing down, he pushes me gently into the apartment, locking the door behind us. I am completely swept up in him, swirling in a fit of hormones and desire.

"Where is your bedroom?" he asks, nuzzling into my neck, sucking gently on my skin.

"This way," I say, guiding him slowly towards my bed. All my hesitant thoughts have disappeared. I want this. I will deal with the consequences in the morning.

The next morning, I awaken to the sound of birds chirping outside my window. The alarm clock reads 7:00 am; it's still early. I roll over smiling, only to find that Mayson is no longer in my bed. My heart sinks. He's left me. How could I have been so stupid? Sitting up quickly, I rub the hair from my forehead. I try my best to hold in my tears, but they are threatening to plummet from the corners of my eyes. Don't do it, Daphne. Do not cry over him, not again.

"Morning," I hear from the doorway. Mayson is standing there, dressed only in his boxer shorts, holding a half eaten banana and a large glass of ice water. Sighing with relief, my pulse starts to return to a normal pace.

"Uh oh," he says. "Are you feeling alright? You look very pale, Daph."

"Yes, I'm fine," I mumble, running my fingers through my

hair, and yanking the sheet up to conceal my exposed breasts.

"No need to cover up for me, Puddin'. I was enjoying the view." He smirks. That smirk will be my undoing. I know that now. "Here, I brought you some water. You had quite a bit of wine last night."

"Thank you." I nod, genuinely appreciative of the small gesture.

"I also went into your medicine cabinet. I hope that's alright. My head was killing me, so I took a couple Advil. I brought two for you, as well."

"Again, thank you," I muster a small, hesitant smile on my lips.

Mayson places the water in my right hand and the Advil in my left. My sheet slips down, but my hands are too occupied to fix it. Mayson grins.

"That's more like it." He chuckles. A small laugh escapes my lips, as well. I am starting to relax; he's still here and taking care of me.

Popping the pills in my mouth, I wash them down with the cold water. Placing the cup on the nightstand, I gasp. Mayson is planting small kisses on my shoulder, breathing deeply and caressing my lower back with his hands.

"Mayson," I say, almost as if I'm asking a question. But, then again, maybe I am.

"Yes, Daphne?" He replies between kisses.

"What are we doing?" Never one to go with the flow, I had to know what on earth he was doing here, stroking my skin, nipping my freckles and being altogether way too charming for my own good.

"Didn't you have a good time last night, Puddin'? You seemed to...." He's still kissing me as he asks. Murmuring into my neck, stroking my hair and caressing his way up to my ears: he knows they are my weakness.

"Yes, of course. It was incredible. Just trying to get my bearings, that's all" I respond honestly. He pulls away, sits up straight and looks me in the eye.

"I want to see you again, if that is alright with you," he says, reaching out to stroke my hair. He twirls several strands in his fingertips as he gazes at me, his green eyes shining in the morning sun. Mayson seems genuine, sincere and looking for my approval of his feelings toward me. "I need to get back to campus later today, but I can come up this weekend. And then, we can take it from there. At least, that's what I'm hoping for." He kisses my hand and smiles warmly.

"That sounds nice, Mayson." And it does.

Chapter 7
Drinks

I have waited three very long, very excruciating days to see Mayson again. Finally, Friday afternoon arrives and he will be here shortly. I've changed my outfit five times, groaning and rolling my eyes at each wardrobe choice. Nothing seems good enough. My nerves are getting the best of me as I anxiously await my houseguest, lover, possible future boyfriend. As always, I'm worried about the future. I'm worried about the distance between us, worried that this means something different to him than it does to me. I am trying so hard to stop the worries, but they creep up again and again as I attempt to clean my apartment for his arrival.

Finally, a car door closes in the small parking lot outside my window. My heart leaps into my throat and I glance at the clock. It's 7:00pm and he is right on time. I hear him climbing my wooden staircase that leads to the back door. Waiting for him to knock (not wanting to seem too eager), I inhale deeply in an attempt to calm my nerves.

I twist the knob and open the door with a smile. Mayson has an enormous grin on his face and a large bouquet of stargazer lilies in his hand. He knows they are my favorite flowers.

"Wow, you remembered," I marvel softly.

"Yep," he smiles, obviously proud of himself, "It was years ago that you mentioned you loved these. I thought it'd be fun to surprise you." He's obviously looking for validation.

"They're perfect, Mayson." I say dreamily, almost in a trance. What is he doing to me?

After a few hours of polite conversation and innocent flirting, we head down to a local bar for dinner and drinks with Morgan and Matt. Morgan has taken it upon herself to assess our current situation to see if she approves of Mayson's intentions towards me. She and I went to different Universities, so she has never met him, even though I have told her so much over the years. With Morgan's determination to keep me safe and happy, this should be an interesting evening.

"So, you're an architect, yes?" Morgan asks before sipping her Long Island Iced Tea, our favorite drink.

"Yes, I am. I love it. Very fulfilling work for me," Mayson replies confidently. If Morgan had planned on making him squirm tonight, it doesn't seem likely to happen. He rubs his hand on my thigh as he elaborates on his career. The nerve endings in my leg spring to life against his fingers; it's exhilarating. I glance at the clock, hoping that soon the evening will come to an end with my cousin and her boyfriend. I am aching for Mayson's touch, and not just on my thigh.

"Speaking of fulfilling careers, Daphne is such a fantastic teacher. Her students love her. Has she told you about any of them?"

"Um…her students?" Mayson asks, taken aback. Morgan

nods assertively, raising a lone eyebrow. "Uh, no, I don't think they have come up in conversation yet."

"Ah," Morgan says, nodding to herself. The subject needs to be changed as tension starts to creep into the space between my cousin and my date.

"Morgan, let's get another round. Everyone's drinks are getting low." I say, standing up and giving her a look that warns her not to protest.

We walk to the bar, arm in arm. "Okay, Morgan, what was that all about back there? Why are you giving him such an attitude?"

"Oh, *c'mon*, Daphne! Of course I'm giving him attitude. You sulked over him for years, and I mean, years. He broke your heart. And if you're not going to be protective of your own heart, then I have to be!"

"He means a lot to me, Morgan. If you don't give him a chance…"

"I didn't say I wouldn't come around eventually, Daphne. But, he has to give me a reason to like him. You are too wrapped up in him to think clearly. Obviously, I have to do your thinking for you!"

"I wouldn't go that far, Morgan. I know that I should be apprehensive," I say defensively.

"But, are you being apprehensive? You look all starry eyed to me. He reached over to touch your leg and you practically swooned!" I look at her in shock. She saw that? "Yeah, I noticed, Daphne. Look, just be careful, please."

When we return to the table, Mayson and Matt are engaged in polite conversation. Clearly, my buddy Matt is attempting to repair the damage his girlfriend may have created. I always knew he was on my side. Morgan slides in next to Matt who wraps his arms around her. Feeling a bit uneasy, I sit down next to Mayson, waiting for some sort of indication that everything is ok. He kisses me gently on the lips and whispers into my ear.

"You were gone so long. I missed you."

Resisting the urge to tease him about how my little trip to the bar is nothing compared to a four-hour flight to Denver, I hold back. In this moment, I realize how terrified I am to scare this man away. Whether by Morgan's grilling, my teasing or anything else that might come about, I am sick with worry that things will come to an end before I even get a real chance with Mayson. Quickly I finish my drink to escape the anxiety.

The rest of the evening is more relaxed, aided mostly by the increase of alcohol in our systems. Morgan pulls me on the dance floor and Mayson is happy to watch me as I sing and dance, swiveling my hips to the music. I feel so alive and nothing can spoil it. I gesture for Mayson to join me and he shakes his head and mouths the word "no" with a large smile on his masculine lips. My mouth forms a dramatic pout but I continue dancing with Morgan.

Two more songs come and go as Morgan and I continue to laugh, twist, shake and act like complete fools on the dance floor. I glance back at the table and see that Mayson is on his phone, no longer watching us. He seems upset, perhaps due to how loud the bar has become. He walks away from the table to complete his call. Wondering who is on the other end of the line, my thoughts get cloudy and turn dark. The thought of him talking to another woman makes me sick to my stomach.

"What's wrong, Daphne?" Morgan yells above the music, "Do you need to sit down?"

"No, I'm fine. I think I'm just getting tired."

Moments later, I feel an arm wrap around my waist, his woodsy scent invading my senses as he nuzzles into my neck.

"Hey, beautiful girl," Mayson whispers into my ear. Morgan takes this as her cue to leave us alone on the dance floor.

"So, you've decided to dance?" I ask as seductively as possible.

"Well, you know I'm not really a dancer, but I couldn't

44

resist how sexy you looked. I had to get out here before someone else beat me to it." He brushes my bangs away from my eyes. "I'm not so good at sharing." He adds.

"Me neither," I reply, staring into his eyes. He glances away briefly and then holds my gaze for what feels like minutes. Cupping my chin in his hands, he kisses me passionately.

"Let's go home, Puddin'"

"Daphne, wake up." Rubbing the sleep from my eyes, I peer at the clock on my nightstand. 5:45 a.m.? Ugh! Why is Mayson awake and fully dressed in my bedroom?

"I have to get back to campus. There's a problem with the plans. They need me back as soon as possible." His tone is a bit dismissive. My heart sinks.

"Really? I thought you might stay the weekend." I'm surprised that he didn't mention anything earlier. Perhaps this was the phone call he received last night. I guess that would explain the look of aggravation on his face.

"I know. I'd hoped to do that. It's just not possible, Daphne. I'm sorry. I have a few more days on campus and then I'm headed back to Denver. I wanted to talk with you more about that while we were together this weekend. I really wish that I could stay here with you." He gazes into my eyes, his tone now sincere and less apprehensive.

"No, I understand. Your project is important. I know it comes first." I reply doing my very best not to seem too disappointed. This is reminding me so much of our differences back in school; Mayson putting architecture first, and me pushing back against his priorities. I was determined to be different this time. After all, this was his career and I had to respect that.

Mayson kisses me goodbye, and just like that, he is gone again, and I'm left wondering what the hell is going on with us. Is Mayson worth the anxiety in my chest, the worries on my brain, the aching in my heart? Time will tell.

I'm tempted to call Elise on her cell phone, but I'd never forgive myself for disturbing her on her honeymoon. I'll just have to wait for her to return as her guidance means so much. For now, sleep calls me once again. Rolling over in my bed, doing my best to block any thought of Mayson from my heart or my head, I slowly fall into a restless sleep.

Chapter 8
Kim

"You don't seriously believe this is going to tell us anything, do you Morgan?"

"Who knows? My friend Cheryl swears by this woman. She goes to see her every year and she always gets the best advice. And so many of her predictions have actually come true."

"Sounds like self fulfilling prophecy to me." My cynicism is so transparent.

"Well, you've been so torn up about what is going on with Mayson. Seriously, this has been going on for years, Daphne. Wouldn't it be good to get a clue as to who you will actually end up with?"

"Yes, Morgan, but that's assuming this psychic knows anything. She could be pulling things out of her ass for all we know."

"Since when did you become such a cynic? You were always the one who read your horoscope and trusted in

Astrology. Hell, you even bought tarot cards in college. I remember you giving 'readings' at your parents' house. You used to use your U of I blanket every time! Now, all of a sudden you don't believe in this stuff?"

"Oh my goodness, I completely forgot about the tarot cards." I laugh, "But, that was just for fun. This is different. You believe this woman is actually going to help me figure out my love life."

"Listen, it's my treat. I have some questions I want to ask anyway about Matt and about my job. I'm not sure I should be staying there much longer. If you feel inclined, we can ask about you. And, if not, you'll be my wing woman."

"Fine, fine," I agree half-heartedly. "I'll go. But, only because you are always there for me."

We arrive at the psychic's home and I'm pleasantly surprised to see that she resides in an incredibly classy (and expensive looking) Victorian estate in upscale Naperville.

"Well, this is quite different from the shacks we've seen along the highway with the signs for Palm Reading." I say, slightly impressed.

"Yeah, maybe she wins the lottery every year to support herself," Morgan giggles as she parks the car in the large driveway. "She doesn't go by a cheesy name like Madame Ruby, either. Her name is Kim, just Kim. Please, be on your best behavior, okay?"

"Of course, I'll behave myself. Now that I've seen where she lives, I'm feeling a lot better about this. Let's go in. I may even ask about Mayson."

Kim is a lovely woman in her late forties. She has gorgeous black hair, pinned up into a bun on the top of her head, her bangs sweeping across the olive skin of her forehead. She is stunning.

"Welcome, ladies," Kim greets us as we enter her large foyer. "And which one of you lovely young women is Morgan?"

"That's me," Morgan extends her hand to shake with Kim. Kim shakes Morgan's hand briefly with one hand, covering it with the other. She holds Morgan's hand for a moment, just long enough for Morgan to look to me, shrug her shoulders and grin. Kim releases Morgan's hands and looks to me.

"So you must be Daphne. I had a feeling when you walked through the door that you would be the one with man trouble." Hmmm, a psychic who 'sensed' something after the answer was already given to her? Wow, how impressive. Before I can even finish my sarcastic thought, Kim gives me a knowing smile,

"Darling, it has nothing to do with my abilities and everything to do with your pained expression. Miss Morgan here looks like she is content, at peace. You on the other hand look uncomfortable and anxious. Come, ladies, let's go to my sitting room and get better acquainted."

Blushing with embarrassment, I follow Morgan and Kim into the sitting room. Morgan takes my hand and whispers, "Just have a little faith, Daphne. You may even get some much needed answers tonight." I nod in submission.

Kim gestures for us to sit in two lovely armchairs, each draped with silken blankets. She sits on a small chaise lounge and again responds to my body language. Clearly I wear my heart on my sleeve. It is difficult for me to disguise my surprise at the atmosphere.

"Were you expecting a crystal ball?" Kim smiles warmly.

"Well, I don't know...maybe?" I respond, again discomfited by the psychic before me who is incredibly astute at reading other's emotions. Or maybe she's just seen it all.

"So, Morgan mentioned that you have some questions about a relationship you have started. Rest assured, I asked Morgan not to tell me any more than that. It can, many times, cloud my abilities if I know too much about a situation. It's always better for me to simply use my senses."

"Yes, well, maybe you could start with Morgan. I'm not really sure if I want to know anything or not." Morgan rolls her eyes at me. Apparently, she was hoping I would just go with the flow. She should know me better than that.

"Well, that is fine with me. So, let's see, Morgan. I can tell from your contented nature that you are currently in a healthy relationship. This is actually your first healthy dating relationship in quite some time. You have had a bit of a rough road with men. One in particular, I see was incredibly tall with several freckles on his nose—"

Morgan gasps and clutches her hand to her mouth. Kim is referring to Morgan's ex-boyfriend Brett. They dated in college and he treated her terribly; insulting her intelligence constantly especially in front of those she cared about. Morgan broke up with him about eight months into their relationship when she discovered he had cheated with three different members of her sorority. She was devastated and subsequently unable to trust the opposite sex for quite some time.

Kim's description was eerie. Brett was obscenely tall, about 6'5, towering over Morgan at only 5'2. He had a large cluster of freckles situated on his nose only, no freckles anywhere else on his body. Even though I haven't showed my surprise as obviously as Morgan, I am blown away. Perhaps I would let Kim talk to me after all.

"Shall I continue?" Kim asks, not at all alarmed by Morgan's response, but testing the comfort level in the room regardless.

"Yes, please," Morgan replies, inching closer to the chaise lounge.

"Alright then," Kim continues, "The man you are with is an incredibly motivated and driven person. He also cares for you immensely and dreams of a future with you. There will be a time when you doubt his motives, but rest assured he has your best interest at heart. He's good for you and his love is unwavering."

Morgan's eyes are wet as she smiles at Kim. This is what she was hoping to hear. She and Matt have been happy for a long time, but with her track record, I know she's afraid of what the future may bring and no amount of reassurance from me or others close to her will change that. Perhaps the predictions this evening will finally be what she needs in order to look towards a future with Matt.

"That's wonderful, Kim. Can you tell me anything about my career?"

"Hmm," Kim begins, "I don't see you continuing with your current company for longer than a few years. After all, you'll be pretty busy with other things."

"What kind of other things?" Morgan asks, confused.

"Are you sure you would like to know the specifics?"

"Yes," Morgan responds with confidence.

"I see you with your hands full, at home. I see you with babies."

"Did you say babies, as in more than one?" Morgan looks panicked.

"That is what I see. But, don't worry. You have several years yet before worrying about that." Kim flashes a knowing smile at Morgan.

"Just continue to live your life. Use your current work situation for what it is: excellent experience that you will come back to when the time is right. But, no, I do not see you there for longer than five years."

"Wow," Morgan looks bewildered, overwhelmed and a bit stunned. Kim smiles and looks to me.

"So, Daphne, have you decided whether or not you would like to talk with me?"

"Yes, I would like to know whatever you can tell me."

"Alright," Kim says. "You are a bit harder to read than Morgan. Do you have a timepiece or any other personal item that I may hold in my hand? This helps me to connect a bit with you. It doesn't always work, but it has helped me previously in cases such as this."

Quickly, I remove my watch and hand it to Kim. She smiles and holds it in the palm of her hand, closing her eyes briefly before looking at me with a smile.

"Puddin'?" She asks with a raised eyebrow. This time it is my turn to gasp.

"What did you say?" My eyes are wide, my mouth agape as I stare at Kim. Morgan giggles nervously.

"The man in your life, he calls you this? It's quite a cute nickname, I must say." She giggles softly.

"Yes, I think so, too." My cheeks grow hot. Shock is still coursing through my brain.

"He's not who I see, though." She sighs, "Not in your future."

My heart tumbles to the floor. This is what I have been dreading. That my anxiety over Mayson is well-founded; that he truly isn't the one for me.

"May I ask who you see?"

"Well, the man you are dating has sandy hair with very brilliant green eyes, yes?" I nod.

"Right, that is definitely not who I am seeing down the road. I am seeing a tall man with dark brown, chestnut hair. He is very handsome and cares deeply for you. He has a wonderful sense of humor and you enjoy one another immensely. He brings you peace and a tremendous amount of happiness, although you may not realize it when the relationship begins. It will take some time, but it will be worth it for you, for him, for both of you. He is the one I see."

Looking to Morgan, I fail to keep the tears from forming. Morgan gives me a sympathetic smile and mouths, "It's okay."

"I'm sorry," Kim says gently. "I know it can be awfully difficult to hear the opposite of what you were hoping for. Remember, not everything I see is 100% correct. However, when it comes to faces, I am confident in my abilities. The man who calls you Puddin' is not the one I see. That doesn't mean that you shouldn't pursue this relationship. Although, I can feel your caution with him and it is not without merit. I encourage you to continue with a reasonable amount of hesitation. But, know that you have a remarkable amount of happiness awaiting you in the future."

Morgan and I spend most of our car ride home in silence. She is grinning from ear to ear and I am more overwhelmed than ever. Finally, Morgan speaks.

"Daphne, this doesn't mean that things won't work out with Mayson. You know that, right? She admitted freely that what she sees isn't always accurate. You have to follow your heart."

"But, am I wasting my time Morgan? Am I just chasing the dream I've had since I was nineteen years old?"

"I have no idea. But, I do know that you need to give things with Mayson a real chance, or you'll never forgive yourself. No regrets, Daphne. You know that I'm not his biggest fan, but I also don't want you to sabotage the entire relationship because Kim, the supposed psychic, doesn't see him in your future."

"Then why have you not been able to stop smiling since we left her home?" I ask accusingly.

Morgan shrugs. "The good stuff is easier to believe."

Chapter 9
Flight

A month has passed since Mayson left my apartment so early in the morning. I haven't seen him in person, but we have Skyped several times and we've talked and texted on the phone almost daily. He's back in Denver now. I've never visited Colorado before, and seeing Mayson would be a great way to escape the boring summer break that I'm having, but I have not yet been invited. Perhaps it's too soon?

Elise has returned from her incredibly long honeymoon and is settled into life as a "Mrs." After waiting weeks to update her about Mayson, I'm thrilled to finally share things with my best friend. Digging into our salads, Elise listens intently as I pour my heart and soul to her. She knows Mayson better than any of my other friends do. If anyone can help me through this, it's Elise.

I don't share my visit to the psychic, partially out of embarrassment, but also because I'm not ready to face what Kim has told me about my impending future. I know Elise would never approve of putting my fate in another's visions of my future, anyway, so it's an easy detail to skip as I fill her in on all of the Mayson drama.

"Wow," she says, gazing at me with large eyes. "You've been quite the busy girl."

"I know! Thank God I haven't had to worry about work. If this was going to happen, I guess summer break is the best time. But, seriously, Elise, what have I gotten myself into?"

"Well, what does Morgan think?"

"She doesn't like him. But, she's doing her best to be supportive because she knows how drawn to him I am. And she doesn't want me to have any regrets." Elise throws me a questioning glance.

"What does your gut tell you? Is he bad news or do you think he is worth taking a gamble for?"

"So, I'm gambling my heart now?" I ask, pouting.

"Perhaps you are, Daphne. You know you two don't exactly have the prettiest track record. You were together, then he broke your heart and you tried to be friends. And, then…"

"True," I agree, interrupting her, "But, at this point, I think I'm too far gone. I want to see him again. I hope to see him again, at least." I stare at my fork, still hovering above my salad.

"What do you mean hope, Daph? Of course he wants to see you! You guys text every damn day!"

"Well, I know that. But, it's pathetic how much I look forward to his texts. I depend on them too much."

"I was afraid you were going to say something like that. Look, Daph, I'm not saying that this thing with Mayson is a bad idea. I haven't seen you two together in years. But, I can say this. I adore you, and your feelings matter to me----I will not stand by and watch you get your heart broken all over again and stay silent. I'm sorry if that's hard for you to hear."

I nod, knowing she's looking out for me.

"Do you promise to, at least, listen to me if I see any red

flags? This guy put you through the ringer. Don't forget that, alright?"

"Of course," I reply truthfully. "Thank you, Elise."

A few hours later, we are pulling into my small parking lot when I hear my phone "ding" — it's a text, and I know exactly who it's from.

"Hmm, wonder who that might be," Elise teases. "Perhaps his ears have been burning this afternoon."

My lips form a curious smile as I read the text. It's from Mayson and it's different from any other text I've received from him.

Check your mailbox.

After showing the text to Elise, we both giggle in surprise and run to my mailbox in front of the building. My heart skips a beat when I see the mail has already arrived. There are no packages. However, at the bottom of my pile of mail there is a large envelope. The postmark is from Denver. A large sticker with "delivery confirmation" flashes in bright green.

"What do you think it could be?" I ask, my heart thumping uncontrollably in my chest.

"There's only one way to find out. C'mon, get it over with!" Elise urges me.

I slowly rip open the envelope and find round trip airline tickets to New York City. If there is one city in this country that I have wanted to visit during my lifetime, it is NYC. My heart is doing flip flops inside of my chest.

"Holy crap, Daphne, you're going to spend a weekend in New York! That is so romantic. Is there anything else in the envelope?"

Tearing into it once again, I find a post-it note that must have fallen from the tickets.

Join me? --M

Still in shock, an enormous grin plastered onto my face, I grab my phone and send Mayson a simple text message: See you there.

Three days later, I arrive at the Four Seasons in New York City. In disbelief as I gaze around the lobby, I can't believe that I will be staying here for the next two days. It is truly a sight to behold, magnificent décor and beautiful flower arrangements placed on every available surface. My nerve endings have been twitching non-stop ever since I received Mayson's cryptic text. Breathing deeply, I search for the man who causes such excitement and anticipation in my heart.

"Daphne!" Mayson pops up from a leather chair. He is grinning, his hair freshly trimmed and face recently shaved. He looks incredible. He walks quickly to me before sweeping me up in his arms and spinning me around.

"Wow," I say, collecting myself when he releases me.

"You're finally here!" he says, sounding ecstatic. He leans in for a soft, gentle kiss. "I feel like I haven't seen you in so long!" he whispers as he presses his forehead to mine.

"It's great to be here," I manage to say, feeling incredibly overwhelmed with joy.

"Come on. Let's get your luggage upstairs. Then we can explore the city together. Some incredible buildings in this town! I want to show you everything. Absolutely everything!"

Mayson is energetic, smiling and humming to himself as we stroll through the streets of New York. As he points out buildings and elements of architecture that he finds remarkable, I am completely wrapped up in him once again. I want these moments to last forever.

When we reach Central Park, I am in awe, unable to stop looking around at all of the lovely scenery before us. Movies have depicted this beautiful park but it's like nothing I have ever seen on screen. Completely enamored and swept up in the moment, I reach up to Mayson and plant a kiss on his cheek.

"You've wanted to come here for a long time. I remember that." He smiles, a dimple forming in his cheek. He wants to please me. All this time, I have been thinking about how on earth I will please him. Is it possible that he is feeling the exact same way? Are we making up for lost time? All those years that we could have been together, but instead were held apart by circumstance, are they finally coming to an end? Will I get my happily ever after?

"You've been remembering a lot of things, Mayson. It's a little unnerving."

"Oh," he looks slightly shamed, as if he has been scolded. I quickly rephrase.

"Don't misunderstand. I love it. Every single thing you have remembered about me, I love. I always felt…" The words hang off my lips. Spoiling this moment would be something I would regret for years to come and I wasn't ready to risk it. I have had enough regret, especially when it comes to this man opposite me.

"Say it, Daphne. Whatever it is, I want to hear it." His eyes are pleading with me. He wants the truth. Taking a quick, deep breath, I am ready to be honest.

"I always felt as if you were the alpha in the relationship and I--"

"You thought I was the what? The *Alpha*? Meaning that I ran the show?"

"Quite simply, yes." I respond honestly. He looks perplexed as I question him, "Can you disagree?"

Mayson sits on a nearby bench, collecting his thoughts. "I guess you have a point. I've always been pretty stubborn. But, you must know by now that I listened, I paid attention."

"Yes, you did, Mayse. You really did." The flowers, the trip to New York, he did remember who I once was. And he does know parts of who I still am. But, it still doesn't feel like enough. There was so much more that I was holding back, afraid of scaring him away, afraid of losing him again.

"Look, Daphne. I'm not perfect. I know that. I can be selfish, inconsiderate and a bunch of other not-so-pleasant things. But, I do care. And I do want to be better."

"Thank you," I muster, completely blown away by his response.

"Now, can I be honest with you?" he asks, gazing into my eyes, a bit of a playful smirk on his lips. God, he is so sexy.

"Of course you can." I brace myself, afraid of what I might hear next.

"You have to stop punishing me for what I did when we were in college. I was nineteen years old when we broke up, and twenty one when we slept together before graduation. I'm not the same person that I was. I'm flawed, of course. But, who isn't? I can't magically make you forget how I behaved, but this relationship isn't going to go anywhere if you're apprehensive to be with me here, right now." His eyes pleading, he leans in to my neck and kisses my earlobe. He whispers softly, "Be with me here. Now. Please, Daphne."

Swept up in the moment, I submit to him. No longer wanting to cling to the past, to think of what could have been. I am ready to be with Mayson here and now. Slowly, holding hands as we walk, we make our way back to our hotel and to the room that has been waiting for us.

"I've missed you," I smile, trying my best not to let my eyes well with tears. My emotions are overwhelming as Mayson and I lay face to face in the large, majestic bed, the silky sheets barely covering us as we gaze at one another with sleepy eyes.

"Me too, beautiful," he responds, caressing my shoulders making me squirm in the best possible way.

It's Sunday morning and soon our fantasy weekend will come to an end. We will board separate planes, headed to separate destinations. With all the strength that I have, I refrain from asking how we'll proceed from here. Desperate to stay in this moment with Mayson, I'm once again pushing away my true wants, my true needs. My heart sinks as I realize just how much of myself I've been keeping from him, simply afraid of making him run for the hills. And so, I cling desperately to this beautiful man before me, and hold back my questions, my concerns, my fears.

"This is one of the most romantic weekends of my life. Thank you, Mayse." I say, stroking his cheek. "Thank you for planning this for me, for us."

"My pleasure, Puddin.'" He smiles. "It has been magnificent. You…you are magnificent." His voice is especially husky with this last sentence, and his passion consumes me. Swept away, yet again, by the surprising emotions of Mayson, I flush and grin from ear to ear.

"I have a confession to make, Mayse."

"Uh oh," he furrows his brow, suddenly looking serious.

"I lied to you when I said that our first time wasn't my first time. It was."

"Thank goodness, I'm not crazy!" he says in relief. "Although, now I really feel like a piece of shit; I took your virginity and never called. Oh, Daph, I'm so sorry. I wish there was something I could do to make it up to you, something I could say."

"Should I have kept that to myself?" I ask, wishing I hadn't said a word. But, I needed to. I needed him to know.

"No, absolutely not, I'm glad you told me. I just wish I hadn't been so, I don't know, thoughtless with you. I wish I had made it special…or that we hadn't done it at all."

"You regret it?" I ask, my heart tearing in shreds. How could he regret it? I certainly don't…only what happened afterward.

"No, Daph, of course not. I just wish your first time had been special."

"But, it was, Mayse. It was with *you*." I smile and he smiles back at me with a large and compassionate grin. With newfound confidence, I decide to ask the question I've been dreading all weekend, "Hey, I have a big favor to ask."

"Um, okay," Mayson says, looking pensive and concerned.

"I have a wedding to attend in a couple of weeks. I would love for you to be my date."

"Where is it?" he asks. Such an odd question, really.

"Um, it's being held in Chicago."

"Who's getting hitched?" he seems to be relaxing at the idea of accompanying me.

"My friend Phillip is marrying a fabulous girl named Janna. It is going to be in Lincoln Park at a very cool locale near Montrose Harbor. It should be beautiful."

"And you don't have a date?" he teases.

"Nope," I say, biting my lip and shaking my head with a pout.

"Of course, Miss Daphne Harper, I would love to be your date." He smiles warmly and kisses me on my shoulder. Breathing a huge sigh of relief, I glance at the clock and quickly bolt back to reality.

"We should get dressed, Mayson. Our flights will be leaving before we know it," I say, glancing back at the clock, wishing the numbers could be frozen for just a little while longer. Slowly, I sit up and throw the sheets off of me.

"Not so fast, Puddin'," he replies with a devilish smirk that makes my toes curl. "I'm not quite finished with you yet." And just like that, I am swept up in Mayson all over again as he kisses me passionately, pulling me back to the bed.

That afternoon, I am extremely close to missing my flight because of our final moments in bed but, it was totally worth it. Nothing can wipe this smile from my face. For five years, I have dreamed of being with Mayson. My dreams are finally coming true. As the plane soars through the sky, my heart is soaring as well, dreaming of my future with Mayson; a future that I hope begins soon.

Chapter 10
Senior Year (Spring Semester)

It's two nights before graduation and all of my friends are gathering at our favorite campus bar, Legends. Unfortunately, Legends holds many memories of Mayson and I and so visiting this bar right before finishing college feels bittersweet. But, I'm determined to celebrate and not to think about him at all. Besides, he's still in France.

Or maybe not.

Mayson is leaning up against the bar, talking with some of his friends who I remember from the dorms. He looks different to me. He's wearing trendy glasses, the kind with the tortoise-shell and rigid angles. He's also wearing a button down shirt with bright vertical stripes and fancy chinos. What happened to my sweatshirt-wearing gorgeous ex-boyfriend? He seems to have been replaced by a stylish new model.

Frozen in my tracks, I'm not sure what to do. As far as I know, he hasn't seen me. But, we're standing only a few feet from one another, so that seems likely to change. Why didn't he get in touch to tell me that he had returned? No call, no email? My heart sinks knowing that he didn't feel the need to contact me. I need to clear my head.

"Is that who I think it is?" asks Elise, stirring her vodka cranberry.

"Yeah," I say, still watching him, admiring him while trying desperately to push the lump in my throat down, down, down.

"He looks different," Elise observes.

"I know," I respond, nodding.

"Are you going to talk to him?"

"I don't think I can handle it, Elise,"

I glance back at him for just a second. In that moment, our eyes meet. The corners of his lips twist a bit in recognition as he nods his head slightly towards me.

"What the hell was that?" Elise asks.

"You saw it, too?" I ask, focusing back on Elise, "I have no idea what to do. I feel like I'm going to have an anxiety attack right here in the middle of the freaking bar."

"He's still staring at you, Daph. He's being really obvious about it, too."

"Are you serious?" My heart is racing, but instead of anxiety, excitement is building slowly in the pit of my stomach. He's staring at me. This is a good thing.

"Dead serious." Elise nods. "You need to look at him. Come on, see for yourself."

With that, I slowly turn my gaze towards Mayson. He smiles as if proud of himself. Our eyes lock for what feels like several minutes.

"Go over there," Elise insists, nudging my arm.

"No way, if he wants to play games with me, I can do that. I'm not giving him control. Who knows how long he's been back on campus. No calls, no emails. So, now, I will wait and see. I'll wait to see how he'll proceed." As I finish talking, Mayson slowly raises his beer towards me, winking. I raise mine in reply and give him a smug smile.

He nudges his friend and walks over towards me. My

mouth is suddenly bone dry. I've won our little game, but now I have no idea what to say. I wonder if I'll even be able to speak.

"Hey there, Puddin'."

When we were together, I always teased him about his South Carolina accent. It is thick tonight. I can tell he has had quite a bit to drink already. Buzzed or not, I'm thrown by his affectionate tone. I hadn't expected to ever hear that nickname again after our break-up. Even though we'd attempted to maintain a "friendship", that friendship was incredibly one-sided. Over this past year, most of my emails to France had gone unanswered…and the ones I did receive were distant and cold. It was only when we chatted online that things were warmer, like they were when we were together.

"Well, if it isn't the world traveler?" I say, trying my very best to sound casual, easy, although my hands are shaking, as are my words. Too many conflicting thoughts are racing through my confused brain. "How was France? I didn't realize you'd be back so soon."

"Yeah, we finished up a few days ago. Administration insisted we arrive back in time for convocation. Can you believe we're done here? In a couple of days we have to join the real world," he declares with that sexy grin of his. God, I love him. Despite everything, I cannot deny how he makes me feel.

"So, will you be headed back to South Carolina?"

"Yep. But, I've sent resumes all over the country, especially to the Denver area. You know how I love to ski. I always imagined that's where I'd live. How about you, Daphne? Where are you headed?"

"Back home to Chicago. I'm going to live with my parents until I hopefully start teaching in the fall. I haven't found anything yet, but I'm trying not to worry."

"Oh, you'll find something," he assures me. I suddenly realize that Mayson is making his way closer to me by the second. Soon, I'll be able to feel his breath on my skin and I'm looking forward to it. I tilt my head in order to be even closer to this boy I've missed for so very long, concern and hesitation be damned.

"So," he continues, "You want to go somewhere less crowded? You know, for old time's sake?"

"Sure, why not?" I answer, giving him the most confident smile I can possibly muster. Secretly, I wonder how much of our encounter has already been fueled by alcohol. After all, I can hear it in his drawl and I can smell it on his breath.

We walk, hand in hand, back to his apartment on Green Street. The entire walk there, we talk about his months spent in France. I've always wanted to go overseas and Mayson is enjoying my enthusiasm. He tells me all about the gorgeous buildings that have been there for centuries, the amazing museums and the incredible culture. Completely fascinated, I find myself hanging on his every syllable.

Back at his apartment, we slip back into old routines very quickly. Snuggling up in his bed, he twirls my hair around his fingers. Rubbing my hands softly on his bare chest, my heart races and adrenaline courses through me. It feels incredible.

"I missed you, you know," he whispers softly. His heart is pounding. I can feel it through his shirt.

"Yeah, me too. You were so far away this year."

"No, I mean, I've missed you since, you know, since we broke up."

"Really, you did?" I sit up with a start. "Then, why...?" I'm unable to finish the sentence. I just sit, bewildered, staring into his green eyes, searching desperately for an answer.

"I don't know, Daph. For some reason, it didn't feel right and it was freaking me out. I thought I needed to be with my buddies and keep my head in the game. It didn't help that my parents had been on my case about how bad my grades got when we were dating. And then when I went home for Spring Break..."

"So, you didn't stop loving me?" I inquire softly. I had convinced myself that he simply lost interest, and that he didn't care. I couldn't believe that I may have been wrong for two years.

"Well, to be honest, I thought I had. I really thought so. But, seeing you tonight, it sort of, I don't know, brings back some really good memories." He chuckles, pushing my hair out of my eyes. He rubs the pad of his thumb on my earlobe, slowly moving his hands down to my neck. His caresses transport me back to a place that I have yearned for, hoped for, wished for.

"So, what do we do now, Mayse?" Deep down, my conscience is screaming at me, knowing that taking this any further would be a terrible idea. He is drunk, and that is all. And I, well, I am unbelievably sensitive, and not quite ready to give up on my first love.

"Well, now, I think we should just see what happens," he murmurs, leaning in to kiss me. Kissing his lips feels inconceivable, and still so much like home. Excited yet panicky, I can't let go. I can't pull away. This magnetic force between us is pulling me to him even though I know I should be running from his apartment screaming. This will not end well, Daphne!

"I've missed you, Daphne. Really missed you," he whispers into my ear, planting delicate kisses along the earlobe he just caressed a moment earlier. His hot breath trails from my ear to my shoulder blade, where he is slowly pulling the neckline of my blouse to the side. He nibbles at and nuzzles my pale skin.

"I've always wanted to count these freckles," he laughs to himself. "Let's see...one...two…"

With each freckle he locates, he plants a tiny kiss, causing the hair on my arms to stand at attention. I find myself accommodating his kisses, unable to stop his quest to count them all. He is so determined, so sexy and so intent on driving me wild.

He fixes his eyes on me and reaches for the hem of my blouse. Gripping the soft, cotton fabric, he fiercely rips it off my body. I gasp, biting my lip, waiting to see what he'll do next.

"I want you, Daphne." His eyes lock with mine and I am completely his, completely willing to do whatever he wishes.

We make love for the first time, my *very first* time. It feels like it'll be the most incredible yet most heart wrenching experience of my life. I know that the morning light will bring disappointment and despair when I have to say goodbye to Mayson, possibly for the rest of our lives. As I drift off to sleep, I convince myself that this is all worth it. I had wanted Mayson to be my first for years. My wish has finally been granted. But, I'm not at all ready to let go of him.

The next morning, I wake up feeling unbelievably awkward. Mayson is snoring quietly beside me. I have no idea what to do. For several minutes, I lay stunned, hoping that he'll to awaken, take me in his arms and make promises for the future, our future.

But, something in the pit of my stomach tells me that this will not work out. Attempting to leave as quietly as possible, so as to avoid an uncomfortable confrontation, I roll quietly to the edge of the bed. The rusty springs in the mattress squeak and Mayson lets out a contented sigh. He is awake. Crap. All at once, I'm terrified that he might not even remember that I'm here.

"Morning," he says, rubbing his eyes aggressively.

"Hi. Sorry to wake you." I say, trying to hide the relief in my voice, "I was trying to be quiet."

"Not a problem. Hey, how are you doing this morning, you know, with everything that happened? No regrets, I hope?"

"No, I don't think so. Last night was very nice. I just can't believe that we're both leaving campus after Graduation tomorrow. We're off to start our lives, huh?" I ramble, pushing my feelings deep down within myself.

"Thank God!" he declares, sitting up in bed, leaning against the wall. I hang my head in shame after hearing those words. Mayson obviously isn't agonizing over our impending separation.

He notices the expression on my face and backpedals, "No, Daphne, I didn't mean it that way. I'm just ready to start my career. After all this work, I need to have something to show for it, ya know?"

"Sure, I get it." My eyes search the room for my shoes. I need to keep them occupied so that tears don't form.

"We'll be in touch, right?" he asks casually. It feels like a knife is piercing straight through my fragile heart. Last night had meant nothing more to him than two old flames rekindling a romance for old time's sake. Even though he had said those same words the night before, almost exactly, it is still a surprise to know that he really meant them. I had hoped for so much more. I had hoped for forever.

"Yes, I'd like that. Listen, I have to head home. I have so much packing to do before my parents arrive tomorrow for the ceremony. But, I have your parents' phone number."

"Oh yeah, I have your parents' address and phone, as well. We should definitely email, though."

Unfortunately, I already know what it was like to have an email relationship with Mayson and I'm in no hurry to revisit that scenario.

"Sure." I lean in to kiss him softly on the cheek, trying to hide the clear disappointment spread across my exhausted and troubled face. Standing, I walk to his front door and say goodbye to the boy I love.

Chapter 11
Wedding (Present Day)

"You're *not* serious," Mayson laughs. "You must be exaggerating!"

"I'm not, I promise," I confirm, shaking my head. We're driving to Phillip and Janna's wedding. It's a gorgeous day; perfect for a wedding ceremony.

"Were you trying to catch every single bouquet? Am I going to stumble upon some crazy collection of dried out bouquets in your kitchen cabinets or something? I don't think I can handle that, Daph." He's cracking himself up. I, on the other hand, don't find it nearly as humorous as Mayson does.

"No, it's the strangest thing. Honestly, aside from the first few that I caught, I deliberately tried *not* to catch the damn things. It's like they had minds of their own."

"Or your friends are trying to mess with you." Mayson is such a theorist. I have a feeling he won't drop this conversation until he feels he's reached a plausible explanation for my extraordinary talent.

"Well, considering I wasn't friends with every single bride, I don't know about that theory, Mayse. It's simply an odd gift, or curse, depending upon how you view it."

"Well, now I can't wait to watch the bride toss her bouquet tonight. I have to see what happens," Mayson teases.

"Hmm, maybe I'll need to visit the ladies room when the DJ announces the toss," I ponder, smiling at the road in front of me.

"Oh no, you don't!" Mayson tickles me on the leg, "I need to see this firsthand! You can't avoid it! I'm fascinated now and want a good show!"

Sure enough, three hours later, Mayson and I are enjoying a couple of glasses of wine when it's time for the garter and bouquet tosses. I groan.

"Show time!" Mayson laughs, pulling me towards the dance floor.

First is the garter toss. All single men are asked to come to the dance floor. When Mayson does not budge, I glare at him.

"What?" he asks incredulously.

"I'm not going to suffer alone," I tease. "Get your ass out there!"

"Oh," he says, "Right, I guess I'd better take one for the team."

Mayson strolls confidently towards the rest of the single men on the dance floor. He's cool, collected, and grinning like hell at me. Phillip seductively strips Janna of her garter and tosses it over his shoulder. It lands right in Mayson's hands. I turn a hundred shades of pink. I can even feel my toes blushing.

Mayson twirls it in his fingers, gives me a naughty grin and says, "I guess it's official. You're sharing your curse."

"Holy crap!" Shocked, I stare at the dainty piece of fabric with an adorable blue charm. "Now, get your sexy ass out there and see if you can avoid the bouquet. I've gotta say, though, I don't see that happening!" Mayson smiles. He's teasing me, so I decide to give it right back to him.

"What makes you think I'm going to avoid it this time? Maybe I want to catch it now." I am no longer the one who's blushing. Mayson glances at the floor and then glances back at me. For some reason, his eyes look conflicted. Perhaps I've gone too far.

"I dare you," he says boldly, staring me straight in the eye. My knees feel weak. He has called my bluff. I didn't expect that at all. Could it be that Mayson is falling as hard for me as I am for him? Is it possible that he isn't afraid of a future with me? Or is he just being a royal, stubborn pain in the ass? I assume it's the latter and head towards the other single ladies congregating behind the bride. It is a big group this time and I secretly wish there was less competition to worry about.

At the last second, I decide to purposely avoid the bundle of flowers and take a couple of steps back, but I'm pushed forward quickly by a couple of giggling teenage girls, just dying to get the bouquet so that they can marry Edward, or Jacob or whoever they're arguing about.

Janna tosses the bouquet in the air. The woman in front of me jumps up like she's going to spike a volleyball, reaching as high as she can. The flowers spring from her fingertips and tumble down, bouncing off the shoulder of a bridesmaid. The air in my lungs escapes me as the bouquet finally lands perfectly in my hands. In shock, I have to grab the base of the handle before it tumbles to the ground. I don't want the teenagers to rumble.

Not knowing whether to feel triumphant or sheepish, I walk towards my date holding the beautiful batch of hot pink gerbera daisies in my hands with a look that screams 'I told you so'. Mayson shakes his head and chuckles to himself.

"Wow," he says, "Maybe the universe really is trying to tell you something, Daphne. But, I--"

Mayson isn't able to finish his sentence as the DJ is ushering us out into the center of the floor to take a picture with the bride and groom, him with his garter, and me with my bouquet. I am embarrassed, but thrilled. Perhaps the universe is speaking to me. And, perhaps it's time to listen.

Mayson and I spend the rest of the reception dancing closely to every song played. He gazes into my eyes and gives me soft kisses. Stroking my face with his hands, he pulls me tight and breathes in deeply.

"Thank you for bringing me, Daph," he says with a serious tone.

"I'm so happy you were able to join me." I muster, suddenly feeling uncomfortable with the look in his eyes.

"Me too. I feel like one day, we may be looking back on this night. What about you?"

Gazing into his gorgeous eyes, his pensive smile and his light pink cheeks, I want so desperately to tell him how I'd like nothing more than to look back on this night, the night he caught the garter and I the bouquet, the night we realized we were meant to be together. But, I can't. I'm still too terrified to believe that any of this is real. I'm waiting for us to crash and burn, and as much as I know that I need to open myself up to loving Mayson again, I just can't.

And so, I smile awkwardly and say, "That would be nice."

Mayson breathes a heavy sigh and holds me close as we sway on the dance floor. I'm in love with this man. I hope to one day be able to tell him how much I care without feeling as if my emotions will swallow me whole, leaving me a lonely and bitter shell of a woman when he inevitably leaves me again. I hope…. I hope.

Chapter 12
Thanksgiving

Mayson and I have been seeing each other for four months now. It hasn't been easy. Being halfway across the country from the man whose touch I yearn for is almost heartbreaking at times. We text, we talk on the phone, but it is never quite enough. We've only seen one another twice since he accompanied me to Phillip's wedding. He was called back to campus to fix structural problems with the project he was running, and each time I was grateful that mistakes had been made. Each time, I dropped everything that I was doing; lesson plans were put on hold, time with friends was postponed, and admittedly, I called in sick one Friday in order to drive three hours to see him.

Our visits have been rushed, there isn't nearly enough time for us to spend together as Mayson balances his relationship with me and the expectations given to him by his firm. I am fully aware that I need to take second seat. I've accepted the role and I'm no longer resentful. It has become my reality. And, in full disclosure, I am pleased to have whatever time I can get with Mayson. Despite my intentions, I am pining for him constantly. Thinking about him when I should be working, daydreaming of a future together when I should be planning my future as an educator. I'm lost in him, happily taking whatever I can get from the relationship I have willingly accepted. This is a long distance situation and at this point, it is too soon to be discussing relocation for either of us. And deep down, I know that if anyone will be uprooting their life, it'll be me. Mayson has always wanted to live in Colorado, and his position is a highly coveted spot. He and I both know that I can teach anywhere.

But, a new school year has begun. It's November, and I'm locked in until at least May of next year. Knowing this, I'm able to relax and not put too much pressure on myself to make any decisions with Mayson regarding our future plans. We are able to move along at a snail's pace, which, for the most part, is quite comfortable and fulfilling; flirty phone conversations, sensual text messages and friendly email banter has become our norm.

The Thanksgiving holiday is quickly approaching and I am excited to have an entire week off of work as our school district traditionally holds a "fall break" for both students and faculty for the entire week of Thanksgiving. I know where I want to be for Thanksgiving, I only hope Mayson will feel the same.

I walk into my apartment, knowing my phone will ring shortly. Mayson calls me from work almost daily, right around 4:00 pm my time. The sound of the telephone ringing each afternoon is the highlight of my day! Just as I finish putting some fresh produce in my refrigerator, I hear the phone ringing. Right on time.

"Hey beautiful," Mayson says in a husky, sexy tone.

"Hi stranger," I reply, "How's work today?"

"Ah, same old, same old. Nothing too exciting. Just a few more hours and I'm going to go for a really long run to relax.

Thanks for those new songs, by the way. They're a little crazy, but they keep me moving."

"I'm glad you like them." I smile, "Nicky Minaj grows on you, doesn't she?"

"Yeah, I guess she does," I can tell he's smirking on the other end of the line. He always thought I had crazy taste in music. Eclectic doesn't even begin to describe me. Raised on the Beatles and Bruce Springsteen, I am a classic rock junkie. But, when I am running, it's an entirely different story---I need loud, seam busting music with ridiculous lyrics. Mayson had never heard of half the artists I listened to until one morning down on campus when he woke up early for a run. He had forgotten his iPod so, he borrowed mine. He said it was the best run he'd had in months. I continued to recommend songs to him. Secretly, I enjoyed influencing his music choices.

"So, Mayson," I begin, "I've mentioned to you that my fall break is coming up at the end of the month." I pause hoping that he'll say something, but there is only silence on the other end of the line. I'm forced to continue, "I would love to spend Thanksgiving with you, Mayse."

For a moment, there is nothing but more silence. Heartbreaking silence that sends uncomfortable flips through my abdomen. Finally, he speaks. "You know I would love that. But, I sort of promised my parents that I would come to South Carolina for Thanksgiving, and they aren't quite, um, ready to meet anyone yet. My mom is big on family-only holidays. My older brother had a habit of bringing around a lot of different girls to family holidays and Mom finally drew the line. I'm really sorry."

His answer, although incredibly plausible, makes me feel uncomfortable. Is he ashamed of me, ashamed of our relationship? Or am I just not important enough to fight for once again? Before allowing myself to get too upset, I remember our conversation in New York.

You have to stop punishing me for what I did when we were in college.

Pulling myself together, I muster up my strength and answer casually, "Oh, alright. That's fine. My mom can be particular about certain things, too. She'll probably be thrilled when she finds out I'll be here."

"Are you okay?" he asks. I can hear the concern in his voice.

"Yes, don't worry. It's totally fine. Besides, I wouldn't want to miss my mom's sweet potato souffle, it's really fantastic."

"Yum. I'd love to taste it someday," he replies, sounding hopeful. I can't figure this man out.

"Listen, Daph, I had better run. I have a meeting with a potential client in a few minutes and I need to get my act together. I'll do my best to call tonight after my run, alright?"

"Good luck with your client, Mayson."

"Thanks, babe."

As I hang up the phone, my heart sinks, but I can't allow it to pull me under. I have to trust Mayson. We've been together for months now, and aside from his admitted self-centered nature, he hasn't done anything to hurt me. No promises have been broken, no betrayal has taken place. We're simply finding our bearings and trudging through long distance as best we can. We're learning together.

Chapter 13
Knock

"Be careful, that ornament belonged to Grandma!" I hiss as Morgan retrieves the fragile glass sphere from the large plastic bin at her feet.

"Wow, you are really edgy today, Daph. What's up with you? Where's your holiday cheer? We're decorating your apartment for the holidays and you're in a snit!"

"I'm sorry. It's not you, honestly. Let me turn on some music. That will help." I need Christmas carols desperately right now. We've been listening to the same CD of carols for decades. It's a special tradition that always manages to get me into the holiday spirit. It's the day after Thanksgiving. Instead of waiting in the insane lines and shopping with the crazies, Morgan and I haul out all of our Christmas décor and decorate one another's places. But, things with Mayson are getting to me and I'm inadvertently taking it out on one of my favorite people in the world.

"It's fine. Do you want to talk about it?" Morgan asks

hesitantly, probably afraid of the possible meltdown that could ensue.

"It's Mayson, obviously. Things are just…off."

"What do you mean?" she asks, seeming genuinely curious by these words.

"He's just different, somehow. Ever since I brought up the possibility of traveling to Denver for Thanksgiving, he's been acting odd."

"Guilt, perhaps?"

"Possibly, but it feels like more. It feels like…"

"College?" Morgan knew me so very well.

"Exactly. He pulled away from me then, and this feels just like that. It's agonizing. The phone calls are shorter. The texts are less affectionate. And I know this sounds silly, but he hasn't called me Puddin' at all since the conversation about Denver. That's exactly what he did last time. It's overwhelming, like an old wound is being opened once again. It's all just too much."

"Can you talk to him about it?"

"I want to, but I can't say anything. He hates when I bring up what happened at school. He made me promise to stop going backwards with us."

"He does have a point. But, that doesn't mean you should ignore your feelings. Just be careful how you express them."

"I can feel myself building a wall to protect myself, to protect my heart. I can't let it get broken again. I have this feeling in the pit of my stomach that I'm going to regret ever dancing with him at Elise's wedding."

"Ok, you are spiraling now, Daph. Take a deep breath. I know this guy has hurt you so much in the past, but that is in the past. You need to leave it there if you're going to have a future with him. The question is, is he worth it?"

"God, I hope so."

That evening, completely exhausted from hours of decorating and holiday cheer with my cousin, I plop myself into my soft, leather reading chair and grab my kindle from the coffee table. It's time to read a nice, relaxing book, forget all about my troubles and lose myself in a story. Delving into the plot of my novel, listening to Damien Rice singing softly, my thoughts drift once again to Mayson. I am falling for him, deeply. And it scares me to death.

A strong knock on my back door startles me and my heart races. Glancing at the clock, I see it's already 9:00 pm. Who could be here at this hour? I glance through the peep hole and see Mayson on the other side of the door. My heart flips into my throat. Completely overwhelmed, I open the door.

"Surprise," he says shakily.

"Wow, Mayson, what are you doing here?"

"I had to see you. May I come in?" He asks, looking unsure of what the answer will be.

"Of course, yes." My pulse is speeding rapidly, completely off the charts. Adrenaline is coursing through my body as I have no idea what to think. For weeks I've been preparing for my demise with Mayson, but here he is, standing in my apartment, shivering from the Midwestern chill.

"You must be freezing," I say, running to get a blanket. Before, I can take two steps, Mayson grabs my hand. He twirls me around into his arms. I giggle, falling backwards into his firm chest.

"I've missed you. I've missed that incredibly sexy laugh." He says, staring into my eyes.

So badly, I want to tell him how much I've missed him, but the words won't come. Terrified of saying too much, of drawing parallels from the past, I muster a small smile.

"It's wonderful to see you, too, Mayse."

Several hours later, we're lounging on the couch, watching a romantic comedy. Feeling a bit more confident, I ask the question I've wanted to ask, needed to ask since he arrived at my door. It's the elephant in the room and we both know it. It's time to get rid of the elephant.

"Did you have a nice Thanksgiving?"

"No, I didn't, Daphne." He says, his eyes darkening. Suddenly, I feel like he's upset with me. But, that doesn't make any sense. After all, I wanted to spend the holiday together.

"Why is that?" I ask, confused.

"I didn't get any of that sweet potato soufflé you told me about. Why do you think I hopped on a plane today? I just had to try it," He winks at me, his rascally grin flashing, causing my cheeks to grow pink.

"Well, you could've had some yesterday. I make a pretty decent soufflé. And I'm sure the grocery stores in South Carolina have all the necessary ingredients." I say, terrified that I've not only exposed the elephant in the room, but also tied a bright pink feather boa to its trunk. Mayson doesn't hesitate. He nods and takes a deep breath. He is clearly prepared for this conversation. Perhaps he knows me better than I give him credit for.

"I know. I'm really sorry. But, I'm here now. And I did a lot of thinking as I sat at my Mother's dining room table last night, wishing you were there with me."

I try to keep the air in my lungs as he says these words, but I cannot. Shock fills me as I stare at him wondering if my bottom lip is on the floor.

"Really?" My voice is soft and hoarse.

"Yes, Daphne, you silly girl. I wish you had been there with me. I wish I could've introduced you to my family. I wish I could've held your hand at the dinner table while my dad carved the bird. I wish a lot of things had been different about that day..." His words fade and he looks away briefly, guilt spread across his face.

He pauses, before continuing, "But, most importantly, I need to tell you something that I realized yesterday." He says softly, gently stroking my cheek with his hand. I look at him expectantly.

"I love you, Daphne...so much." Mayson's eyes are glossy. He looks at me expectantly.

My world stops. I can't believe what I'm hearing. The words I've hoped to hear for so many months, so many years since this gorgeous man walked into my life, have just been spoken. But, now that I'm hearing them, I am beyond conflicted. All of the cold phone calls, the short text messages, everything that has happened since he came back into my life are invading my brain and I'm incapable of ignoring them. Desperately, I try to tear down the wall I've built, but it sticks. It's too strong, I can't break it down. Not yet. And so, I answer him the very best that I can.

"I'm *falling* in love with you, too, Mayson." His eyes sink to the floor and he shrugs.

"I guess I deserved that, Daphne." He shrugs again. "I know I haven't exactly been easy to deal with lately."

Searching for words to erase what I said, to make everything alright, I try desperately to say the three words that he wants to hear...but, I can't. They will not leave my lips. I'm too afraid; too terrified of regretting them after they've been said.

"Give me time, Mayson. You have me on such a roller coaster. When we are up, we are so, so up. Everything is amazing. But, when we are down...I feel absolutely lost and terribly weighed down with conflicted emotions."

My words trail off as I shrug my shoulders and put my hand in his. He clutches my hand tightly and nods, not looking at me. I place my head on his shoulder and we continue to watch the movie on the television screen.

Chapter 14
Mistake

I wake up the next morning and there is no sign of Mayson. His duffel bag is gone, his tooth brush is not on my sink, and I can no longer smell his woodsy scent in my bedroom. He has left me. I couldn't say the words that he needed to hear, and now he is gone.

Besieged with sadness, I throw myself on the couch, sobbing until I can no longer summon the energy to cry. Completely destroyed, I realize that this is all my own doing. I call Morgan, desperately needing someone to console me; to comfort me as I digest the fact that I've made the biggest mistake of my life.

"Honey, what happened?" she asks, walking into my apartment and wrapping her arms around me.

"Mayson showed up at my door last night. He told me he loved me," I say between sobs.

"Well, that's wonderful. Why on earth are you crying? And where's Mayson?"

"No, you don't get it. I couldn't do it. I couldn't say it back."

"But, you do love him, Daph. He should know that by now, even if you couldn't say the words. You've always loved that man." She rubs my back reassuringly as she speaks.

"I've messed it all up, Morgan. I put up a wall and I've blocked him out. And now, he's gone. He's just…gone."

"Honey, let me make you a cup of tea. Have you eaten anything?"

"No, I haven't. Tea would be nice, though." She nods, gives me a gentle smile and walks towards the kitchen, stopping as she glances at the counter top.

"Daph, have you been in here yet today?" Confused, I try desperately to dissect the look on her face. She holds up a simple piece of paper. It is a note from Mayson.

Dear Daphne,
I feel terrible that I'm leaving while you are still asleep. I have some things to think about. I promise I'll call you tomorrow. Please forgive me.
Love,
Mayson

"Well, at least he feels bad about leaving," Morgan places the notebook paper on my coffee table as I stare into space. "Honey, I don't want to make this any worse, but may I ask what you did say when he professed his love to you?"

"I told him that I was *falling* in love with him…." I say, glancing up at her with a sheepish expression.

"Ouch," she grimaces.

"I know," I reply, hanging my head. "You have no idea how badly I wanted to tell him that I love him. I do, I love him desperately. That's what terrifies me."

"So, why didn't you just say it?"

"Did you not hear what I said, Morgan? I'm afraid; so afraid that he will break my heart."

"But, he professed his love first. Wasn't that thrilling?"

"Yes, of course, but so confusing. He's basically been avoiding me since I asked to be with him at Thanksgiving. And now, he shows up and confesses his love. I panicked. What can I say?"

"Maybe you should call him. Tell him now. Better late than never?"

"No, in his note, he said he'd call me tomorrow. I know him well enough to know that he doesn't want me to contact him before then. Besides, he says he has to think things through." Hanging my head, I continue, "Maybe this is just too much for me, Morgan. Maybe I need something simpler, someone who doesn't make me feel like this."

"Like *what*, in love?" Morgan asks, surprised.

"No, of course I want to be in love. But, you have no idea how tortured this 'love' makes me feel. We're up, we're down. We're on, we're off. I can't keep up. I am constantly confused, bewildered, overwhelmed and panicked. I trust him one minute, but can't rely on him the next. Yes, he has said he loves me, but I have no idea what that even means to him. Maybe I should be with someone who doesn't make me feel so uneasy."

"Maybe," Morgan says unconvincingly. "Listen, I know you are feeling awful, but Matt and his friends are having a get together at the Cubby Bear. Maybe you'd feel better if you came out with us tonight. It could get your mind off of things with Mayson."

"But, what if he calls?"

"That's simple. Just bring your cell. You can step outside and talk to him if he calls. I hate to think of you sitting around in this apartment feeling like this. You look awful, Daph."

"Wow, thanks."

"He'll come around, Daph. He loves you. It will all work itself out. Let's go get your mind off of things, even if it's only for a few hours."

"Alright," I agree begrudgingly.

Later that evening, I'm finishing my third Long Island iced tea and dancing with Morgan to a local band. Buzzed is an understatement to describe my level of intoxication at this moment. I am feeling no pain whatsoever as I sway and bounce to the blaring music. Eventually, Matt and his friend, Evan, begin dancing with us. Matt swoops in and wraps his arms around Morgan. She leans in seductively and places her head on his shoulder. As they dance, Evan stands behind me and we dance and sway to the music together.

I can feel Evan closing the gap between us, placing his hands gently on my hips. His breath is hot against my neck as we begin to fall into rhythm with one another. I rock from left to right, inching closer and closer to him as the music pounds. Slowly, he twists me until we are face to face.

Evan is handsome in a frat-boy kind of way. His short brown hair spikes a bit at the front. His deep brown eyes are warm, but sexy, and I find myself wanting to attach myself to him, attach myself to something easier, something simpler than what I have with Mayson.

"You're really hot when you dance, Daphne." Evan says, looking deep into my eyes.

"Thanks, you're not so bad yourself." I reply, raising an eyebrow.

"I was hoping I'd see you here. Matt mentioned you've been seeing someone, but you seem pretty available tonight..."

Evan and I have crossed paths in the past, usually in settings such as these, but I've never paid him much attention. He's a laid back guy who seems to always be single. His sense of humor is sarcastic and he makes me laugh but, until tonight, I've never felt any type of spark with him. Whether it's the Long Island making its way through my bloodstream or the heartbreak that's consuming me, it doesn't matter. All I know is that this perfectly attractive and friendly guy has his hands on my hips and his eyes locked with mine. He's interested in more than just chit-chat or dancing. He wants me.

"Yeah, I'm available," I flirt.

Through my drunken haze, I'm jerked back to my meeting with Kim the psychic. She mentioned the man I would be with in the future. He would have brown hair. She also said it would take time for us to fall in love, to be happy. Overcome with emotion, I tell Evan that I need to use the washroom.

"Hurry back," he smiles.

Running to Morgan, I yank her from Matt's arms and drag her to the Ladies Room.

"What the hell is going on, Daphne?" Morgan is tipsy too. This conversation could be a challenge.

"What if Evan's the one, Morgan?" I shriek, clasping my hands together.

"What? You hardly seemed interested in him, Daphne. What are you talking about?"

"The psychic, Morgan! Remember the psychic? She said I was going to end up with a guy with chestnut hair. His hair is *dark brown*! That's chestnut, right?" I ask, staring into space. The Long Islands are disturbing the processing in my fuzzy brain.

"Yes, Daphne, chestnut is dark brown," Morgan rolls her eyes. "But, you don't even like him. You're just humoring him because you're upset about Mayson."

"But, remember, she said it would take some time for us to be happy!" The other women in the restroom are starting to look annoyed with my noise level but, we're in a bar, it's awfully loud and I've had way too much to drink, so I honestly do not care.

"Daphne, I don't know." Morgan shakes her head.

"I feel like this could be a sign."

"What kind of sign?" Morgan looks apprehensive.

"That Evan is the one for me. I need to give him time, that's all!"

"Look, Daph. I like Evan. He's actually a really cool guy. I would love it if you dated him. Hell, I'd be thrilled if you two fell in love. So, do whatever feels right. I'm done defending Mayson, especially since I don't even like the guy." I frown at her.

"Sorry, truth serum talking," she sighs, shrugging her shoulders, holding up her Long Island. "Look, let's go back to the guys and have funnn, Daphne." She slurs, looking up at the bathroom ceiling and stomping her right foot just a bit.

"Alright, let's go. But, if Evan and I fall in love, you and I will remember this night as the evening my future changed forever!"

"If we can remember it," she giggles.

Evan locks his hands with mine when I return to the dance floor. Placing them on his shoulders, I intertwine my fingers behind his neck and draw him closer. My lips part and he presses his mouth to mine. Our tongues dance along with our bodies on the dance floor. A little voice inside my head is yelling at the top of her lungs, begging me to stop, to check my cell phone, to call a cab back to my apartment, anything to pry myself off of this eager young man in front of me. But, I have no interest in listening to that voice. Evan is my escape. My intoxication and my yearning for something real, pull me towards him. He's my antidote for the pain and heartache that is Mayson.

We stumble into my apartment around 3:00 am, giggling and knocking things over as we make our way to my bedroom.

"God, Daphne, I've wanted you for so long," Evan mumbles into my neck.

"You have?" I pull away, looking into his eyes, searching for a sign that he's the man for me, desperately wishing that Kim had given me more information. I'm still incredibly intoxicated but am doing my best to justify this sudden attraction to a guy I've practically ignored for months.

"Well, yeah. I've been pestering Matt to set us up, but he told me the time wasn't right. I'm so glad things are finally happening with us." He runs his fingers through my hair and nibbles on my earlobe, before gazing into my eyes. The crease in his brow shows concern. "But, are you sure this is what you want? You're such a sweet girl. I don't want to ruin things by moving too fast if that's not what you're ready for."

"No, I want this, I promise," I insist, running my fingers through his hair. Evan smiles and scoops me up in his strong, muscular arms and carries me to my bed, placing me gently on top of the covers. He lies down slowly, drinking me in with his eyes. He looks positively elated and I'm instantly wrapped up in his happiness and his desire for me.

"Do you believe in soul mates?" I ask as Evan slowly opens the first three buttons of my top and slips his hand over the delicate lace of my bra.

"I'm not sure, Daphne. But, I'm definitely open to the idea." He strokes the skin of my breasts tenderly as he nibbles and sucks at my neck. His touch is extraordinary and he sends tiny shivers down my spine as his fingers continue to explore my breasts, my stomach, and my sides. Soon, all of my clothes are on the floor and I am pulling at Evan's pants, urging him to go further. Within a few short moments, we are twisting and turning beneath my cotton sheets. Evan pulls a condom from his wallet and hands it to me with a playful grin.

"I'm terrible with these things. Will you help me?" He looks so innocent in this moment, so sweet. Could he be the one? Could he be my soul mate?

I rip the foil package open and carefully roll the condom onto Evan. He groans and pushes me forward onto the bed with a sudden urgency. He enters me and I slowly become lost in his embrace, lost in the beautiful rhythm that our bodies are creating. His movements are fluid, sexy, tantalizing. My skin tingles with every touch of his hands, every twist of his hips and every kiss he plants on my lips.

The next morning, my room is spinning. I wish I could say that I have no memory of what happened last night, but that would be a blatant lie. I know he's still here; I can hear him breathing softly just a few inches away. Tears begin to pour from my eyes. What have I done? Somehow, in my drunken state, I thought that Evan was the dark haired man that Kim had predicted. But, deep within my soul, I know this isn't right. Staring at him as he sleeps, I know I feel nothing for Evan, absolutely no spark, no emotion, *nothing*. It was simply a mixture of alcohol, desire and very bad decisions that led me to having this man in my bed.

Mayson promised to call today and I'll have to decide whether or not to share what I've done. But, how can I possibly do that? How can I hurt him more than I already have? I will, most certainly, lose him if he knows about my drunken fling with Evan. The thought of that makes my stomach flip uncontrollably and I feel as if I'm about to vomit.

Running to the bathroom, I grasp the toilet seat, pushing it away from myself as I heave uncontrollably. Regret spills from my eyes with my tears. Sobbing into the toilet I can think of nothing but Mayson. Eventually I'm able to catch my breath.

After brushing my teeth, I sit back down on the bathroom floor, not wanting to go back to my room. I'm sure Evan is awake by now and I'm mortified; I don't want to confront my drunken mistake. Pressing the back of my head against the wall, I look up at the ceiling, wishing for a way out of all of this. How had I allowed things to become such an inconceivable mess?

A soft knock on the door startles me. "Daphne, are you okay? Can I get you anything?" he asks on the other side of the door. I reach up to open the door slightly and Evan peeks in. He's dressed in his clothes from last night and the tone of his voice tells me he's worried.

"Hey," he says softly. His face looks just as handsome as it did last night. If only that was enough.

"I'm so sorry," I reply, tears forming in my eyes.

Evan steps in and sits down next to me, putting his head

against the wall. He turns towards me and gently pushes the bangs from my eyes. I feel genuine warmth coming from his deep brown irises.

"You have nothing to be sorry for, Daphne. If anything, I should be the one who's apologizing. You were drunk last night, clearly," he says gesturing towards the toilet.

I can't help but giggle at his ability to find humor in this situation. He continues as he pats my knee lightly with his hand, "I feel like maybe I messed up my chances with you and that really sucks. You're such a great girl and I've liked you for a while."

"It's not you, Evan. I'm just really confused right now."

"I hear you," he says gently. His eyes skim over my body from head to toe, as he continues, "Aside from all of the emotional stuff, how are you feeling physically? I always drink a can of coke for a hangover because it settles the stomach. Toast helps, too. Can I make you some toast?"

Evan is attempting to take care of me. Knowing just how thoughtful, just how considerate this man is multiplies the guilt that continues to build inside of me.

"No, I'll be okay. I think I just need to be alone. Is that alright?"

Evan nods solemnly, "Sure, I understand. I'll leave my phone number on your counter, you know, in case you need anything."

"Thank you so much. Really, I--" tears are building in my eyes and I'm not really sure what to say to this man who wants to comfort me, who wants a chance with me. I'm unable to give him the reassurance he seeks.

"It's going to be okay. Really it is," Evan says.

Slowly, I muster up enough energy to walk him to the door. When he leaves, relief sweeps through me. Doing my best to push the clouds from my head, I'm determined to think clearly, to keep my relationship with Mayson intact. I refuse to lose him over this. Today, I'll do whatever it takes to make things right. I'll tell him that I love him, beg for

90

forgiveness, and tear down my wall. I hope it's not too late.

Chapter 15
Call

"So, how long has it been, Daph?" Elise asks. We are sitting at a local Chinese restaurant. She holds her chopsticks in anticipation, waiting for me to tell her the last time I heard from Mayson.

"Two weeks. It's killing me. I was finally ready, Elise. I was ready to tell him everything that I've been feeling about him, about us. I keep sending him text messages and calling his cell, but I get nothing in return. He must be so hurt. I feel like maybe he's ending this."

"No," Elise responds, shaking her head. "There must be a good reason why you haven't heard from him. Maybe he's super busy with work, or he's not ready to talk. I'm sure you will hear from him soon, Daph. He loves you, for goodness sake!"

Begrudgingly, I raise my chopsticks towards my mouth, forcing in another bite of beef and broccoli. Just as the food touches my lips, I hear the familiar ring tone of my cell phone. My stomach does a cartwheel as I dig through my purse, searching for the phone, praying that I can find it before he hangs up.

"Mayson? Mayse?" The pause on the other end of the line makes the hair on the back of my neck stand up.

"Daphne, hello. My name is Cecelia Holt. I'm Mayson's mother." Why on earth would Mayson's mother be calling me? I can't think of any possible reason unless, unless.... "I've received all of your messages and texts. Mayson is not ignoring you, Daphne. He has been in a very serious accident."

My body grows numb. I cannot feel my fingers, my toes. Panic overwhelms me as I wait for Mrs. Holt to continue, but there is silence.

"Is he alright? Is Mayson alright?" my voice is cracking with anticipation and worry. Tears well in my eyes and my hands begin to quiver. Elise places her chopsticks on the table, looking at me with questioning concern.

"No, Daphne. He's not alright. He's on life support. We're hoping that he'll recover from his injuries, but right now, his outlook is...well, it's not good." Her voice cracks and she clears her throat.

"Can I see him?"

"Of course, dear, that's why I called. It's obvious that you two are close, and I wanted you to have the opportunity to visit him, to know where he is."

The walls are closing in all around me as I write down the address of the hospital. My life will never be the same after this phone call. That realization disturbs me to my core. Hanging up with Mrs. Holt, I slump in my chair, staring into space.

"Daphne? Daph! Honey, what's going on? You are as pale as a ghost." I can barely hear Elise. All I can hear is the sound of my heart pumping blood through my veins. Her arms wrap around me as tears flood my eyes, streaming down my face and neck.

"I could lose him, Elise. I could lose him and he'd never know how I feel about him. He'll never know that he's the love of my life. I thought he was ignoring me…but, he wasn't. Instead, he's lying helpless in a hospital bed. God knows how long he's been there."

"Mayson? What do you mean? He's in a hospital bed? Was he hurt?"

Nodding, I reply, "He was in an accident."

We sit in silence for several minutes. Elise slowly strokes my arms with her fingertips, trying desperately to comfort me as best she can.

"What on earth am I going to do, Elise?" I ask solemnly, feeling completely defeated.

"You're getting on the next plane to Denver. And I'm going with you," Elise replies confidently as she strokes my hair. "You're not going to lose him, Daph. You're going to sit by his bed, talk to him and help him wake up. And then, you're going to spill your guts and get your damn happily ever after." I nod, wiping away the tears on my cheeks.

We arrive in Denver the following day. The hotel we've booked is only a few blocks away from St. Joseph's Hospital, so we quickly check in to the hotel and start walking. It's early afternoon and Elise suggests stopping for lunch, but I can't. I must get to Mayson. She holds my hand as we ride the elevator to his floor. The nurse directs us towards his room and I feel like I'm swaying through a dream. This can't actually be happening. The only man I've ever loved can't possibly be here fighting for his life.

"Deep breaths, Daphne, it's going to be okay." Elise says softly, "I'm going to wait in the elevator lobby. You go ahead inside," she continues as we approach his room. I see Mayson through the glass. His beautiful, sandy brown hair is no more. His head has been shaved and a long cut lingers across the right side of his head. His eyes are closed and he's hooked up to several machines, IV bags giving him much needed nourishment. He looks like he's lost a significant amount of weight and I wonder how long he's been like this. When did this happen? Did it happen while I was so carelessly kissing Evan on the dance floor? Did it happen when I was in bed with Evan, trying desperately to forget Mayson? Or did it happen when I was saying goodbye to Evan awkwardly at my back door wishing I could take it all back? Guilt plagues me and I can think only of the betrayal that I've committed. I am a horrible person, a horrible girlfriend. I do not deserve him.

I scan the room, and I'm relieved to find it empty, for I feel my guilt is a being in and of itself, standing next to me, shouting my betrayals to the world. Mayson is lying lifeless in the small bed. His arms are stretched out at his sides, and tubes are in his mouth. His chest rises and falls in a hypnotic rhythm. Tears pull at my eyes as I stare at him from the foot of the bed. My once strong and vibrant love is now so still, so calm, so broken.

My legs feel uneasy so I grab an armchair from the corner of the room. Bringing it to the side of the bed, I sit and lock my hand with Mayson's. I am powerless to stop the tears that pour from my eyes. I am kissing his hand, stroking it and looking at him through swollen eyes.

"Oh, Mayse. What the hell happened?" I weep, stroking his thumb, his fingers, his wrist, hoping that somehow, my touch will magically bring him back to me. But, it doesn't. His chest continues to rise and fall with the machines. The IV continues to drip softly into his veins, and the guilt in my heart continues to haunt me. It is time to confess my sins.

"I did something horrible, Mayse. I betrayed you in the worst possible way. But, if you can just wake up; just wake up and talk with me about it, I know things can get better. I can be better…for you. Please, Mayse…" I sob uncontrollably into his limp hand.

"I know that I don't deserve you. But, the past few months have been the best and worst of my life. They've been awful because I've been fighting with myself; not wanting to be hurt again. But, I'm done with that, Mayse, because you are the best thing that has ever happened to me. You make me feel things that no one else ever has. I'm ready to tear down my wall, Mayse. I'm ready to be with you, here, now. Won't you please wake up and be with me? Please? I love you, Mayson. Come back to me, please."

I'm interrupted by a sharp voice. "*Come back to you?*" A young woman with long, silky blond hair is staring at me from the doorway. Her piercing blue eyes are angry, stabbing. She cocks her head to the side and hisses, "Who the *hell* are you? And why on earth are you telling *my fiancé* that you love him?"

Chapter 16

Brynn

"Your fiancé?" I ask, feeling the sting of her words all over my body. Shocked, confused and alone, I stand up and look down at Mayson. Betrayal is consuming me. He couldn't. He wouldn't. Would he? I feel as if I may be sick. "What are you talking about?"

"Mayson, that's who I'm talking about!" she screeches, dramatically pointing down at him. "The man I'm going to marry!" She takes a deep breath, her eyes narrowing slightly. "Who *are* you? I want an answer!" She crosses the room until she is only inches away from my face. My pulse is out of control and my heart is breaking. Mayson is not mine, he is someone else's. He is not at all who I think he is.

"I'm Daphne. Mayson and I went to college together. We dated then, but reconnected this summer. We've been dating for a few months now." My voice trails off at the end. I'm terrified to find out where this conversation is leading and what will be revealed in its wake.

"Well, isn't that just fantastic?" the young woman says, her voice dripping with anger and sarcasm. She glares at Mayson with a look that shows she is no longer surprised by the sight of me.

"I'm Brynn." She says, raising her eyebrows, looking for some recognition of her name. But, I've never heard it before and she rolls her eyes at that realization. "I don't know why that doesn't surprise me. I know who you are, Daphne. I know all about you…at least, I did years ago in college. What I didn't know is that you two have been having a fling right under my nose."

"It wasn't a fling," I reply angrily, defending myself. Her icy blue eyes continue to overwhelm me, but I will not give up without a fight. "It was much *more* than that. He told me he loved me."

"Well, obviously he told both of us *a lot* of things," she snaps defiantly, crossing her arms, her gorgeous amber mane falling past her shoulders.

I narrow my eyes, looking at her and reflecting on what she has said, "How do you know my name?"

"I grew up with Mayson in Charleston. We went to different Universities. We started dating in college when we he came back home during spring break of sophomore year. You know, right before you two broke up. Put the pieces together, Daphne."

"He *what*?" My thoughts are racing. He broke up with me for her? He lied to me in college, told me he needed to get his priorities straight, focus on his future. I feel helpless, scared and out of control. I look desperately to Brynn for more answers. I need more pieces of the puzzle in order to make them fit.

"You heard me," she hisses, "He ended your relationship in order to be with me and we've been together ever since."

"No. No." I can't see straight. My world is collapsing in front of me.

"Well, maybe I was able to give him something that you

were unwilling to give?" Her words burn through my body.

"What are you talking about?" All at once, it dawns on me, "Did he sleep with you during spring break?" I'm praying that Brynn will say no, but deep down I know what her response is before she even utters the words.

"What did you expect, Daphne? He was a nineteen year old boy! They live and breathe sex and he was stuck dating little miss prim and proper, refusing to give it up," she sneers, "He was going out of his mind. No wonder he came looking for me."

"Oh my god…I can't believe this is happening," I say, trying to catch my breath, to wrap my brain around the past.

"How do you think *I* feel right now? I've been with Mayson for years…years. I uprooted my entire life to be with him. I moved to Denver in order to have a future with him. I spend holidays with his family. I take care of his dog while he travels for work. Trust me, Daphne, you and he were nothing but a fling. And as pissed off as I am right now, I am not walking away from him. So, I suggest you get the hell out of here. You have no business being near him or his family right now. And the sight of you is making me sick!"

My stomach turns and instinctively I run out of the room, tears spilling from my eyes. People walk by, looking at me with curiosity and concern.

Planning a future together? Holidays with his family? Things are starting to make sense. Brynn is the reason why I was not welcome at Thanksgiving. His fiancé was already with him, eating turkey and mashed potatoes with his family. Mayson has betrayed me…again. Everything that I thought I knew about him, about us, was a lie. A few short weeks ago, he was professing his love and now? Now I have no idea what to do or where I stand. Should I board the next possible flight? Should I stay by his side? Thoughts race through my head as sweat collects on my furrowed brow, tears streaming uncontrollably down my cheeks. I have to get out of this hospital or I fear it will swallow me whole. I have to get out.

Now.

Elise is sitting quietly in a chair near the elevator lobby, iPod buds nestled deep within her ears. When she sees me, she hops out of her seat and runs to my side.

"Daphne, are you ok? What's the matter?"

"He...I...he has a...I'm not...Oh my god, Elise." I fall apart completely in her arms as she pulls me down to a nearby chair. She strokes my hair gently as she softly whispers, "Shhh" into my ear. But, a few moments later I feel Elise's body tense and all of a sudden she is quiet.

"Excuse me, are you Daphne?" I look up to see a woman in her fifties. She is beautiful despite the dark circles under her eyes. She looks so much like Mayson. I know she must be his mother. She must be Cecelia Holt. Wiping the tears away, I do my best to compose myself.

"Yes, I'm Daphne." I nod, rubbing my eyes roughly with the backs of my hands.

"Hello. I'm Cecilia, Mayson's mother. We spoke on the phone. May I sit?" she asks gingerly. I nod uncomfortably and she sits down next to me. Elise presses her arm around my shoulder even tighter than before, protecting me from another possible confrontation. Cecelia notices the gesture and nods in understanding.

"I saw you running out of Mayson's room and hoped I might catch you before you left the hospital. I would hate to think that girl chased you off."

"But, she's his fiancé." I say in confusion. Cecelia's eyes widen.

"Did she *say* that?" shaking her head in disgust she continues, "Yes, of course she would. In truth Daphne they are dating, but my son is not engaged...to anyone," she rolls her eyes, "And he certainly isn't engaged to Brynn. If he were, I would know it. Brynn has always been ten steps ahead of Mayson. She's just staking her claim is all."

"So, he's not engaged?" I ask, feeling some relief.

"No, dear, he's not. Why don't you come back to the

room and we can talk further."

"I'm not sure I can, Mrs. Holt." My apprehension is clear in my shaky voice.

"Please, call me Cece. And, don't worry, I've sent Brynn home to cool down. You won't have to worry about her; not today anyway."

I nod my head in agreement and slowly we make our way back to Mayson's room. When we enter, she pulls two chairs together next to his bed and we sit in silence for a few minutes, both watching the rise and fall of Mayson's chest.

"Brynn told me you've been seeing Mayson for several months. She's infuriated, to say the least."

"Yes, I know and she has every right to be, I guess." Cece shrugs in a non-committal gesture towards Brynn. "Mayson and I started dating this summer," I continue.

"So, you're the reason that Mayson was always so happy when he returned home from his Chicago business trips?" she smiles. I blush, but return her sentiment with a soft smile.

"I like to think so." I reply, my cheeks turning crimson.

"Aha, a mother always knows when something unusual is happening with her children. Mayson has been," she pauses, "different for a while now. I couldn't quite put my finger on it. But, seeing you here is making everything a little clearer for me."

"To be honest, Mrs. Holt, I'm more confused than I have ever been in my life. I know that, technically, I'm 'the other woman,' but I didn't know that was my role. I thought Mayson was my...well, my boyfriend." She nods compassionately with a knowing smile.

"I love my son. God, I love my son. But, he's always been a bit impulsive, and extremely self absorbed. I'm sure he never meant to hurt you or Brynn, for that matter. Knowing Mayson, he must've had some "plan." And now, he's lying in a hospital bed and his secrets are revealed." She shakes her head, laughing sadly. "He's a good boy, Daphne...a good, good boy. Please don't give up on him, not yet."

"I'll try not to, ma'am. But, it is difficult at the moment."

"I can only imagine," she says, wiping her eyes and looking quickly at the door, "Look, I've never been a big fan of Brynn. She is simply not the type of woman I want my Mayson to be with. But, when I told you something was different with him, I meant it. He's been happier, kinder, and gentler these past few months. He's been a joy to be around…until Thanksgiving, that is. He was a royal pain in the ass on that holiday," she laughs, stroking his arm gently and patting his wrist lightly.

"He did tell me that day was difficult." I reply, remembering our ill-fated conversation the following day. She raises a curious eyebrow before continuing.

"He and Brynn arrived on Wednesday and he hardly spoke a word during their entire stay. He sat on the couch with his brothers, watching football, drinking beer. Normally, he stands in the kitchen with me while I cook the bird. He tells me stories about all the projects he's working on, the buildings he has a hand in designing. But, not this year, this year he hung with the men and left Brynn and I alone in the kitchen. Couples have their ups and downs. Although, I secretly hoped he was finally going to break up with her, I assumed this was one of their downs."

Mayson's words creep into my head, *I did a lot of thinking as I sat at my mother's dining room table last night, wishing you were there with me.* I was the reason; the reason that Mayson was not himself with his family, the reason he kept to himself on the couch watching football. But, was I merely a distraction from a down cycle with Brynn? After all, I was the other woman in this equation. I couldn't let myself forget that.

"Cece, everything happened so fast earlier. I wasn't able to ask what happened to Mayson. I know he was in an accident, but I don't have any other details. Will you please tell me what happened?"

"Mayson went out for a morning run about two weeks

ago. He had his iPod going way too loud, as always. Ever since he was a boy, he's always had a thing for ear deafening decibels. I always thought he'd lose his hearing, but this was so much worse."

"Was he hit by a car?"

"Yes, a stupid teenager was texting and didn't see him jogging into the intersection. By the time she saw him, it was too late. Thank God she did know well enough to call 911 before even getting out of her car. The doctors were able to get him into surgery quickly and that has saved his life up until this point. But, I could just kill that girl." Tears stream down her face as she continues to stroke Mayson's hand. All I can think about is that damn iPod and the songs *I* picked out for him.

Cece wipes her tears away with a stroke of her hand and continues, "You need to prepare yourself. His outlook is not good. Of course, as his mother, I remain in complete denial. I can tell you to prepare yourself, but I'll never be prepared to lose my baby."

"I'm so sorry," I cry, my heart sinking for her, for me, for Mayson.

"The doctors say there is a 50 percent chance that he may never be able to breathe on his own. I doubt my son would approve of being kept alive by machines."

"But, there is a 50 percent chance that he'll be ok?" I ask, wiping my tears with a tissue.

"There is always a chance, but the doctors are warning us not to be too hopeful. They call it a traumatic brain hemorrhage. His kind is one of the worst, an acute subdural hematoma." She says, reading from the chart placed by Mayson's feet. "I can never remember the exact term on my own, I always need to look at the chart. Mother's defense mechanism, I think."

She shrugs. My heart breaks for this lovely and kind woman who has opened herself up to me despite our circumstances. I wish so badly that I had the power to take her pain away. Selfishly, I want to see Mayson's stunning green eyes again. I want to tell him that I love him and know that he can hear me. I want to be with him, despite everything that has happened. I want him to live.

Being with his mother has made me fall in love with him all over again. Despite his deceit, despite his lies, in this moment I am bound to him, to his mother, to his family.

Later that afternoon, I return to Elise who is patiently waiting for me in the uncomfortable hospital chairs. She has waited for me and instantly I feel relieved by her presence. Elise stares at me in disbelief as I finish explaining everything that has transpired in Mayson's hospital room.

"What do I do, Elise? Please, tell me…tell me what I should do." I search her face for answers, but cannot find any. She shrugs her shoulders compassionately and rubs my forearm softly before speaking.

"Daphne, things with Mayson have always been complicated. You've never seemed quite comfortable with him, not quite yourself. I've noticed that for years."

"Why didn't you say anything?" I ask, my eyes burning, my nose painfully red.

"It wasn't my place," she says, shaking her head "You loved him, you still do. You're my best friend in the entire world and I want so desperately for you to be happy."

"You said I'm not myself with him. What did you mean by that?"

"You always seem so unsure of yourself when you're with him. As if you are always on your very best behavior. And honestly, that's not how love should be. Just ask Henry! I'm myself with him, completely and utterly myself. Sometimes it sucks to be my husband, I assure you. But, he loves me anyway. He loves me when I'm bitchy, when I'm moody, or when I'm jealous. He just loves me."

"Mayson told me he loved me…"

"Yes, I know, honey. But, how well does Mayson actually know you, the real you? Please don't misunderstand me. You are wonderful. You're funny, kind and sensitive. You light up a room. I know he sees that! But, when you've had a bad day, do you let him see it? When you're pissed off at him, do you let him have it? I *know* you don't. And to be with someone, *really* be with someone, he has to know you inside and out, the good and the bad." I hang my head in shame, knowing that she is absolutely right. I held back my feelings with Mayson. I built my wall in order to keep myself safe. How could he possibly love someone he doesn't really know?

"I still love him. But, this kind of betrayal, I don't know that I can ever forgive this. I don't know that I can move forward even if I am the one that he wants to be with."

"Daph, if you want to leave, we'll go. If you want to stay, that's what we'll do. Give yourself some time to decide." Elise takes my hand in hers and squeezes it tight. "You're stronger than you give yourself credit for. Remember that." She smiles gently, squeezes my hand one more time and gestures towards the door.

"Let's get you out of here. You need to clear your head and you can't be here any longer. You need some distance from Mayson, from Brynn and even from his family. You need to figure out what *you* want, my friend.

Chapter 17
Return

It's been six weeks since I sat with Cece in Mayson's hospital room. Mayson's condition has not changed at all. Cece has warned me that the doctors are starting to become more and more pessimistic about his outlook. Christmas was awful without him. Not that we had ever spent any holidays together but, I'd been so hopeful that this would be our first. I had called Cece that morning to wish her a Merry Christmas. In my gut, I knew she would be with Mayson in his hospital room. She couldn't bear to leave him. The rest of the family returned to South Carolina as she decorated his sterile room with garland and some of his favorite childhood ornaments. It didn't make a difference.

I'm back at home, trying my best to live my life. Occasionally, a student will stay after class and ask me if I'm doing okay. Other faculty members have also taken notice of my rather melancholy disposition. I've chosen to keep most of this private, especially because I'm embarrassed that, technically, Mayson and I were having an affair. Afraid of judgment, I've kept my mouth shut, only revealing the details of my misery to Morgan and Elise.

Morgan and I are making popcorn, preparing to watch a crazy reality show when my cell phone rings. My heart jumps when I see that it's Cece. Cece usually sends text messages to let me know that Mayson has stayed the same in his condition. Perhaps she's calling with good news!

"Hello, dear," she says. Her voice is sullen and instantly I'm terrified.

"Cece, hi, how are you?"

"Daphne, I don't know how to say this..." her voice trails.

"Cece, what is it? Is Mayson ok?"

"No, Daphne. My husband found some documents in Mayson's safe along with his life insurance policy. He left a will and it states rather emphatically that we are not to, under any circumstances, allow him to persist in a situation like this. He has no interest in being kept alive by machines. His lawyer drafted him a DNR document, 'do not resuscitate.' There's nothing more that we are legally allowed to do."

"So, what are you saying? Are they making you turn off the machines?" No, this can't be happening. I can't lose him. Cece sobs into the phone. I feel terrible for being so selfish.

"I am so, so sorry. I shouldn't be thinking of myself. I can't even imagine how hard it must be for you to make these phone calls. What can I do?"

"Come and say goodbye, Daphne. We're turning the machines off tomorrow. I begged the doctors to wait until then, so that his brothers can be here. But, I have no idea how long he will still... be with us when they turn them off."

"Of course," I reply, my voice weak and frail. Tears are streaming down my cheeks. This is a nightmare and, rather than waking up from this wretched dream, I now have to force myself to get on an airplane and continue the agony. But, I need to be there, for Mayson and for Cece. I need to say goodbye, to kiss his cheek and tell him, again, how much I love him.

Morgan and I arrive at the hotel in Denver the following morning. I'm grateful that my cousin has dropped everything, called in sick and accompanied me here. If not for her, I don't know if I'd have made it. As it was, I was in tears at the airport and on the plane.

"I'm going to stay here if that's ok, Daph." Morgan says, pulling her laptop from her briefcase. "I didn't know Mayson and I don't want to intrude upon his family. They deserve to be surrounded by those who truly love their son."

"Of course, Morgan, you're here for me and I'm so thankful. I'll call or text you to let you know when I'll be back."

Walking through the hospital doors feels surreal. I'm returning after a few long, excruciating weeks, and yet it feels as if I never left. The elevator delivers me to Mayson's floor and I'm flooded with memories, the good and the bad, the kisses and the tears, the wonderful conversations and the things left unsaid.

Mayson's room approaches and my heart catapults into my throat. Overcome with emotion, I'm terrified that Brynn will be inside the room. I don't want to cause her any more pain, but I also want to have my own goodbye with Mayson without her watching and judging my every word.

Brynn is nowhere to be found as I enter the room. I let out a huge sigh of relief, but the tears erupt from my eyes as I see Mayson lying helplessly in the bed. The hum of the respirator is absent and the silence is maddening. Cece is sitting next to Mayson and she gestures for me to join her. She strokes his hand lovingly and it's clear that he's still with us for the time being.

"Daphne, I'm so relieved that you're here. Dr. Peterson doesn't think he has much longer. His pulse has slowed significantly since they disconnected the machines two hours ago. I'm going to step outside and let you have a moment. I will be back, though. I need to be with my baby when he goes," she wipes a lone tear from her cheek. I offer her a sympathetic smile while rubbing her arm gently. She squeezes my hand briefly before walking out of the room.

I slide the chair next to Mayson's side and hold both his hands in mine. I need to say goodbye, even though I cannot possibly imagine a world without Mayson in it.

"I'm so glad I got to see you one last time, Mayse. I would've regretted it forever if I hadn't. I know I should be angry with you. I should be furious, but I'm not. I'm too devastated to be angry. I thought this was it, Mayse. I thought it'd be you and me." I sob, wiping my tears with my sleeve.

"But, I have to let you go now. It's time for you to be at peace. I will always wonder what could've been for us, Mayson. I will always treasure those lovely moments that we shared. And I will always do my very best to not let my memories be clouded by your mistakes," I stop to take a deep breath before I continue speaking, "I need you to hear me, Mayson. I need you to hear me when I say that I love you. Because I do, Mayse, no matter what happened, no matter what you did or didn't do...I love you."

Choking on the words and tears, I feel Cece's delicate hand on my shoulder. I stand and hug her tightly before releasing her. She needs to be with her son now. Her husband is standing by the door, watching us stoically. It's the first time I've ever seen him. His face is pained, but he does not cry. I turn back to Cece.

"I need to allow you time with your son. Besides, I can't bear to be here when he goes. Thank you for giving me that time. I needed it more than you will ever know." Somehow, I muster the strength to leave the room, knowing that Mayson will be gone in a matter of hours, minutes or even seconds. The thought is unbearable and I can't be here.

Walking towards the elevator, I see a blond woman slumped over a garbage can, her hair pulled back weakly by her own hands.

"Brynn?" I ask weakly. Brynn stands up, wiping her mouth with the back of her hand.

"Ugh! Not you. Please go...just go away. I don't want to be near you right now, not today." She hisses, leaning over to clutch the trash can once again. I can smell alcohol on her breath.

"Please, Brynn. Let me help you. There is a restroom right around the corner. I'll help you get cleaned up before you..." I summon the words, but they will not leave my mouth.

"Before I lose the man I'm supposed to marry? Before he dies? God, I don't want to be talking about this with you, his *whore*, of all people."

"I'm not his whore, Brynn, just like you aren't his fiancé." I say matter-of-factly. Her blotchy, red eyes widen as she looks at me in shock. "Yes," I continue, "I know." Brynn opens her mouth as if to speak, but simply stares at me, wide eyed, looking ashamed.

"He doesn't have much time, Brynn. And if you don't say goodbye, you'll always regret it."

"How *dare* you?" she spits the words as if they're venom, "You know absolutely *nothing* about me. You don't know the years I've spent loving that man, planning our future and worshipping the ground he walked on. Don't you get it? I wasn't enough. I wasn't enough to keep him faithful. He went looking for something more. He went looking for you!" She sobs as she yells at me. I take the lashing, for I know that on some level she's right. I stand up straight and prepare for more abuse. But, instead, she takes my hand and sinks into my arms.

"I will never, ever forgive him. I wish you'd never showed up here, Daphne. At least then I could've said goodbye; I could've loved him when he died. I could've...I could've...this can't be happening! Why is this happening?"

"Brynn, I'm begging you to please say goodbye to him. Neither of us asked for this to happen. Neither of us wants to feel like we weren't enough for him. But, the truth is, we will never feel anything else. He's leaving us. He's going soon. You need to make peace, Brynn. You need to forgive him."

"Do you?" she asks, incredulously, pulling away from me. She looks bewildered. "Do *you* forgive him?"

"Right now, yes, I've forgiven him. I don't know how I'll feel tomorrow. But, I know I have to be here with him right now. I said goodbye and gave him my forgiveness. I needed to do that. I needed to let him go. I have no idea how I'll feel in the future but I don't think I will ever regret saying goodbye to the love of my life."

"Is that who he was to you, the love of your life?'

"Yes," I whisper, afraid of hurting her.

"He was mine, too," she responds. "Damn him!"

"Look, Brynn, I don't know why he kept us both around. I really don't. But, I have to believe that it was because he loved us, both of us. We both know Mayson could be selfish, and maybe this was his ultimate act of selfishness. He couldn't bear to let either of us go."

"Maybe," she nods reluctantly, "I wish I could get the world to stop spinning for a minute. There's no way that I can face his parents like this. I need to sober up."

"So, you've decided to see him?" I ask, hopeful.

"Yes, I need to."

"Are you a coffee drinker, Brynn?" she nods in response.

"Alright, sit down for a minute. I'll get you a cup of coffee and perhaps the world will start to straighten out for you. Then, you can go to him. You can say goodbye to the man we love." A sad smile crosses my lips as I gaze at her. She is so wounded.

"Why are you being so nice to me, Daphne? Why don't you hate me the way I have always hated you?"

"I'm not sure," I answer, shrugging. And, it's the truth.

As much as her words sting, it has never occurred to me to hate Brynn.

"Mayson's deception was his alone, Brynn. I'm not going to hate you for loving him. He was pretty irresistible."

"Yes, he was...is...was." She sobs again into my already soaked sleeve.

Chapter 18
Goodbye

Mayson's services are lovely; devastating, depressing, heartbreaking and unbelievably sad, but lovely. Morgan and I sit quietly in the back of the church as Brynn sits with Mayson's family.

After a small service led by the pastor, Mayson's father walks to the podium to deliver his son's eulogy. Pain spreads across the man's face. His brow furrows and it's obvious he's attempting to hold back his tears, hold back all of the emotion that is brimming from the loss of his son. Before speaking, he brushes the stray gray hairs from his face and breathes in deeply.

"One of the most difficult things to imagine in this world is the idea of losing one's child. I have three boys. They've always been a challenge for my wife and I, as boys usually are. We had our fair share of permanent marker on the walls, ER visits due to broken bones and other things of that nature.

Mayson was the youngest, and with that, came extra

challenges for him and for us. He was always trying to keep up with his older brothers, always trying to prove to the world that he was just as fast, just as strong, and just as talented.

But, there was so much to my son, Mayson.

He was passionate about architecture, even as a small child. We'd take him into Charleston and he was fascinated by the buildings, the modern as well as those built so long ago. He knew he wanted to build things; he wanted to create. He was driven yet free-spirited. He was focused, yet so carefree.

My son was not perfect. Something I've been reminded of recently. But, he had a very large heart and he never set out to purposely hurt a soul." Mr. Holt pauses and glances at Brynn. His eyes then leave her and search the chapel until they land on me. My heart jumps. Brynn turns in the pew and glares at me. A chill runs down my spine as her arctic glare reminds me of how much my presence still hurts, and will always hurt, her.

"So, today, I am choosing to remember my son as the free spirited man who wanted to build, who wanted to create. Today I am choosing to remember my son as the man that he was becoming. He was building a future for himself, one that I wish I could've seen. For, I know, as I've always known, Mayson was meant for greatness." He pauses, turns to the large statue of Christ on the crucifix, and gesturing to Jesus adds, "Perhaps he still is, perhaps his greatness will emerge in the Kingdom of Heaven. Goodbye, Mayson. Make me proud, son, as you always have."

Mr. Holt chokes on his words and grasps the edge of the podium, his eyes staring downward as if to shield the congregation from his tears, from his pain. My eyes grow hot as the tears stream down my face. He wipes his cheek with his handkerchief, gives a weak smile to the congregants and sits back down next to Cece for the remainder of the services.

I cannot endure the burial so, after the church services, I

quickly head to Mayson's family in order to pay my respects and to say goodbye. After hugging each of his brothers, I turn to Cece, my lip quivering from the sadness that has enveloped my soul. She embraces me and I sob once again, no longer able to feel my soaked cheeks.

"Dear, I'm so sorry that we met this way. I know this may seem like an odd thing to say, but I will miss you." Cece says, lightly touching my cheek. Brynn flinches watching our exchange.

"I wish we could've met on different terms, Cece. If there is anything that I can ever do, please let me know," I say reassuringly as I rub her shoulder softly. I nod at Mayson's father, his face once again lacking emotion. I imagine that he's trying to stay strong for his wife, but my heart breaks for him. His son has died and he appears to have gone numb. Perhaps he is.

The next morning, I'm packing my suitcase, preparing for the flight back home when my cell phone rings. Without even glancing at the screen, I answer. The voice on the other line is unexpected, especially so soon after Mayson's services.

"Hello, dear, it's Cece."

"Hi, it's so nice to hear from you." So nice, but so soon.

"Listen, Daphne, I'm sure that you're planning to head back to Chicago sometime soon. But, I'm wondering if you might be able to meet me before you leave. I have something rather important to discuss with you."

"Of course I can meet you." My reply is hesitant. I have no idea what she would possibly want to discuss. But, I'm happy to have the chance to spend time with her nonetheless, "My flight leaves this afternoon, but I'm free until then. My cousin, Morgan, had to head back earlier, so I'm available any time."

"I remember you mentioned that your hotel was near the hospital. There is a lovely cafe just around the corner from St. Joseph's called Bon Apetit. Let's meet there in, say, an hour?" Her voice is shaky, almost nervous.

"Yes, that would be fine. I hope everything is alright, Cece."

"I'll see you soon, Daphne." Her voice sounds agitated. My nerve endings sizzle as my brain ponders the sudden change in her demeanor. On edge, I somehow manage to finish packing my suitcases and head to the cafe.

Cece is waiting for me when I enter the restaurant. Large, dark circles sit beneath her eyes. She looks as though she's barely slept. My heart aches for her.

"Good morning, Daphne," she greets me, pulling me in for a warm embrace. "Thank you so much for seeing me on such short notice. This would've been so much harder to do over the phone..." her eyes leave mine as she returns to her seat. Sitting down, my heart thumps frantically in my chest.

"Cece, I have to be honest. You're making me incredibly uneasy." I say, hoping she'll reassure me that everything is ok, that I've just misunderstood her behavior. Grief can masquerade in many forms, after all. Some can become angry, defiant, or edgy. I hope that Cece is exhausted and elusive due to her anguish. But, there's no change in her disposition. Instead, she hangs her head and begins her confession.

"I've been up all night, Daphne. I wasn't sure if this was the right thing to do, but...I had to see you. I had to tell you what I know."

"What you know? Did you learn something about Mayson?"

"Yes, well, I found something, something of Mayson's. But, I believe it was meant for you," she says, reaching into her purse. "Please forgive me for showing this to you, but I had to...I needed you to know." What could possibly be inside that purse? What other betrayal had Mayson committed against me? The suspense was absolutely horrendous. Forcing myself to breathe deeply, I wait for Cece to reveal her discovery.

My jaw feels like it's dropped to the table as she places a

small velvet box in front of me.

"This can't possibly be what I think it is," I gasp in horror.

"Open it, Daphne." Holding my breath, I slowly open the elegant box. A large solitaire diamond is nestled into a gorgeous platinum setting. There is no doubt it's an engagement ring. Its beauty forces a large sigh from my throat.

"I don't understand, Cece. This must be for Brynn. Why on earth are you showing this...to me? I can't bear the idea of knowing I was cheating with a man who was about to propose to another woman." Cece shakes her head defiantly.

"This is the reaction I was afraid of, Daphne. I know that Mayson and Brynn were together a long time. But, every fiber of my being tells me that this ring was meant for you." Her eyes are pleading with me to listen.

"For me? Why? What makes you think that, Cece? I'm struggling to wrap my mind around all of this." Completely besieged, I reach into my purse to find a tissue. My eyes are swelling with tears and I'm angry with myself for crying again over Mayson's unfaithfulness. These feelings of anger are also directed at Cece for sharing this with me, for pouring lemon juice on the paper cut inside my heart. Why would she do this to me? Why?

"I didn't exaggerate when I told you that Mayson had been different lately. He was different the entire time he was seeing you, Daphne. He was lighthearted, carefree, *in love*. I could see it, I could feel it. I had never seen him like that, not in all the years that he and Brynn were together. Of course, they seemed happy, but he was not enchanted by her. She did not bring out the best in him. But, I think you did. And I think Mayson knew that. In my heart, I believe he was planning to end it with Brynn, but then...the accident..."

"Cece, I'm sorry, but this is too much for me to process right now," I say, hanging my head, wiping my tears, wishing for this dreadful conversation to end.

"Maybe this was a mistake, Daphne. I'm so sorry. You

are such a sweet and loving person. I thought this would give you peace. I thought this would help you to know just how much Mayson loved you."

"But, I don't know that this ring is for me, Cece. That's the problem. Yes, you feel it in your gut. But that's simply not enough. There is no engraving with my name, no note inside the box, nothing. And so I'm forced to reconcile the fact that the man I loved purchased a ring that may have been meant for me. But, I will never know for sure...ever."

"There is a receipt," Cece says, her voice commanding that I listen.

"What?" I muster weakly.

"Does this date mean anything to you?" she asks, handing me the small piece of paper with the name of a jewelry store at the top. It's dated Saturday, November 27, the Saturday after Thanksgiving.

"Yes, it does." I say, my heart creeping into my throat.

"Well?" Cece asks in anticipation.

"The night before, he told me he loved me." I say softly. Cece gasps and smiles widely.

"So, it must be for you," she exclaims while releasing a large sigh of relief.

"No, you don't understand. He said he loved me on Friday evening, but then he left me the next morning. He purchased it the day he left me with no goodbye."

"He left you? That doesn't make sense. The two of you expressed your love for the first time."

"No, I didn't say that, Cece. I told you that Mayson expressed his love."

"You didn't return the sentiment? I'm so confused. You seem to care so deeply for him, I assumed you loved him, too." Cece looks panicked.

"I do love him, Cece. I just couldn't find the words that night. It was complicated and I was overwhelmed. The point is, he left the next morning, leaving only a note. He said he had things to think about. I can only imagine he had decided to end things with me and pursue a future with Brynn."

"Or perhaps, he was making the ultimate gesture to win your love." Cece suggests, raising one eyebrow. She reminds me of her charismatic son. Does she truly believe this or is she only telling me what she thinks I need to hear in this moment. Did Mayson think I needed an engagement ring in order to return his love? Or had he simply given up on me? More questions without answers. Another mystery that will plague my soul.

"Maybe," I say, staring at the table, my heart pulsing painfully inside my chest, "or maybe not."

"Oh, Daphne, I would never want to hurt you." She sighs, reaching out to touch my hand. Without thinking, I pull away from her. She looks so much like Mayson, that I can't bear her touch. I can't bear to be hurt again. When I see her expression, her eyes wide and wounded, I'm immediately filled with regret for hurting her.

"I know that, Cece. You've been through so much. I haven't forgotten that. But, I was finally coming to terms with everything and now...now it's worse than I ever could've imagined. I dreamed of a future with Mayson, fantasized about it. I dreamed of moving to Denver, of buying a home, of getting married. And now, you're telling me that he may have shared that dream with me. But then again, he may have decided to pursue those things with someone else."

Abruptly, Cece stands up and wipes the tears from her eyes. "Words cannot begin to express how sorry I am, Daphne. I thought I was doing the right thing. As a mother, I wanted to comfort you, to let you know that my Mayson was capable of more. But, like my son, I have hurt you and I'll always regret that. I need to go, Daphne." She stands and places the ring box in the middle of the table.

"This ring belongs to you. I am certain of it, Daphne. Even if you can't see that right now. Do what you will with it. You can leave it here, throw it in the nearest trash bin... whatever you feel you need to do. But, I know in my heart that it's yours."

"Wait, Cece--" I jump up, but it's too late. She has left me standing next to the table in the cafe, patrons staring at me with curiosity. Unsteadily, I grab the velvet box, place it in my purse and head towards the door, back to the safety of my hotel room. My flight can't leave soon enough. I must leave Denver as soon as humanly possible.

Chapter 19
Questions

"Daph, honey, please get out of bed," I hear Morgan talking into my answering machine. She knows me too well. I glance at the clock and groan seeing it's already noon. I know that I should get up and start my Saturday, but I feel as if I'm permanently adhered to my bed when I'm not at work. I've done my very best to keep up a positive front when teaching my students, after all my personal life should not affect their education. But, at the end of each day, I'm completely spent and yearn for the comfort and solitude of my bedroom.

Mayson's ring calls to me from the top drawer of my dresser. I can't bring myself to open the box, afraid I will fall apart completely but, the thought of parting with it is equally painful. Morgan doesn't know about the ring. In fact, no one knows it's in my possession apart from Cece.

Morgan continues to speak into my machine, "It's been weeks now, Daph. I'm getting tempted to use my spare key and drag you out of bed...Daph. Daph!" Slowly, I pull myself out from under my cotton comforter and walk to my phone.

"Hi, Morgan." Simply uttering these words takes a massive amount of effort and restraint. Lately, whenever I speak outside of school, my voice quivers and cracks and I feel helpless to stop the tears that inevitably pour from my eyes.

"Thank God. I was about to come over there this time. I mean it."

"That's what you said last weekend, Morgan. I'm fine. I just need to be alone."

"Nope, I'm not accepting that answer today, Daph. We're spending the day together whether you like it or not. Get dressed. I'll be right over."

Five minutes later, Morgan is knocking at the back door. I somehow muster up the will to answer, knowing her face will show pity and concern, two emotions I'm avoiding like the plague. I hate when people feel sorry for me. I hate feeling helpless. It's almost as awful as feeling heartbroken...almost.

Luckily, when I open the door, her face shows none of these emotions. Rather, her beautiful blond hair is pinned up in a pony-tail, a powder blue scarf that matches her eyes is wrapped around her neck and she's smiling from ear to ear. I'm instantly annoyed at her chipper demeanor, yet relieved at the lack of worry on her face. The first thing she does is stroll over to my CD player, removing my Andrew Belle disc. I've had the song "In My Veins" on repeat ever since I left Denver. Cringing, I watch as Morgan lifts the disc out gingerly, places it in its plastic case and into her purse. The lyrics echo in my mind even after silence fills the air.

"I need that," I mutter. "It's the only way I feel connected to him." Morgan ignores me completely.

"Oh good, you managed to get dressed. I can see you didn't shower, though."

"You didn't say that I had to bathe. From now on if you're going to order me around, you'll need to be more specific. You know I can just burn another mix off iTunes," I

122

hiss.

"I'm going to ignore that remark since you're my cousin and I love you. But, Daph, enough is enough. It's been two months since Mayson's funeral. It's time, honey. It's time to let go just a little bit. That song pulls you right back within yourself, right back into the pain and I won't let you get pulled in anymore. I'm doing this for you. You must know that."

"Morgan, I *do* know that. I'm just filled with so many emotions that I'm powerless to manage them right now. I still need to feel connected to him somehow. He's gone and I know that, but I'm left thinking about Brynn and about his family, especially Cece. We left things so badly--"

"Daph, she must've known that seeing the engagement ring would leave you upset. How could she not? It was an act of selfishness, if you ask me."

"Selfishness?" How could Cece have been acting selfish? The thought had never occurred to me.

"Yes, Daph, I've given this quite a bit of thought. Cece wanted to tell you about the ring because it would give her peace, it would give her the closure that she so desperately needed. She wanted to believe that his terrible behavior was all for a noble reason, all for a positive end result.

She said he was behaving differently while seeing you. As a mother, she wanted to envision him proposing to you, to making you his wife, to living happily ever after with the woman that she instantly connected with in the hospital. She didn't want to believe that he was seeing another woman only to propose to a person like Brynn."

"Brynn didn't do anything wrong, Morgan. She loved Mayson. She trusted him just like I did."

"That's not what I mean. I'm not blaming Brynn. Although I'm shocked that you're somehow able to look the other way knowing he cheated on you with her during college."

I cringe as she brings up this painful memory that I've

chosen to submerge deep within my consciousness. Morgan continues as she lovingly strokes my shoulder, "What I'm saying is that Brynn obviously did not have the same positive effect on Mayson. Cece felt that. She wanted her son to be happy, to be kind, and to be generous. And she observed her son taking on all of these attributes when you entered his life, not Brynn. They had been together for years. It wasn't until you showed up that she saw the change.

So, she wanted to see him as being a man who would risk everything for the right person. She was able to forgive him cheating on Brynn. It sounds as if she couldn't bear to have him cheat on *you*. In her eyes, you were the one for him."

Slowly, Morgan's words settle into my brain. Deep down, I know she's right. But, I can't bear to blame Cece. She was a victim in all of this, losing her son and not knowing what his true intentions were. Part of her must be ashamed of his behavior, but the other part was hopeful; I must've represented the hope that she felt. She'd hoped that Mayson could be the man she had envisioned. Without warning, my eyes begin to burn, and deep, guttural sobs escape my lips. Morgan quickly wraps her arm around me and holds me tight as I weep uncontrollably for what feels like eternity.

For eight long, excruciating weeks, I've been swirling in doubt and confusion. I would never know if Cece was correct about Mayson's intentions towards me or to Brynn. I would never know for whom he purchased the ring that sits inside my dresser. The conversation in the cafe has haunted me as I've desperately clung to Cece's words, hoping she was right. But, those words have also caused me to retreat like a reclusive hermit, wishing I could turn back the clocks and prevent the accident that stole my love.

"Talk to me, Daphne, please. I feel like I've caused you to break apart and I hate myself right now."

"No, no, Morgan. You're right," I say between sobs, "For weeks now, I've been laying here daydreaming about Mayson, imagining he was still here. I've been playing scenarios in my head; how would he have proposed? When would we have married? Would he have taken me to France for our honeymoon? Would we have started a family? How would that ring look upon my finger?"

"Oh, Daph." Morgan's eyes moisten as she stares at me with the look I've dreaded for weeks, the look of pity.

"Stop looking at me like that, please. You don't get it. What you just said is what I needed to hear. I need to move on. I need to let those scenarios go. Just because Cece felt that the ring was for me, doesn't mean that it was. I understand that now. I need to get past this. I need to say goodbye to him...for real, this time."

"Wow," Morgan gulps. "I don't think I've ever been more proud of you in my life."

"Thanks. I hope I can stay true to what I just said. Moving on is going to be really hard."

"I know, but you have me and you have Elise. We'll help you through this, I promise. The man of your dreams, the love of your life, he's still out there. I know it."

"God, I hope you're right," I laugh, feeling hopeful for the very first time. "I'm going to take a shower and then we can get the hell out of here. I need some fresh air."

"Thank goodness. I'll do a little clean up while you get ready. This place is a pit, Daph."

"Thanks," I smile, my first one in months. "I'm so lucky to have you."

Morgan's crystal eyes sparkle as she begins picking up Diet Coke cans from my coffee table, "We're both lucky, Daph. Now, take a shower. The department stores won't wait forever!"

"Good, I have a paycheck waiting to be burned. I've hardly spent money in months. Oh, and Morgan?"

"Yeah?"

"You can keep the CD." I smile, shrugging my shoulders. Morgan looks shocked before I turn quickly towards the bathroom. Little does she know that although the music will be gone, the ring will still be here, calling to me from my dresser drawer.

Chapter 20
Dating

It's a rainy Sunday afternoon and I'm spending way too much time on the internet, checking my email and Facebook page. On a whim, I log into my dating profile on the site Morgan set up for me ages ago.

Shocked, I stare at the welcome page with my mouth agape. Twenty two "date requests" are waiting for me, many dating back to last summer when I was completely wrapped up in Mayson. Curious, I begin to sift through the requests. Surprisingly, many of my potential suitors are quite handsome and seem to have steady careers. Clicking on the latest date request, sent just this weekend, I'm surprised to find an unbelievably gorgeous face staring back at me.

Name: Brock Gallino
Age: 30
Body Type: Athletic
Career: Lawyer

Relationship Status: Never Married
Seeking: A relationship

Intrigued, I read further about Mr. Gallino. Brock loves his career as a lawyer, but is even more passionate about his favorite sport, hockey. He's a devoted Chicago Blackhawks fan and has season tickets to the games. He seems to be a true "guy's guy" with spiky hair, a deep tan and tattoos on his forearms. In his message, he tells me that I'm "cute" and that he "loves my red hair and blue eye combo." He wants to get together for a drink or perhaps dinner if I'm interested.

My curiosity, combined with a smidge of loneliness, motivate me to hit "reply" and accept Brock's invitation for a date. It's time for Daphne to move on and this would have to be the first step. Brock seems attractive, successful and interesting. Perhaps this will be a great way to get my feet wet in the dating pool.

The following weekend, I meet Brock for dinner at a French Bistro that he suggested. Not usually my type of cuisine, but willing to try something new, I agree to dinner and drinks. I recognize Brock as I walk in the front door of the restaurant. He walks over to greet me and I'm immediately consumed by the scent of his musky cologne. Brock is dressed in a button down linen shirt and khaki pants and he's as good looking in person as his profile suggested. He kisses me on the cheek and smiles widely, "Daphne, it's so great to meet you in person. You look lovely."

My heart flutters as we make our way to the table. I'm definitely attracted to this guy, but need to see if his personality matches his physique.

The conversation is a bit awkward. He talks about himself...a lot. I'm not used to men who are so consumed by themselves. It's a little troubling to find that even by the time we've finished our meal and are sharing a piece of chocolate cake, he has only asked me one question about myself. I could probably write an entire essay about him, though. I learned about his childhood, his career at his law firm, where he got each of his tattoos and why, his apartment downtown, etc. etc. etc. His one and only question to me, "So, Daphne, do you like French food?"

Just as I'm ready to thank him for the date and retreat to the comfort of my corduroy sofa, our waiter delivers the bill to the table. Out of habit, I offer to help pay for the bill. I've been doing this for years, dating back to high school when boys struggled to afford dinners out with their girlfriends. No one had ever let me pay on a first date, ever. But, I guess there's a first time for everything.

"Yeah, that sounds great." He says, "Your share will be $37.50"

Seriously? He already divided it in his head? Who was this guy? This wealthy lawyer who suggested the French restaurant is letting his date pay for exactly half of the bill. Thank goodness I had already placed cash in my wallet, just in case. Begrudgingly, I drop $38 on the table, testing to see if he will give me 50 cents in return. He does not. That confirms it, Brock is a cheap ass.

After paying our bill, we walk out to our respective vehicles. As I'm unlocking my car, Brock says, "Wait, Daphne, the night is still young."

Taken aback, I respond, "Well, what did you have in mind?"

"Well, I thought maybe you'd like to come back to my place," he smiles with a sexy grin that I imagine has worked well for him in the past. I do my best to hide my disgust at his proposition.

"I'm thinking I should call it a night, Brock. I have a busy day tomorrow."

Brock looks disappointed but doesn't ask to see me again. Suddenly, his intentions for the evening have become transparent and I can't get into my car fast enough. Morgan calls me within minutes of my drive home.

"Seriously?" she asks incredulously, "The dude is a

lawyer and he didn't pay for dinner? He asked you out and he chose the place. What a cheap ass!"

"Those were my thoughts exactly. But, that's not the worst part. The guy had absolutely no interest in getting to know me, but had every intention of getting me back to his place. Geez, Morgan, is this what dating is going to be like? Going dutch for dinner followed by one night stands with douchebag guys who don't even try to sound interested in me?"

"No, not at all, Daph. This is just one date with one guy. Don't give up yet. You said you had plenty of other date requests on the website."

"Yeah, okay." I agree. "But, you need to pick the next date. I chose Brock and look how that turned out."

"Alright, I remember your password. I'll choose the next guy. No lawyers this time."

"And no tattoos," I add.

"Why not? Matt has a tattoo," Morgan says defensively.

"I know. I just want to get as far away from Brock's type as I possibly can."

"I understand," Morgan concedes. "I'll get to work right away."

By the time I arrive home, there's already an email from Morgan telling me the name of my next date.

Name: Abram Moore
Age: 35
Body Type: Athletic
Career: Teacher
Relationship Status: Never Married
Seeking: A relationship

In his profile picture, the blond haired blue eyed Abram is smiling wide while riding a bicycle. He lists his pride in his athleticism, his love of all things culinary and his desire to one day write a hit screenplay. Morgan definitely did a decent job. He sounds nothing at all like Brock.

When Abram calls later that evening to schedule our date, I'm immediately drawn to his voice. It's soft and silky and I can tell he has done this many times before. I must admit that the thought of ending up with another teacher sounds wonderful. He's an English teacher and loves to talk about literature and the classics. In addition to screenplays, he writes poetry and has a real artistic streak to him.

Unlike Brock, Abram asks me many questions about myself. He inquires about my job, my family, and my students. He seems genuinely interested in my answers. We have many things in common such as our love of the theater and for books written by Hemingway and Twain. When he asks me out for the following weekend, I realize that I'm genuinely looking forward to learning more about him, wondering if maybe this could amount to something.

Abram suggests we meet at a restaurant in between our two suburbs, an Irish Pub that sits on the outskirts of a movie theater. He writes screenplays and I love movies so I assume we'll be heading there if all goes well at dinner.

"Wow, you're even prettier in person, Daphne," Abram says, greeting me at the door to the pub.

"Thank you," I smile. "You look very handsome yourself."

Abram's light blond hair is short and spiky in the front. His hipster glasses complement his sapphire eyes and I'm instantly drawn to the freckles that adorn his pale cheeks. He takes my hand gently and leads me to our table.

"Would you like something to drink? They have really great microbrews here," he says as he hands me the drink menu.

"I think I'll have some wine. Moscato is my favorite."

"What is that?"

"It's a sparkling white wine. It's slightly bubbly and I just love it."

"Well, then, let's get you a glass," he smirks.

The waitress arrives and Abram orders our drinks, "The Lady will have a glass of Moscato, and I'd like the Lemon Shandy House Brew." At once I'm wooed by him referring to me as "the lady"---definitely a first for me while on a date. But, as our waitress walks away, I catch him staring at her ass! He turns back to me, a cocky grin spread about his face and winks, as if I should enjoy his wandering eye. I want to lash out, call him a pig and throw my drink (which has not yet arrived) square in his face. Instead, I hold my head high and convince myself to stay calm. All guys have roaming eyes, Abram just isn't afraid to hide his.

When our waitress arrives with our drinks, Abram focuses his attention completely on me once again so I decide to give him another chance. He is rather cute, after all.

"To our first date," he toasts, "I hope to get to know you much better during this meal, Daphne. So far, I'm very impressed." He winks again. What is it with this guy and winking? Does he have some kind of twitch?

"So, what is your all time favorite movie?" Abram asks, leaning in closer to me.

"Hmm," I ponder. "I would have to say Rocky."

"Really, that's an interesting choice. Do you have a thing for inarticulate boxers?" he laughs in a mocking tone.

"No, I love to root for the underdog. I also love the relationship between Rocky and Adrian. I'm a sucker for subtle romance."

"Wow," he leans back into his side of the booth, seemingly disgusted by my movie choice. He acts as if I've harmed him in some way by having an opinion that doesn't coincide with his own. Perhaps there is more to Abram than it seems.

"What about you? What is your favorite movie?"

"Well, I like to see *films*. Most of what is out there is complete drivel. It's really hard for me to find a movie that I can tolerate. But, if I had to choose a film, it would be Citizen

Kane."

"Oh," I say simply. The way he enunciates the word film makes my skin crawl.

"Is there a problem with Citizen Kane?" he asks defensively.

"No," I reply, "It's just that I've never seen it."

"You can't be serious, Daphne. Where have you been living, under a rock?"

"Excuse me?" I ask, stunned. "That was uncalled for, Abram. I must say, you seem to be a bit of a movie snob."

"You'd better believe I am," he retorts, "I don't buy into the whole Hollywood trap where movies like Rocky are given Oscars and ridiculous actors like Stallone are able to rise to stardom. That guy sounds like he's been punched in the face way too many times. Seriously, the guy can barely act his way out of a paper bag.

What other movies do you like--Weekend at Bernie's? The Muppets Take Manhattan?" He laughs into his beer, evidently amusing himself. I'm wishing that I hadn't finished my Moscato so quickly so that I could, in fact, toss it into his smug little face, smudging his perfect glasses. Although he'd probably insist they are called "spectacles." What an asshole.

"As a matter of fact," I say, grabbing my purse and standing next to the table, "I happen to love "Weekend at Bernie's". My cousin Morgan and I can recite half that damn movie and I'm not ashamed of it. As for "The Muppets Take Manhattan", it is one of my very favorite films from childhood and I'd be ashamed to date any man who thought it ridiculous. The Muppets are an American institution, one that should be celebrated, not mocked. You could learn a thing or two from men like Jason Segel--,"

Abram interrupts me sarcastically, "You mean the idiot who developed the new Muppet Movie? Are you serious? That guy's a joke."

"You know, for someone who wants to write a hit screenplay some day, you have an extraordinarily limited view on what is acceptable and what is not."

"It's called having taste. Let me guess, you probably love to see Jennifer Aniston 'rom-coms' with your girlfriends, don't you? You probably love those hideously developed plotlines. Wake up Daphne, get a clue."

"Oh, I'm awake, Abram. And I've already gotten my clue. It's obvious that you are a snob, plain and simple, and you have no respect for other people's tastes or opinions. Because of that, I will be leaving now. Thank you for the drink and the enlightening discussion on *films*."

"Seriously, you're leaving because I don't like your taste in movies? Or should I say your *lack* of taste in movies," he laughs again to himself. He is ridiculously smug.

"Well, yes, as a matter of fact, I am. And my parting words to you will be from another one of my favorite movies that I'm sure you despise...'Pardon my French, but you're an asshole!' Good night, Abram."

"Ferris? Did you seriously just quote Ferris Bueller?"

"You'd better believe it. This "Rocky" loving, Bernie reciting, Muppet fan has quoted Ferris Bueller. I hope you are able to find the right girl, Abram, because she sure as hell ain't me!"

And with that, I proudly make my way towards the exit of the pub. Our waitress pulls me aside as I'm nearing the oak of the bar.

"Girl, that was awesome. That guy is a total dick. He comes in here all the time with dates, but I never see him with the same girl more than once. I always thought he was a bit of a player. But, after overhearing the tail end of your conversation, I realize it's because he's just a jerk and no one can stand to go out with him more than once!"

"Thanks," I smile, genuinely grateful for the reinforcement that I didn't overreact. Abram really is an asshole.

"I would suggest you come back another night and meet some of our regulars, but unfortunately your hipster, holierthan-thou date seems to always be here."

"That's sweet of you. Just between you and me, I've been on two really bad dates in the last few weeks. I think I'm ready to throw in the towel."

"No, don't. You're really adorable, and I think your taste in movies is awesome. My name is Mallory, by the way. Come in some other time and I'll buy you a drink, introduce you to some nice guys who won't insult you."

"I'm Daphne. Thanks for being the tiny silver lining in my storm cloud of a date."

"Anytime! We girls need to stick together against jackasses like him. Want me to spill a drink in his lap? I've done it before. I'm really good at making things like that look like accidents." Mallory's grin is devilish but sweet.

"No, that's alright. Let's let him sit there all by himself with nothing but his snobbery to keep him company. My couch is waiting for me at home. I think I'll indulge in a cheesy romantic comedy just to spite the asshole." I laugh, hug my new friend and leave the bar.

Once again, Morgan calls as I'm driving home. After sharing a few details of my horrendous date, I tell her to meet me at my apartment so I can fill her in on Asshole #2. She shows up at my door with an assortment of Jennifer Aniston romantic comedies (all of which I've seen several times).

"Let's do it up right, girl." She smiles, referring to her stack of movies, "And after these, we've got to watch Weekend at Bernie's in order to properly celebrate you walking out on that fucker!"

Popping in the DVD, I'm grateful for Morgan and Mallory. Dating is going to be tough, but at least these jerks have been a distraction from my sadness. I can only hope that soon I'll meet someone who will actually matter to me. Deep down I know I deserve to meet someone who will make me feel as sexy, as beautiful and as loved as Mayson had…perhaps even more.

Chapter 21
Rings

"Ugh," I groan to myself, looking at the clock. "Two more class periods to go." Even though I know I should be utilizing my lunch period as productively as possible, I find myself lurking in my email box. Just as I'm about to log off and get some grading done, I notice an email pop up in my inbox. It's from a familiar name, Matt Renbeck, Morgan's boyfriend.

Hi Daphne

I was hoping that you could do me a huge favor. I'd like you to help me choose a ring for Morgan---that's right, I'm planning to propose! I have no idea what she'd like, though. You know her better than anyone.....will you please help me?

Thanks,

Matt

"Holy crap!" I think to myself. Morgan is getting engaged, and I get to help pick the ring. Excitement boils up in my chest as I quickly type a reply to Matt telling him that I'd be honored to assist him, knowing that my cousin will absolutely say yes. And now, I'm feeling the pressure to find the right cut, style, etc. for her ring. Wow, this is going to be tough, but I'm up for the challenge!

I'm so thrilled for Morgan that the rest of my day flies by quickly. I spend the rest of my plan period searching for rings on the internet, remembering Morgan's desire for a solitaire diamond in a platinum setting. I'm certain that Matt and I can find something stunning.

Luckily, Matt and I are able to schedule our shopping excursion for the very next day. Keeping secrets has never been a talent of mine and I'm utterly relieved that he kept Morgan busy the night before so that I would not have to put on my best poker face.

"You know, you'll have to keep the secret even after we find the ring, right Daphne?" Matt asks, nervous. It's obvious he thinks I'll crack under pressure.

"I know," I say, trying my best to reassure him, "But, at least once you purchase the ring, I can relax. I'm so excited right now I can hardly stand it."

"Oh good. I was worried this would be awkward for you. Because of, well, you know..."

Hesitating briefly before speaking, I take a deep breath, trying my best not to cry. "It is a little awkward after seeing Mayson's ring. But, my happiness for Morgan means so much more. Just bear with me if I start to cry in the jewelry stores, okay?"

Matt cringes and I laugh nervously, "I promise it won't last long. My emotions seem to get the better of me whenever I think of him."

"Look, Daphne. I know I only met the guy once, but I

have to say I wasn't that impressed. He seemed, I don't know..." Matt's brow furrows and he breaks our eye contact, clearly conflicted.

"What? How did he seem, Matt? I'm interested to hear a male perspective."

"I don't know, Daph." Matt's frown deepens, "He just didn't seem good enough for you. You seemed kind of ill at ease around him. I'm so used to seeing you as such a jokester with Morgan and all of your friends. You weren't like that around him. He was kind of a buzz kill."

Wow, struck by Matt's words, I feel stunned. Matt is normally the laid back, never-has-strong opinions about stuff, kind of guy. But, clearly he had a strong impression of Mayson, and quite an undesirable one at that.

"I'm sorry, Daphne. Maybe I shouldn't have said anything. But, I know how much Morgan wants you to be happy with someone who really loves you."

"And Morgan doesn't think Mayson loved me?" Tears are forming and beginning to stream down my face. Matt looks like he's ready to run as far away from me as possible.

"I don't know how to answer that, Daphne. I think we just agreed that something was off with the guy. That's all. I'm really sorry that I brought it up. You're doing me such a favor and I feel awful that I brought you back to that nightmare."

"To be honest, it would've happened the second they pulled the first ring out of the case. At least, this way, I can try to get my crying over with instead of freaking out the salespeople." Matt and I share an uncomfortable laugh. "Look, this day is not about Mayson. It's about you, Morgan and your future together. Let's not go backwards anymore tonight. Instead, let's move forward."

"Alright, let's do this," Matt says, taking a deep breath and offering me his arm. I wipe the last few tears off my cheeks and smile up at him.

The jewelry store Matt has selected is intimidating.

Several salespeople are standing nearby and each of them turn their attention quickly towards us as we enter the store. We find ourselves seated in front of a large case of platinum engagement rings. I share Morgan's preferences with a saleswoman named Lisa who immediately begins pulling ring after ring out of the case. Matt's face becomes increasingly pale as several rings sit before him.

"Take a deep breath, Matt. We're going to find the right one." I reassure him, patting his arm softly.

"So, tell me about your girlfriend," Lisa says, "Sometimes it helps me to find the right ring."

"Well, she's awesome...so, so awesome," Matt says, color returning to his cheeks as he thinks of Morgan. Lisa winks at me. "She's sweet and beautiful and the sassiest chick on the planet. She's really loyal and fun and I'm incredibly lucky."

"That's wonderful," Lisa replies.

"I've been planning to do this for a while. In fact, I should've done it months ago and I'm not sure what was holding me back. But, I don't want to let any more time go by." Looking at Matt with true admiration, I notice his eyes are slowly glossing over as he thinks about Morgan and his commitment to her. I wish I could record this moment in time for Morgan as I know she'd love to see it.

After two hours looking at rings from three different shops, we find ourselves back at the first shop with Lisa our saleswoman. Matt keeps focusing his attention back to two similar bands. Both have large solitaire diamonds on platinum settings, but one is a true solitaire with sculpting in the band. The other has a gorgeous, unique border around the diamond which reminds me so much of Morgan. It's striking yet whimsical, not your average engagement ring. My gut tells me that Morgan will fall in love instantly when Matt places this exquisite band on her finger.

"This is the ring, Matt," I say with complete confidence.

"I was hoping you would say that. I couldn't agree more. Both of these rings are really nice, Lisa. But, this is the one.

This is the one that I can see on her finger." Matt is beaming with pride as he hands the band to Lisa.

"Congratulations. We can have it ready for you in the next week if you'd like to purchase it now."

"Absolutely, I stole one of her rings from her apartment so that you could size it properly." Matt says proudly.

"Excellent," Lisa nods as she proceeds with the sale. Matt breathes a sigh of relief and I bask in his excitement, pushing down my feelings of sadness. Several of the rings we viewed looked so much like the ring Cece gave to me. But, now that the shopping is complete, I feel drained and need to retreat to the comforts of home in order to find solace. Tonight was a reminder of how wounded I still am.

Chapter 22
Dancing

"I don't understand why you won't give the guy a chance. He's been interested in you for so long. Give him a break!" Morgan yells at me.

"Morgan, I'm embarrassed. That morning, when I found Evan in my bed, I regretted it instantly. All I wanted to do was be with Mayson again. I practically pushed him out the door. How on earth could I possibly start dating him now? He'll think I'm only with him because Mayson is, well, no longer in the picture." I still can't articulate the words. I still can't acknowledge verbally that Mayson has died.

"Well, when you say it like that, yes, it does sound pretty bad. But, he knows all of this and yet he's *still* interested in you. He asked about calling you, but he wants to give you time to grieve."

"That's really nice," I say, pursing my lips together, grateful for Evan's obvious forgiveness.

"I don't get it, Daphne. That night at the bar, you were

open to the possibility that Evan was your soul mate, that he was the one Kim told you about. But, the moment you woke up, you went right back to Mayson."

"It was just the alcohol, Morgan. I was being ridiculous."

"Maybe," she shrugs. "But, then again, maybe you're afraid, Daphne."

"Afraid? Of Evan? That's ridiculous."

"No, afraid of something that might actually work out. He likes you and you like him. It's easy, it works and it could lead somewhere. Mayson was difficult. Perhaps you were drawn to that."

"You think I liked being treated poorly? You think I liked the crazy ups and downs?" I ask incredulously, bordering on tears.

"Don't get upset, Daphne. I'm not saying you liked it. I'm saying you might be afraid of actually finding your soul mate, of actually finding the right guy. Maybe you're not ready for the next step."

"Are you?" I ask, "Are you ready for the next step with Matt?"

"Yes, I am. If you asked me that same question six months ago, my answer may have been different. Am I saying that Evan is definitely the one for you? No. I have no idea. But, I do know that you two were drawn to each other that night and there's no harm in seeing if there is something there. I'm asking you to give it one date, just one little date. Forgive yourself for the one night stand and let the man take you out to dinner."

"Alright, give me his number and I'll call him."

"Good girl," Morgan smiles, writing his number down on a post-it note.

That night, I pull out the bright pink post-it, take a deep breath and dial Evan's number. He picks up right away.

"Hello?" he says expectantly.

"Hi, Evan, it's Daphne Harper."

"Hey, Daphne. How are you?"

"I'm fine, thanks for asking. I got your number from Morgan. I hope that's alright."

"Oh yeah, sure that's okay. I'm glad to hear from you. I was hoping you would call sometime. But, I know you've had a rough go of it lately. I'm sorry about everything that happened to you."

"Wow, thanks. I wasn't sure if it would be alright to call, you know, after how I behaved. I'm sorry, Evan. I'm not normally like that."

"I know. I've paid attention since I first met you. You're a nice girl, Daphne. I know you were dealing with the hand you'd been dealt. No worries." He's so carefree, so quick to forgive. It's nice.

"Well, I was wondering if we could start fresh. Maybe grab dinner sometime?"

"I'd like that, Daphne. In fact, I have an extra ticket for the House of Blues this Saturday night. My buddy blew me off and left me hanging. I'd hate to go alone. Do you like the Black Keys? They're one of my favorites!"

"That sounds awesome. I could use a fun night out."

"It's settled then. I'll pick you up at 7:00 and we'll head down for the show." I hang up the phone and smile. I'm definitely looking forward to my evening with the laid back, understanding Evan.

Evan arrives right on time, looking just as I remember him, trimmed short brown hair, hazel eyes, a chiseled chin and defined features. He really is attractive and the idea of another shot with him is becoming more and more desirable by the minute.

"You look great, Daphne. It's really good to see you again."

"Thanks, right back 'atcha! Shall we go?"

Evan and I have no trouble making small talk as we drive downtown to the House of Blues. He smiles frequently at me and I notice an exceptionally cute little dimple on his left cheek. He's so confident, so attractive and easy to be around. Still, as attractive as I find Evan, I'm not feeling any sort of electricity. Perhaps it's all of the inept feelings that have surrounded me since that morning we said goodbye at my back door. Deep down I wonder if it could be more but, I worry we are just incompatible and no amount of drunken sexual attraction can fix that.

We arrive at the House of Blues right as The Black Keys take the stage.

"Come on, Daphne. Let's do what we do best. Dance with me," Evan says, with a sly smile. My heart skips a beat. I'm sober and not feeling attracted to him like I did the last time we joined each other on a dance floor.

Evan studies my face and sighs, "No, I didn't mean that. We did actually do some dancing the last time we were together. Come on, dance with me!" He teases and extends his hand to me. I relax and join him on the dance floor.

We laugh and dance as we listen to the music. He sings many of the lyrics aloud as he twirls me around, his strong hands making only chaste movements toward me. I can tell he's trying to prove a point. He isn't looking for a dance floor make out session. Knowing this, my body language changes and I'm free to be myself, to relax with him, swaying my hips to the music and singing along to the lyrics as I learn them. Evan raises my arms above me, swaying from side to side and I find myself laughing harder than I have in months. I'm having fun for the first time in so long. I wish I could bottle up this feeling and keep it forever. Endorphins stream through my body as we dance to song after song.

Hours later, Evan suggests stopping for a drink on our way back to the suburbs.

"It was so loud in there, Daphne. We didn't really get a chance to hang out and chat. Plus, I'm thirsty as hell. How about it? You up for a nightcap?"

"Definitely," I nod, not ready for our night to be over, the buzz of the club still lingering in my limbs. Even if I tried to go home and go to sleep, I wouldn't be able to. One more drink won't hurt.

Shortly after sitting down at the bar and ordering our drinks, Evan surprises me by bringing up the one topic I had thought he'd avoid.

"So, tell me about him," he says, giving me a knowing smile.

Taken aback, I reply, "Who?" But, I know exactly to whom he is referring.

"You know…the guy." Evan smiles warmly, attempting to ease my obvious anxiety over the topic at hand.

"Mayson?" He nods in reply. "Well, I'm not really sure what to tell you. He was very important to me, but he also hurt me quite a bit, left a lot of mental scars. I'm trying my best to move on, but it's complicated."

"I understand. I've been burned before, too." He nods as the bartender sets our drinks in front of us. Evan passes my sangria to me and clutches his bottle of Corona.

"Really, who was she?" I ask before taking a sip of the fruity wine.

"Her name was Kate. God, I was so in love with that girl. We dated for about three years and I was working up the nerve to look at rings." Evan spins his beer bottle, pursing his lips. "But, then she got really weird on me. She started to avoid me and was always making excuses not to stay over or spend time together. I'm sure you can probably guess what happened next."

"Was she cheating on you?" I ask, hoping I'm wrong.

"You guessed it." Evan says with a bit of an edge. He looks slightly uncomfortable as he continues to whirl his drink. His eyes are locked on mine.

"So, you know what it feels like…" my voice lowers, finally understanding why Evan has been so patient with me. Why he has still wanted to be involved with me even after knowing all of the facts about Mayson.

"Yep. You know, when I first left your apartment that

morning, I was really put off. I didn't understand why you shut down. I thought we had a really great time that night," he blushes as he laughs, scratching the back of his head, showing me that adorable dimple on his cheek once again.

"We did, Evan. It was such a fun night. I was in a really bad place and it just kept getting worse."

"I know, Daphne. Matt told me everything that was going on before I even approached you that night. I knew what I was getting into, believe me. I don't blame you at all. I knew that you were a nice girl who happened to be wrapped up in a lot of deep emotional shit. I know what it's like to have someone play with your emotions. Kate played with my heart for months before I finally discovered that she had moved on with someone else. I never understood why she didn't just choose. She could have let me go before betraying me instead of making me feel like such a chump."

"I'm glad you're opening up to me, Evan. You're giving my conscience some much needed relief. I've felt terrible about how I treated you because I never wanted you to feel used."

"Nah," he shakes his head, "No worries. Honestly, I'm a big boy." He smiles, his hazel eyes a bit damp from the memories of Kate.

"Listen, why don't we forget about Kate and Mayson for the rest of the evening and just enjoy each other's company?"

"That sounds awesome, Daphne. I guess I needed you to know that I get it, I understand. I don't want there to be any weirdness between us. I genuinely like you."

"I like you, too, Evan. And tonight was so much fun. You have no idea how much I needed it. I feel really comfortable with you, like we've known each other for a really long time."

"Wow, that was romantic, Daphne," Evan says sarcastically, but with a warm smile that keeps me from feeling apprehensive.

"What do you mean?" I press him.

"Well, guys don't want to be comfortable for a girl. We

146

want to turn you on, make you tick, make you *feel* things. And, I have to admit that I'm not feeling that from you tonight." His brow furrows a bit. And instantly, I'm remorseful for the lack of passion I feel towards this wonderful man.

"Look, Daphne, it's alright. Really, it is. To be honest, I'm really attracted to you. I think you're gorgeous and you're not even my type." He laughs. I raise an eyebrow, wondering if I should feel offended. "What I mean is, I tend to date women who have a bit of an edge to them and most of the time it gets me into trouble."

"Ah ha," I say, "Like Kate?"

"Exactly," he raises his beer. "You're different, Daphne. You're sweet and kind and so much fun to be around. But, I get it. We aren't exactly made for one another." He takes a swig of his beer and shrugs his shoulders.

"But, I do love being around you." I say, pleading a bit for more of his company.

"As do I, Daphne. Maybe we could try to be friends and see how it goes."

A huge grin crosses my face, "I would love that."

"Cool," he says, tapping my glass with his beer bottle. "Now, let's relax already and enjoy our drinks. How awesome was the band tonight? I'm so glad you were able to hear them live. And I can't believe that was your first time at the House of Blues."

"Yep, it was. I'm a teacher, remember? I don't get out much," I tease.

"Yeah, yeah," Evan scrunches his forehead in disbelief, "Well, if you ever want to go see another band, you know who to call. Music is my addiction and I can't get enough of live shows."

"I can see why. I haven't felt that alive in a long time!" I nod.

"It's pretty thrilling, isn't it?" He asks, his eyes widening.

"I'll make you some mixes, Daphne. I'll introduce you to all of the local Chicago bands that are worth listening to. Then you can let me know if you want to see any of them live. I'll be your music guru," he chuckles.

"Are you making fun of me, Evan?" I ask, not feeling any need to flirt. After all, we've decided to be friends and nothing more.

"Yeah, a little bit," he admits, "But, if we're going to hang out, you'll have to get used to that. It's in my nature to tease, especially my friends. I don't mean anything by it."

"Okay." I smile, "I feel like I'm starting to understand you a lot better, Evan."

"Really?" he laughs, "well, let me know when you have me all figured out!"

"I'll do that," I say, raising my glass.

"Cheers," we say in unison, and continue the evening with playful conversation. I'm no longer nervous or apprehensive around Evan and I'm hoping to continue this friendship. I don't want to cling to my apartment. I want to experience things and live my life, even if Mayson is no longer with me. Even if I haven't yet found my happily ever after, I need to keep living. I need to keep *dancing*.

Chapter 23
Flirtation

"So this is what married people do on the weekends, huh? Invite their friends over for dinner on their beautiful registered dishes?" Teasing Elise, I nudge her as she sets her dining room table.

"This is our first official dinner party as a married couple. Henry and I are excited to have everyone here together tonight. Please try to go with the flow, Daph. There are some people who I would love for you to meet. One in particular, actually."

"And who might that be, dear friend?" It has been over a month since Morgan forced me out of my apartment and helped me to envision a future for myself that did not include Mayson. I've been hanging out occasionally with Evan but haven't seen anyone romantically. I'm hoping that Elise has not been plotting my future behind my back since I'm not really sure I can handle any complications in my life. I'm enjoying being carefree and not having any expectations placed upon me at the end of the night.

"His name is Tanner Finley. You may remember him. He was one of Henry's groomsmen." Instantly, I'm flooded with hazy pictures of the handsome Tanner. I recall his brown hair, goatee and rather sexy smile. I also remember, however, the disenchanted look on his face when I walked to the bar with Mayson, ignoring my promise to have a drink with him. As Elise begins to rattle off his qualifications as a potential boyfriend, I secretly hope to finally have that extremely belated drink. Suddenly, butterflies are flipping in my stomach, the good kind.

Elise and Henry's guests slowly arrive at the dinner party. I glance at the door each time I hear the bell, hoping Tanner will walk in, see me and smile as he did at the wedding. When he does enter, he's not alone and my heart sinks. Why would Elise admit to setting me up with someone if he was already bringing a date?

"That's his sister, Maggie," Elise whispers into my ear.

"Geez, I had no idea you were even standing there, Elise," I say, startled, but relieved that Tanner has arrived dateless. My nerves begin to settle.

Elise gives me a knowing smile and walks back to the dining room to present a few of her guests with cocktails. Henry welcomes Tanner and Maggie into the living room area, where I happen to be standing, pretending to admire the countless silver picture frames from their big day. As I turn to sneak a peek at Tanner, I notice that he's already looking at me. I blush as we make eye contact, embarrassed and stifled by my terrible behavior last summer. As much as I'd like to cross the room and re-introduce myself, I'm secretly terrified of being rejected by the handsome groomsman.

Tanner smiles warmly at me before leading his sister into the dining room. My heart sinks as I feel the tiniest bit of rejection from this moment. Reminding myself that I have many hours in which to get to know Tanner, I casually ease my way over to a few of Elise's girlfriends from work. They are pleasant and fun and immediately draw me into their conversation. I'm grateful for the distraction.

"Hey Daphne," Henry says approaching, "I'd like for you to meet my buddy, Tanner. Tanner, this is Daphne. She was one of Elise's bridesmaids."

Tanner smiles as if he knows exactly what Henry is doing. Elise and Henry have never been known for their subtlety. "Yes, of course. Daphne, how are you?" Tanner leans forward and gives me a rather tight hug. His cologne is light and woodsy, almost like Mayson's. I push that thought to the back of my head. I must stop thinking about him. I need to focus on the indisputably handsome man before me who's giving me another chance when I so obviously blew him off last year.

"I'm doing well. I'm so glad to see you."

"Really?" Tanner seems genuinely surprised.

"Yes, I'd love to get that rain check we talked about at the wedding."

"Ah, you remembered." He grins, "What are you drinking this evening?"

"Surprise me," I say, obviously flirting.

"Okay, back in a sec," he grins.

Henry raises a knowing eyebrow as he walks away and I giggle softly to myself. I know Henry and Elise would love nothing more than to have Tanner and me as permanent guests at their dinner parties. But, I can't get ahead of myself, especially with the dates I've had lately. I need to be cautious and get to know this guy first.

A few minutes later, Tanner strolls back holding two delicious looking martinis in the glasses I had purchased for Elise's bridal shower.

"Elise said they are pomegranate martinis with a twist of lime. They sounded too good to pass up," Tanner says, placing one glass in my hand.

"Delicious," I say, sipping Elise's concoction.

"So, Henry mentioned that you're a teacher. That's really cool, and junior high kids to boot. You deserve some kind of medal for dealing with all those hormones on a day to day basis!" Tanner laughs.

"You don't know the half of it. The stories I could tell. Believe me, they would make you cringe."

"I bet they would. I'm a software engineer, so I don't deal with many hormonal situations in my line of work."

"A computer geek, huh?" I tease.

"Guilty as charged," Tanner laughs, raising his glass to me.

"Well, that could come in handy. I'm terrible with computers."

"Ah, I get it. So, you'll just string me along and then call me in the middle of the night to fix your hard drive, huh?" I love this effortless banter. Secretly I wonder if he meant something else by 'hard drive.'

"Of course," I nod. "Don't forget, I'll also need help with my cell phone."

"We may be able to work something out," Tanner smiles. His eyes are such a gorgeous brown with little specks of light green. I'm fascinated by them. After a moment of my blatant staring, Tanner seems self-conscious.

"Do I have something on my face?" he laughs.

"No, no. I was noticing your eyes. They're really fascinating."

"Wow, pulling out the big guns, huh, Daphne? You beat me to the punch. I was going to compliment your eyes later this evening."

"The night's still young," I raise my glass and smile. I've never had someone catch on to my sense of humor so quickly before. It's fantastic and I find myself even more drawn to the handsome groomsman as we continue to joke lightheartedly over martinis.

When dinner is served, Tanner and I walk together to the dining room. We are the last to arrive and my heart sinks as I notice the only two chairs at the dining table are nowhere near one another. Tanner pulls the first chair out for me to sit. He's such a gentleman.

"See you on the other side," he whispers mischievously. I think I'm smitten.

Somehow I manage to get through this dinner rather painlessly. Henry's friend, Weston is seated beside me and he's a pleasant guy. He cracks corny jokes and keeps me adequately entertained as we dine on Elise's delicious meal. Every so often, I sneak a quick glance at Tanner while he's talking with Maggie and Henry. Almost every time I look up, he's glancing at me as well.

The electricity that I feel between us is growing. We're only a few feet away from one another, yet the distance is causing an unbearable amount of delicious tension. I'm so excited to speak with him again. I can't wait to get a closer look at those gorgeous eyes. I find myself wanting to count those green specks.

"Earth to Daphne," I hear Weston say, using a cheesy astronaut voice. I'm snapped out of my Tanner infatuation and must rejoin the conversation. I glance up at Tanner who is chuckling softly to himself. My stomach flips excitedly as I return my attention to Weston who's happy to regale me with more silly jokes. I smile obliging at my dinner companion, quietly yearning for the smarty pants at the other end of the table. Finally, the meal has ended and the dinner guests retreat with their dishes to the kitchen area.

"That was the longest meal of my life," Tanner's voice is in my ear as I carry my plate to the kitchen. In a split second, the electricity increases.

"Oh really?" I flirt. "Dinner conversation wasn't the best?"

"No, the conversation was fine, but I was hoping to talk more with you. And now that I finally have the chance, my sister isn't feeling well and wants to head home. Unfortunately, I gave her a lift, so I'll have to be going. Damn family." He jokes.

"That's a shame," I say, honestly disappointed that he's leaving. I'm hoping he will ask for my number in the next few seconds.

"So," he asks, "I was wondering if you're free next Saturday night."

A slow smile crosses my lips, "Nothing set in stone just yet."

"Would you like to join me for an evening out?" Tanner asks, leaning in closer. I entertain the thought of counting those green specks in his gorgeous eyes once more.

"That sounds lovely." Writing down my phone number on one of Elise's refrigerator notepads, I smile at him affectionately. As much fun as our teasing banter has been, I want him to know that I'm genuinely looking forward to seeing him again.

"So, it's a date," he smiles proudly. "It was really great to see you again, Daphne. Until Saturday, then?"

He turns away, takes a few steps then heads back. "By the way," he smiles, "I love your eyes. They're as beautiful as the open sea."

I laugh, "Ah, so now who's pulling out the big guns, Mr. Finley?"

"Yeah, you stole my line earlier. But, I had to tell you before leaving. They really are lovely." He takes my hand in his for just a second before turning away.

As Tanner walks out of the kitchen, he turns back and gives me a small wave. For the first time all evening, I notice that he's blushing. Elise leans in close to me, puts her head on my shoulder and says, "Told ya."

Chapter 24

Fireflies

"You're really not going to tell me where we're going tonight?" I giggle, turning my head towards Tanner as he smiles proudly to himself, like he's holding all the secrets of the universe. Dusk is approaching and we've been driving in the car for what feels like hours, not that I'm complaining. I could do this all night.

"No, I'm really not going to tell you. You'll have to be patient," he replies, patting my hand gently. His skin feels warm. "We'll be there soon, though. I can tell you don't do very well with anticipation."

"You're right," I laugh, "I'm the worst. I was the kid who would try to open my Christmas presents ahead of time and re-wrap them so my parents wouldn't notice."

"You're kidding, right? You'd go to all that trouble just to see what was under the tree?"

"Yep. You said it yourself; I don't do well with anticipation."

"I'm starting to think that was a giant understatement," Tanner teases. His brown eyes are captivating me once again and I find myself staring at him for the remainder of the ride.

A few minutes later, he pulls the car up to a small park. Still intrigued, I'm not sure what to think.

"Oh, I love playgrounds!" I tease, "But, I must warn you, I get sick on the merry-go-round."

"Not so fast, Daphne, I have to grab a few things from the trunk first." He thinks he's so clever. Well, maybe he is.

Strolling confidently to the back of his Jeep, he opens the trunk and retrieves an old fashioned picnic basket, a checkered blanket and a grocery sack. Goosebumps rise on my arms as I wonder what's inside them. Trying to conceal my excitement, I follow Tanner to the open field behind the playground.

"Will you help me with this?" Tanner asks, handing me one end of the checkered blanket.

"It's the least I can do." I smile, "So....what's in the basket, Mr. Finley?"

"Hmm, I'm thinking I should make you wait a bit now that you've revealed your true nature. Making you wait could be so much fun," he smirks. I do my best to pout dramatically and he smiles. "Okay, okay! I see you're bringing out the big guns once again. Have a seat, and I'll show you." Giggling, I pounce on the blanket so I'm seated next to the large wicker basket.

Tanner opens the top of the basket and places two plates on the blanket, followed by wine glasses and several small plastic containers filled with cheese, grapes, and bread.

Finally, Tanner places a bottle of wine on the blanket and I practically swoon. Observing my reaction to the bottle of Moscato di Asti, my absolute favorite, he looks sheepish and a bit uncomfortable.

"I have a confession to make," he says, gazing thoughtfully into my eyes, "I knew that Moscato was your favorite wine. It wasn't some lucky guess or an act of fate or anything like that."

"A-ha, so you gathered intel?" I grin, "I'm guessing Elise is responsible for this?"

"Yep. I'd never even heard of it. The plan was not to confess and instead pretend it was my favorite. I'm a terrible liar, though, and didn't want to impress you under any false pretenses."

"You did impress me, though," I reassure him.

"Really? Even though I cheated a bit?"

"Yep. I love that you cared enough to go to Elise. I think that's awesome." I'm having trouble containing my enthusiasm. "No one has ever done that for me before. I know it may seem like something minor, but trust me when I say that it's not."

Tanner takes my hand, raises it to his lips and plants a delicate kiss on the tips of my fingers. My pulse quickens and my mouth starts to feel dry as my nerve endings dance. It's been so long since I've felt like this, it's a bit unsettling. I resist the urge to pull my hand away. Heat is gathering at my fingertips and flooding the rest of my body. I'm aching for him to kiss me, to stroke my hair and caress my neck. His gentle, simple gesture has sent me into a beautiful frenzy. Every bit of my body is yearning for him. Who knew a computer geek could be so hot?

"Okay, are you ready for rapid fire dating questions?" My confidence is growing and I'm eager to know about my handsome date.

"Go for it," he sits up, giving me his undivided attention.

"Favorite movie?"

"Say Anything."

"Seriously? I love that movie so much," I'm practically gushing. I can't believe Tanner loves one of my all-time favorite movies, usually deemed a chick-flick. Abram would be horrified.

"Yeah, I guess I'm a big sap. I think it's a great movie. I love the boom-box scene where he's standing outside her window. John Cusack, who's my favorite actor by the way, really nails it."

"I agree," I smile. Wow, this guy is getting under my skin.

"So much for rapid fire questions," Tanner teases as he pops a grape into his mouth, snapping me back to reality and to the task at hand.

"Oh, right, sorry. Okay, favorite book?"

"1984," he says confidently.

"George Orwell, huh? I love that book as well. I'm a dystopia junkie."

"Wow, we have something else in common, Miss Harper."

"Yep. All right, stop distracting me! Favorite band?"

"The Rolling Stones," he says matter-of-factly. "Paint it Black is my all-time favorite song."

"Ahh, so you have a dark side, too?" Shamelessly flirting with my date, I can't help myself. His answers are blowing me away.

"Favorite way to spend an evening?" I ask.

"Um, I'd say a picnic with a beautiful woman sounds like the perfect evening to me." Tanner answers, handing me a slice of cheese and a handful of grapes.

We sip the wine, nibbling on the cheese and bread while laughing again and again. Telling one another ridiculous dating stories, I'm at a bit of a disadvantage since he's friends with Henry and already knows some of my mishaps.

"So, wait, hold on...." Tanner laughs, trying to catch his breath, "the guy sent you a YouTube video of Van Halen?"

"Yep, he sent me the "Hot for Teacher" video. He was hoping it would score him a date."

"Well, did it?"

"Nope," I state proudly.

"Good girl," Tanner nods, seemingly reassured by my taste in men.

"Well, the YouTube video isn't the reason that I turned

him down."

"Oh, really? I'm intrigued. Please tell, what was the reason, dear Daphne?"

"He was divorced and he had four kids. I'm not ready to be the mother of one, let alone the stepmother to four! It was way too much pressure at the time."

"Oh wow. Yeah, I'm thinking you may have dodged a bullet on that one." Tanner nods. Just then, my cell phone dings. Glancing quickly, I see Cece has sent me a text. I quickly put my cell phone away.

"It's ok. You can read your message," Tanner says reassuringly.

"Nah, it can wait." A bit shaken, I try to refocus my attention completely on my date, "So, tell me, Tanner. What's the craziest thing a girl ever did to be with you?"

"Hmm, believe it or not, I'm drawing a blank. Don't get me wrong, I've had my share of dates and even a few girlfriends. But, I've never had anyone chase me around. Computer guys aren't exactly known for making the ladies swoon."

"Well, I'm swooning." Raising my eyebrow, I look him straight in the eye.

"Are you?" Tanner asks with a sexy smile.

"Yep, big time. This is a very romantic first date, you know."

"You ain't seen nothing yet." He is so confident. I love it. "Turn around. It's time for the sunset."

I turn just in time to see the glowing orange sun sinking slowly into the clearing. It's gorgeous and unbelievably romantic. Tanner wraps a small blanket over my shoulders, slides in next to me and takes my hand in his. When I turn to smile at him, he kisses me softly on the lips. My chest flutters. I'm tired of the polite kisses, I want more. A lot more.

Eventually, the sun has set completely and the twilight sky is nearing darkness. Just as I mentally prepare for the end of our picnic, Tanner reaches into his bag and pulls out several candles. Smiling wide, he shrugs his shoulders, "Citronella, to keep the bugs away. I'm not quite ready to let you go. When was the last time you looked up at a sky full of stars?"

Tanner carefully lights all of the candles and places them carefully around our blanket. He lies down and I follow his lead, placing my head next to his. We're so close that I wonder if he can hear the thunderous thumping of my heart. He places his hand into mine, threading our fingers together tightly.

We gaze at the stars for hours. Tanner points out several constellations to me and I'm captivated by his knowledge of the sky.

"I was fascinated by the stars as a kid. I had a telescope in my room and everything. Maggie and I used to stare up at the heavens on clear summer nights."

"I think the stars are incredibly romantic," I whisper, "I love that you know so much about them. I feel like I'm learning a little more about you."

"I'd like you to know a lot more about me…when you're ready."

Puzzled by this response, I press him, "What do you mean, when I'm ready? What did I miss here?" I lean up on my elbows and stare into his eyes, expectantly.

"I wasn't going to say anything. But, this night has been…well, it's been pretty incredible. I want to make sure that we move at a pace that works for you and I know you've been through a lot this past year, Daphne. I don't want to mess anything up."

"Oh," I say, taken aback, "So, you know about Mayson?"

"Yes, Henry told me. He wanted to make sure I was careful, you know, with your feelings. And, he was right. So, we'll take it slow. Just know that I like you, a lot, and I'd love to keep seeing you."

"I like you a lot too, Tanner. You really don't need to worry about me, though. I'm a big girl. Yes, Mayson put me through a lot. And it was incredibly painful to lose him in the way that I did, but I'm doing my best to move past it."

"Okay, I'm sorry I brought it up."

"No, I'm impressed that you brought it up. I love that you are straightforward and you say what you are feeling. I used to be like that, too. It's refreshing."

"You used to be? What made you change?"

"Well, let's just say that Mayson didn't appreciate brutal honesty."

"Ah, I see. Well, just so we're clear, I do. I would much rather we talk things through openly, without holding back, than to have unspoken things fester between us. I've always lived my life that way and I really don't have any plans to change."

"I'll work on it," I promise. "Habits can be hard to break sometimes."

"Ok, now lie back down and let's look at some stars. It looks like the fireflies are coming out."

"Oh, I love lightning bugs."

"Lightning bugs?" Tanner asks incredulously before laughing hysterically.

"You heard me. What's so funny?" All of a sudden, I remember Citizen Ass, Abram, laughing at me and I cringe. I don't want to be with another guy who takes pleasure in thinking less of me.

"I'm sorry, I've never heard that term before. It's cute, very endearing," he grins and instantly I remember that he is nothing like Abram. Relaxing and regaining my confidence, I tease him in return.

"Well, you, Mr. Finley, must've been raised under a rock. Everyone in the Chicago area knows they're called lightning bugs."

"Well, that explains it. I grew up in Michigan. I relocated when I was offered a job at my company. I've been living here for about five years."

"Well, you're a Chicagoan now, so you had better get used to calling them by their proper name." I tease.

"Fireflies," he nods assertively, giving me an irresistible smile that I'm pretty sure will be my undoing.

"Alright, alright, I give in," I put my hands over my head in surrender.

"You're incredibly sexy, you know that?" Tanner asks quietly, his cheeks redden slightly.

"No, I don't," I say, taken aback at this sudden compliment.

"It's true. You've got to be the sweetest and sexiest woman I have ever had the pleasure to watch lightning bugs with."

"Ah ha, you said it properly!" I laugh, throwing back my head in delight. I turn to face my date and before I know it, Tanner is kissing me. Not a soft, delicate kiss like earlier in the evening, but a hungry kiss full of desire. His hands cup my cheeks as I ease effortlessly into his embrace. His touch feels so natural, as if we've been doing this for years. Tanner's tongue enters my mouth and every nerve in my body stands hungrily at attention. His kisses are graceful, deliberate and smooth. My toes tingle as he presses me into the checkered blanket, our legs twisted together in a beautiful, private knot. His hands thread through my hair seductively as he continues to kiss my lips, my chin, my throat. I slip my hands underneath his polo shirt and he moans softly into the crook of my neck.

Just as his hands wander underneath my cotton tunic, my phone rings, startling us both. I recognize the ring tone, even though I haven't heard it in months. It's Cece...again. First a text and now a phone call. I haven't seen or heard from Cece since we met at the coffee shop months prior to this night. Something must be wrong.

"I'm so sorry, Tanner. This might be an emergency. I should take it."

"Of course," Tanner says, out of breath. He looks flustered.

"I'll be right back." Tanner nods and hands me a candle.

162

"So you can find your way back," he whispers.

I offer a weak smile, guilt flooding me as I answer the phone. I'm walking away from my gorgeous and thoughtful date in order to talk to the mother of my ex-boyfriend. Something does not add up. But, I must take the call.

"Cece, hi."

"Daphne, I'm so sorry, is this a bad time?" Cece asks quizzically.

"Well, I'm...not at home at the moment. Are you alright?" I can't handle telling Cece that I'm on a date, the first date that I've enjoyed since losing her son. I feel guilty, as if somehow my dating Tanner and moving on might cause her pain.

"Oh no, dear, I'm fine. I've been thinking about you so much and finally decided that I needed to get in touch," my body calms as I hear these words, knowing she's alright. This bond I feel towards Cece is unexplainable, yet so strong.

I glance back at Tanner who is drinking another glass of wine and running his fingers through his hair. His brow is furrowed in concern and I know he's worried. But, as guilty as I feel for leaving him on the picnic blanket alone, I'm so relieved to hear Cece's voice.

"Well, I'm so glad that you did. I felt terrible with how we left things."

"Oh, Daphne, you have no idea what that means to me. This may seem strange, but I feel such a connection with you. Perhaps it's what we went through together, losing our Mayson. I don't know, but I just called to say that I'm here if you ever need me. I care for you deeply, almost as if we've known each other for years. Is that terribly strange?"

"Well, maybe, but I don't care," I laugh, tears filling my eyes. "I feel the same way. Listen, I do have to go, but I will call tomorrow and we can catch up."

"Fantastic," I can tell she is smiling on the other end of the line. "You take care now."

"You do the same, Cece."

"Oh, and Daphne, thanks for answering my call. I wasn't

sure that you would after, well, after the cafe."

"I'll always answer. I will speak to you tomorrow."

Walking back to Tanner, a spectrum of emotion floods through my brain. Cece referred to Mayson as "our Mayson." How could I possibly tell her about Tanner? How could I tell her that he intrigues me in a way that no one else has since her son? I can't. If she asks about my love life, I'll have to lie. I must protect her feelings. She's been through enough.

"Is everything alright?" Tanner's concerned eyes find mine.

"Yes, everything is fine. I'm sorry about that," I try my best to sound casual.

"No emergency then?" I can tell Tanner is fishing for information and I can't blame him. We were in the middle of an extremely hot make out session and I stopped to take a phone call. Pangs of guilt shoot through me, knowing I may have hurt Tanner's feelings, and possibly his ego.

"No. Just someone I hadn't talked to in a very long time, an old friend. She had texted earlier so when I saw that she called, well, I thought maybe she was in some kind of trouble." Tanner nods, listening intently. "I'm so sorry that I spoiled the moment."

"That's alright. I'm hoping there will be many other moments in our future," he teases. I smile widely back at him. He quickly glances at his watch.

"Let's get you home before the cops bust us for being in the park this late."

"Ah, so you're a rule follower, eh?" I ask, realizing just how much I love teasing Tanner Finley.

"Not all the rules, but I really don't want this date to end in the back of a police car. So, yes, in this case, let's behave ourselves." Inside, I pout a bit, not wanting to leave this near perfect date. But, knowing that there will be more nights like this puts the smile back on my face as we drive to my apartment for a slow and sensual good night kiss.

Swooning over a computer geek? Hell yeah!

Chapter 25
Interrogation

"So, what on earth do you talk about with her?" Morgan asks skeptically over a slice of pizza. We're sitting on my apartment floor watching a romantic comedy (Abram would be so proud) and chatting over dinner. I've somehow managed to reveal my ongoing friendship with Cece.

"Everything really. Well, almost everything. I can't bring myself to tell her about Tanner. It would crush her."

"But, you said yourself that you're talking to her a couple of times a week. Tanner has become a huge part of your life. How could you not tell her about him? If Cece's really your friend, you wouldn't hide it from her."

"In theory, I agree with you. I know I shouldn't be hiding him from anyone. I adore him but, she's still in mourning. If she knows I'm starting to move on, she may pull away from me."

"And why would that be so terrible? What is so special about this friendship? You have plenty of friends already." I can hear the obvious disdain in her voice.

"I don't know how to explain it, Morgan. It's a bond that I've never felt with another human being. Maybe it's because we both lost Mayson, maybe it's because we comforted each other in a way that no one else has. All I know is that I treasure her and really look forward to our talks every few days. She's become like a second mom to me."

"And what about Tanner? Does he know about Cece?"

"Not exactly," I mutter, looking at the floor.

"Daphne!" Her mouth is agape, her eyes open so wide I can see white all around her bright blue irises.

"I know, I know. It's just so odd. I don't know how to explain it to him."

"But, he knows about your friendship with Evan, right?"

"Yeah, I told him about Evan from the start. He doesn't mind. Besides, he knows that Evan talks with me about the women he's interested in. We've even talked about possible double dates. But, his relationships don't last long. Evan is very fickle."

"And Tanner's okay with it?"

"Yes, he seems to be. I think he knows that Evan and I don't have feelings for one another. We just go to concerts and hang out occasionally. I try to convince him to date nice girls while he entertains me with stories of the troublemakers he's trying to date. Besides, Tanner likes him. My friendship with Evan is so different from my relationship with Cece."

"Well, with everything I know about Tanner, he wouldn't appreciate you hiding this from him, never mind the fact that you haven't told Cece yet. That's deceptive, Daphne. It's *so* not you." Morgan looks terribly disappointed in me. "Look, you told me how much he appreciates honesty and dealing with things as they come about. He doesn't like secrets. You're playing with fire, my dear."

Morgan's words sting. I'm simply not ready to reveal anything yet to Tanner or to Cece. They both mean so much to me, both relationships so new, so fragile. The thought of

166

hurting either of them is unbearable. Cece continues to be a living, breathing connection to the man I loved for years. Tanner is absolutely fantastic, so different from my first love in many ways, yet he evokes many similar feelings. I'm falling for him quickly. It terrifies me; just as my feelings for Mayson once did. It's simply not the time for me to reveal either of them to the other. Yes, it is a risky choice, but I must live with it, at least for now.

"Ok, changing subjects. I need to talk to you about Matt." Uh oh.

"What about him?" I do my best to remain casual as I take a bite of pizza.

"He's acting really, really strange lately. I'm worried he's getting ready to break up with me." Morgan looks alarmed. I need to calm her fears without giving away any potential engagement information.

"Why on earth would you think that?"

"Lately he seems to be working even longer hours than usual. We're supposed to be taking a trip to the Bahamas next month and all of a sudden, he doesn't want to talk about it at all. We've been planning this trip for months. I'm terrified that he's going to break things off right before we're supposed to leave. You know, like Carrie did to Mr. Big in the first season of Sex and the City." It's hard for me to not laugh at Morgan. She's definitely over thinking this.

"My guess is that he's working really hard before your trip. You know Matt is a hard worker and I'm sure he's just trying to get ahead of the game before traveling. Morgan, I see the way he looks at you. Regardless of his recent behavior, I'm certain he is still very much in love with you."

"Hmph," Morgan utters. She's not convinced. Crap. I'm not sure what else to say without being obvious that I have more information than she does on the matter.

"Promise me you'll wait until after your trip before saying something to him, Morgan. The last thing you want to do is put a damper on something you've been planning for so long.

If he acts strangely on the trip, then bring it up when you get home. I know you'd regret it if you brought things up too soon. And if he cancels the trip, I'll kick his ass. Okay?"

Morgan stares at her food for a moment before answering, "You're right. Maybe he *is* trying to get ahead of his work load. That does sound like Matt. Besides, he hasn't been cold towards me or anything like that."

"Does he just seem preoccupied?" I ask, knowing that Matt is absolutely preoccupied. Knowing him, he's excited to propose while on their vacation and is able to think of nothing else. His longer hours at work are probably a desperate measure in order to keep his poker face intact.

"Yes." Morgan nods, wide-eyed, relieved that I understand.

I'm also pleased, knowing that I've convinced her not to confront Matt before they leave on vacation. In a few short weeks, they'll be boarding a plane, headed towards an incredible getaway; one that will include a proposal. Morgan has no idea what's in store for her, but I do and I'm thrilled!

Chapter 26

Firsts

After an incredibly long school year, summer vacation has finally arrived. Unlike past years, I've declined to teach summer school so that I may enjoy these several weeks with Tanner. On this lazy Sunday afternoon we are snuggled up in my bed. He's reading the Sunday business section of the newspaper as I lay my head on his chest, enjoying the rise and fall of his ribcage. Gently, my fingers wander up and down his thigh in an attempt to finally find a ticklish spot on his body.

"It's no use, sweetheart," Tanner insists, "I've told you I'm not ticklish."

"Everyone has a weak spot, Tanner." I say confidently.

"That's true, Daphne. But, not everyone's weak spot is a ticklish one." I get the feeling Tanner is talking about his feelings for me. Perhaps I'm his weak spot.

I sit up and stare deeply into his speckled eyes. His cheeks quickly turn a deep shade of crimson. He knows I have him figured out. Instead of glancing away or making a joke, Tanner simply shrugs his shoulders and smiles.

"Come on, you know I'm crazy about you," Tanner says.

"Really? I thought you were just using me for my Sunday paper?" I tease, avoiding his straightforward nature. I wonder if I used to make Mayson feel like this when I was blunt and to the point with him. Did I make him feel ill at ease the way that Tanner does? Did I make him tongue tied as I feel right now?

"Well, I do like a good business section," he jokes, "But, no Daphne, you are, in fact, my weakness. You must know that by now. Sometimes it's hard for me to think clearly when you look at me like that." He lovingly strokes my cheek with his knuckles. I close my eyes, enjoying his tender touch.

"Like what, exactly?" I goad Tanner, not to torment him or make him uncomfortable, but because it drives me crazy knowing how much I excite him.

"Well, for example, when you tease me and act like a little jokester. It's adorable and sexy and I can hardly stand it. C'mon, you know you drive me senseless, Daphne."

"Senseless? Well, that doesn't sound very pleasant," I say, pouting slightly. As hard as it now is for me to express myself, I love hearing Tanner confess his feelings for me and want to hear more, so much more.

"Oh, it's better than pleasant. You drive me insane in a way that no one else ever has. The way you glance at me when you think I might be looking your way is one of my favorite things in the world," he says dreamily, stroking my hair with his fingers. "Sitting across the table from you at Henry and Elise's dinner party was the best possible torture. You kept glancing my way, thinking I might be looking back at you. What you didn't realize is that I *never stopped* looking at you that night. You were all I could think about."

"I felt the same way," I finally admit, not wanting Tanner to think his confessions are the least bit one sided. Reaching out, I gently play with the whiskers of his goatee. Tanner responds as he always does, by breathing in deeply and closing his eyes tight. I know how to turn him on and I love it. I can't get enough of this feeling, this feeling of having power over another person's emotions and desires. I'm wrapped up in Tanner in a way that is new yet somewhat familiar. He is so unlike Mayson, honest and direct.

"God, you're gorgeous." Tanner says as he opens his eyes. He looks at my cheeks, my forehead and my nose, exploring every curve of my face.

"Thank you," I giggle, "But, you don't have to butter me up to get in my pants."

Tanner looks hopeful as he gazes into my eyes. "I want you so badly. Are you sure you're ready? We can stop if you want to wait. It's alright. Really, it is," he says, his voice strong yet cracking a bit with emotion. His brown eyes are sweet in their expression as he attempts to suppress the building desire within his body. We've been dating for several weeks. We agreed to take it slow and we have. But, today things are different.

"No, I'm so ready for this. I've never been so sure of anything in my life. Please, Tanner, I need you, every bit of you." I pull him back down to me and his mouth is once again pressed to mine. Parting my lips, I invite his tongue back into my mouth. Just as he begins to submit to my kiss, I tug swiftly on his shoulders and flip him to his back. Leaning my hands into his chest, I smile giddily. His muscles are tense and firm as a look of astonishment spreads across his handsome face.

"Wow, you're pretty determined, aren't you?"

"I told you, I'm ready. And I won't let you talk me out of this."

"I wouldn't dare," he laughs as I slowly nibble on his neck.

Cupping his face with my hands, I press my lips against his, letting him know that I'm in no mood to stop. I want him desperately. He shifts himself slowly and moans quietly into my mouth. Message received.

I rock into him again and again until he pulls his mouth from mine. His eyes sear as he flips me onto my back and kisses me passionately, holding my arms above my head with one hand. With the other, he slowly traces an invisible line down to my shoulder blade and a delicious shiver runs up my spine. He is driving me wild and he knows it. He pulls away and gazes down at me lovingly. He pushes my bangs from my eyes and caresses my cheek with his strong hand. This sweet, simple gesture sends me into a frenzy. I want him.

Our tongues and bodies dance and twist together in a rhythm I've never experienced with another man. It's so passionate yet so effortless. I can't seem to get enough as he moves tenderly above me, stopping every so often to gaze into my eyes with absolute love and devotion. I stare at him in awe, urging him to continue as the pressure builds inside of me. It is agonizing, yet beautiful and I never want it to end. Tanner pushes me to the edge and I feel myself breaking apart as I cry out his name. His body tightens above me as he finds his own release. He lays down beside me, both of us speechless. Every part of me tingles from my fingers to my toes. As I struggle to catch my breath, he slowly traces the curves of my side with his fingers, leaning in to plant tiny kisses in the small of my back. After several minutes, I finally find the energy to speak.

"That was...wow,"

"I know," Tanner says, clearly proud of his accomplishments.

"That was honestly, the best 'first time' I've ever had."

"That's awesome," Tanner says, astounded. "You, you're awesome. That was, by far, my best experience...ever. I'm so wrapped up in you, it's ridiculous." He says, lovingly threading his fingers through my hair.

"I haven't been this wrapped up in someone since...well, it's been a long time."

His brow furrows knowingly as I almost mention

172

Mayson. "Look, I know it must be really hard with everything you went through, but I need to know something."

My nerves stand on edge as I await his question. "I must know. Am I a rebound? You mean so much to me and the thought of coming in second with you is excruciating."

"Tanner, that's not fair. There's no comparison."

Tanner sits up quickly; his eyes bore into mine. He's obviously not happy with my answer. "I'm not asking you to compare us. But, I need to know that I'm not your recovery guy, the one who simply helps you get your groove back. I need to know that you actually want something real with me, because I've never wanted anything more."

"Of course I want something real with you. You're fantastic. I love being with you, love spending time with you. Yes, I loved Mayson. But, he's gone and I'm ready to move on."

"Are you?" Tanner questions, his eyes turning frustrated.

"Yes! We just made love, for God's sake! Do you think I do that with every guy I date? Please, stop this. I want to be with you and I don't know what else you want me to say." Gazing into his eyes, pleading for patience, I reach out to run my fingers through his beautiful chocolate-brown hair. He presses his eyelids tight and takes a deep breath.

"Alright," he nods, "I'll work on it. Just know that I'm not giving up on you. I will fight for you, sweetheart."

"I hope so," I shiver, pulling Tanner's arms around me, regrettably thinking of Mayson.

Chapter 27

Rooftop

"Are you sure you're ready for this?" I tease Tanner, knowing full well he is ready to meet my family. We are joining them at a rooftop Cubs game along with several of my other relatives. As we stand on the platform, waiting for the train that will take us down to the city, I stop to admire my handsome boyfriend.

"What are you doing, sweetheart?" Tanner tilts his head to the side curiously.

"Just admiring you," I smirk.

"Hmmm," he says, pulling me into his arms, "I could get used to that."

"Me too," I say, planting a small kiss on his full lips.

"So, remind me again, what are the topics I should avoid with your Dad? Politics, religion...anything else?"

"Hmm, stick to talking about baseball and you should be all set." I laugh. "No, seriously, everyone will love you. Just don't mention that you're a White Sox fan."

"I'll keep it a secret, that's for sure." Tanner laughs. "How long do we need to be dating before I'll be able to reveal my true nature?"

"Hmm, it may be a few years yet." I smile.

"A few years? Nah, they'll love me right away and I'll convert them."

"You think so, huh? That's another sign that you're not from Chicago. There are no converts in this town."

After a short train ride, we arrive at the Sheffield Building to watch the Cubs game. As we climb the three flights of stairs, I fend off Tanner's roaming hands as he tickles and pinches my bottom. We reach the entrance and see my Dad waiting for us at the top. I turn to look at Tanner who grins sheepishly.

"Daphne, honey, you're here." My dad smiles and extends his hand to Tanner.

"Mr. Harper, it's great to finally meet you. I'm Tanner."

"Yes, Tanner, I'm glad you were able to join us today. We've been waiting for Daphne to bring you around. Come on, let's grab a beer." He pats Tanner on the back and gives me a wink. As they walk away, I hear my Dad ask, "So, Tanner, tell me, are you a Cubs fan?"

"Daph, honey, you made it!" I turn to see my Mom headed towards me. She is radiant in her Cubs visor and top; she'd live at the ball field if we'd let her. "I saw your father talking with Tanner. He's very cute, sweetie."

"Yes, he is. And he's also funny. His sense of humor is one of my favorite things about him. Mom, I'm so excited for you to get to know him. He's positively amazing."

My mom runs her fingers through my long hair, giving me a warm smile. "Oh, darling, you have no idea how lovely it is to see you happy. Your father and I have been worried about you. You've gone through so much. But, the look on your face tells me all I need to know. I'm certain I'll adore Tanner. He's making you glow with such happiness. Come on, let's catch up with those guys and have a drink."

Several hours later, Tanner and I are sitting on the train headed back to the suburbs. I've had a few too many beers so I'm leaning on Tanner's shoulder for support. His hand caresses my leg gently, drawing shapes on my thigh with his fingers.

"Your family is such a blast," Tanner reminisces. "Your aunts, uncles, cousins, everyone was really nice to me. They welcomed me with open arms. My family isn't quite so..."

"Loud?" I ask, giggling. Tanner gives me a fake scowl before continuing.

"What I meant to say was that they are boisterous."

"That's just a smart word for loud." I shrug.

"Yeah, ok, they are loud. But, I love that. Don't get me wrong, my family is great, but they are definitely reserved. My mom won't be offering you a beer the moment she meets you. I think your cousin Trevor offered me a beer about every ten minutes. If I'd accepted each one, you'd be dragging me home right now. But, he's a hell of a guy. I'm really looking forward to seeing your relatives again."

Sighing with satisfaction, I mentally replay scenes from the baseball game in my head; Tanner joking so easily with my Dad, charming my mother and my Aunt, drinking beer with my cousins. He fit so beautifully into my family, into my world. With each passing day, my feelings for Tanner are getting stronger. Remembering what my Mom had said to me earlier, I smile knowing that Tanner has made all the difference in my life.

Chapter 28

Engagement

Tanner and I are cuddled up on my sofa, eating Chinese food and watching a romantic comedy (take that, Abram!) when the phone rings. Glancing at the caller ID, I see it's Morgan calling from the Bahamas.

"Hello?"

"Daphne, you stinker!" Morgan laughs into the phone. "You knew Matt was going to propose! You helped pick the ring!"

"Yes, I did, Morgan. Did you say yes?"

"Well, of course I said yes!"

"Tell me all about it."

"Oh, Daph, it was so wonderful. He arranged to have a private dinner set up for us on the beach at sunset. We had our own little canopy draped over the table and there were candles everywhere. It was so incredible. He got down on one knee as soon as we reached the table. It was adorable. He couldn't even wait for us to eat."

"I'm so thrilled for you! I'm dying to know, do you like your ring?" The awkward pause that follows makes my heart sink.

"No." Morgan says, sounding sad.

"Oh," I respond, dumbfounded.

"I LOVE it!

"Ah!" I yell into the phone, "Who's the stinker now?"

Morgan laughs, "I had to do that, just to even the score! Seriously, though, it's breathtaking. I don't think I could've chosen anything better. Thank you so very much for helping Matt."

"It was my pleasure."

"I need to get back to my fiancé," She giggles, "We're going to go for a long walk to discuss our plans for the wedding. But, before I go, I have an important question to ask you."

"Yes?" I reply.

"Will you be my Maid of Honor?"

"Of course!" I shriek, bouncing up and down on the couch, causing Tanner to drop his chopsticks.

"Hooray! Thank you for everything, Daph. We'll be home in a few days. I can't wait to see you."

"I can't wait to see that ring on your finger! Enjoy the rest of your vacation." Hanging up with Morgan, I let out a contented sigh.

"So, he asked her, huh?" Tanner questions, "He was really nervous before the trip. He was convinced that Morgan would see the ring at the airport."

"Matt planned to put it on the conveyor inside his shoes, ring box and all. I knew Morgan would be so distracted by her own things going through the conveyor, she wouldn't pay any attention."

"Obviously it worked or he would've gone down on one knee right there in airport security," Tanner smiles.

"Really? Is that what he told you?"

"Yeah, Matt and I have hung out a few times." Tanner

admits. I had no idea.

"I think that's great, Tanner."

"He's a cool guy. I like him."

"Ooh, do I feel a 'bromance' brewing?"

"Well, he is my type," Tanner jokes. "I was actually thinking of asking Matt to be my date at my cousin's wedding next month, but I think he might be busy. I guess I'll have to ask you." Tanner pretends to look disappointed, his brow furrowed, his mouth forming a pout.

"A wedding, huh?" I ask. Ugh, I haven't shared my bouquet catching abilities with Tanner yet. I figured I had until Morgan's nuptials to share that about myself.

"Yes, it's in Door County Wisconsin. My parents and sister will be going, as well. I hope that doesn't scare you off." Tanner looks hesitant, but relaxes once I raise an eyebrow at him.

"Are you kidding?" I ask, climbing into his lap, "I would love to meet your family."

"Phew, wasn't sure if it was too soon." Tanner admitted.

"Well, you've met my family. Why is this different?" I ask, confused.

"I don't know. Your parents live only a couple of towns over. Obviously I knew I'd meet them pretty early in our relationship. My family is out of state. I'm guessing you thought you had more time before, you know, being introduced."

"I would love to meet the rest of the Finley clan. Besides, we've been dating for a few months now; I think it's time, don't you?" I purr softly into his neck, planting small kisses along the neckline of his t-shirt. Overjoyed by Tanner's willingness to introduce me to his family, I'm suddenly feeling quite amorous.

"I'm glad, Daphne. They're excited to meet you...very excited, in fact. Every time I speak to my Mom, she asks if I've invited you yet. I've been keeping her at bay for a while now, but figured I'd better ask before you made other plans. My folks are renting a large condo. There is plenty of room for all of us....that is, if you're comfortable staying there. We can always get a hotel room if you prefer."

"Hmm," I say, pretending to ponder the alternative, "Let's stay with your folks." Sitting up, I look Tanner in the eye and smile seductively. "Now, will you please stop talking and take me to my bedroom?"

"Oh, of course, what was I thinking?" Tanner laughs, scooping me up and carrying me down the hall. We collapse onto my bed and he showers me with sensual kisses. His body language reveals his relief. I have passed a test. Positively flattered that he wants me to be such an open part of his life, I bask in his seductive kisses, completely enamored.

Tanner's kisses grow more urgent and I'm instantly swept up in his need for me. Running my fingers through his hair, my tongue sweeps eagerly through his mouth and he moans softly. Slowly, I suck on his bottom lip pulling it between my teeth and biting down gently. Tanner lets out another moan. Pulling down his pants at a feverish pace, I'm overwhelmed by my desire to connect with him physically. Voracious, Tanner yanks my top off and explores each breast with the tip of his tongue. Swept up by every delicious flick of his tongue, I move with him in a graceful motion. Needy yet smooth; hungry yet sweet. Every physical move he makes, I'm certain is driven by his emotions, by his devotion to me. This is not just sex, this is love. Real love.

Basking in the afterglow, Tanner runs his fingers through my hair and caresses my back lovingly.

"I swear, your hands are going to ruin me forever."

"How do you mean," Tanner inquires, shifting slightly.

"Your touch is unique. I'm not sure how to describe it. You seem to know exactly what to do and when you want to do it. When you want to excite me, you're able to do that within seconds. And when all is said and done and we are relaxing here, your touch is so sweet. You send shivers down my spine. It's lovely."

"I just have trouble keeping my hands off you. That's all." Tanner says, making little circles on my lower back with his fingers.

Just then, the phone rings. I start to sit up, but Tanner pulls me back down towards him. "No, stay here with me. Pretend it's not ringing."

"Alright, I say. Whoever it is can wait." I smile, snuggling into Tanner's embrace, placing my head on his chest. He smiles warmly and pulls me closer as I hear my answering machine pick up the phone call. My heart skips a beat when I hear a familiar voice travel through the air waves into my bedroom.

"Daphne, dear, it's Cece. I'm calling to say hello and to see what's new with you. I found a really great article on middle school lesson planning and was wondering if you had seen it. I know you mentioned you'll be looking for some new ideas this year. Anyway, just give me a call. I'll be home. Sending you my love."

"She sounded nice. Who was that?" Panic pulses through my body. My heart races and beads of sweat form on my hairline. I'm not ready to tell Tanner about Cece, especially after we've just been so intimate. She seems to have ridiculous timing. Maybe I should silence my answering machine.

"Daphne?" Tanner's voice startles me and I realize I haven't yet told him who Cece is. He is waiting.

Thinking on my feet, I muster, "She's my aunt." I feel downright awful for lying to him, but I'm lost on what else I can do. Tanner would not understand my continued friendship with Mayson's mother and might pressure me to put an end to it. I know I can't do that. Not yet.

"Oh, I don't remember an Aunt Cece at the ballgame," he mutters suspiciously. My heart skips a beat. I hadn't planned on expanding my lie. It is killing me to lie to Tanner.

"She lives in South Carolina and wasn't able to make it." Tanner is silent.

Plagued with guilt, I press my face into Tanner's chest, unable to look him in the eye. Within a few minutes, his breathing slows as he drifts off to sleep. Unable to close my eyes for even a moment, I am utterly ashamed of myself. Just minutes after realizing the depth of my feelings for Tanner, I have once again deceived him by hiding my relationship with Cece. The thought of losing Tanner makes my stomach drop to my knees with panic. I am in love with him, a feeling I've dreaded and yearned for all at the same time. Knowing my behavior is deplorable, but unable to tell the truth, I listen to the beat of Tanner's heart, listen to his shallow breaths and hope to one day redeem myself.

Chapter 29
Cherries

"Wow, it's so beautiful up here. I've never seen the bay." I say, looking out the window of Tanner's SUV, admiring the beautiful atmosphere of Door County on our drive to his parent's rental in Egg Harbor. We pass several billboards advertising wineries, restaurants and cheese shops. The water along the shore glistens in the sunlight and I hope we will be staying on the water.

"The skies are so blue today," Tanner says in agreement, a contented smile upon his face. He pulls my hand into his, giving it a quick kiss before placing it on his thigh. Sighing softly to myself, I continue to admire the view from outside my window.

Soon, we arrive at the resort of condominiums. It's enormous and appears to be situated right on the bay. I'm thrilled. Tanner carries our bags to his parent's unit. My chest tightens as we approach the door. I've never been so nervous to meet a man's family before. I want them to like me, desperately. It would kill me if they didn't. Tanner squeezes my hand tightly and gives me a reassuring smile. It's like he can read my mind. I return his smile with an apprehensive face, and he shakes his head as if to stop me from any negative thoughts. I take a deep breath and nod confidently as he knocks on the door.

A tall man with gray hair opens the door and greets us with kind eyes.

"You made it," his father says, holding the door open wide. I follow Tanner into the unit as he places our bags on the floor.

"You must be Daphne. I'm Paul, Tanner's father." I offer him my hand to shake it, but he pulls me in for a hug. I breathe a sigh of relief, truly feeling welcome. "We've heard so much about you, Daphne. I'm so glad you were able to make it."

"Thank you so much for having me, Mr. Finley. I'm thrilled to be here. Door County is so beautiful."

"Please, call me Paul," he raises a playful eyebrow at me. "Have you ever been up to Egg Harbor before?"

"No, sir, this is my first time in Door County, in fact."

"Well, you're going to love it," he smiles exuberantly. "It's Lily's favorite place on earth. Oh, here she is now," Paul gestures towards the long hallway. I hear the clicking of heels and know that Tanner's mother is approaching. Holding my breath, I hope she'll be as kind as her husband.

"Tanner, Daphne, you're here!" She practically squeals as she strolls over to Tanner and embraces him tightly. Tanner smiles lovingly at his mother and I'm impressed with their rapport.

"Mom, I'd like for you to meet my girlfriend, Daphne."

"Daphne, honey, thanks for coming," she says as she pulls me into a tight embrace. Who knew the Finleys would be so affectionate? They are calming my fears with their obvious good nature.

"Here, honey, come on in. You must be thirsty after such a

long car trip. Can I get you anything? Iced tea? Lemonade?" Mrs. Finley asks as we walk into the kitchen.

"An iced tea would be lovely. Thanks so much, Mrs. Finley."

"Please, it's Lily. My mother-in-law is Mrs. Finley. In fact, you'll be meeting quite a few Mrs. Finleys this weekend at the wedding. There are a lot of men in this family."

"I'm looking forward to it," I say, raising my iced tea to my lips as I follow Lily onto the deck. Paul and Tanner are sitting on the rustic patio furniture, looking at the incredible view. Large pine trees tower over our condo and the bay sparkles in the late afternoon sun. A slight breeze blows through the summer heat making it a little more bearable.

Tanner pats the seat next to him. He smiles and places his arm around me as I sit and snuggle up to him. His mom notices this touch of intimacy and seems pleased.

"So, Tanner tells us that you're a teacher. Middle school, is that right?" Lily asks.

"Yes. He mentioned that you volunteer at a local elementary school. I think that's wonderful."

"I really enjoy it. I participate in the Reading Buddies program. The best part is that I'm allowed to bring in books myself. I have so many books from Tanner and Maggie's childhood and it's fun to introduce them to the children."

"Which is your favorite?" I ask, genuinely interested in Lily's involvement with school children.

"That would definitely be 'Miss Nelson is Missing.' Do you remember that, Tanner? You were so afraid of her when she was wearing that costume."

"How could I forget?" Tanner practically shudders next to me, "Miss Viola Swamp used to give me nightmares." His admission makes me smile. He is so open, so honest and so damn adorable that I can hardly stand it.

In this moment, I know I must tell Tanner that I love him. The emotion is welling up inside of me, filling me from head to toe. I know he loves me in return, so I'm not afraid of that.

But, I want to find the right moment; the exact moment in which to say the words.

"I love that book, too," I say, placing Tanner's hand in mine as I look him in the eyes. I decide to use the word 'love' a lot this weekend in order to mentally prepare him for that conversation.

"Well, Daphne, I must say I think it is wonderful that Tanner is dating a teacher. I've always had the utmost respect and appreciation for that profession."

"Thank you so much, Lily. That means a lot to me." I reply. She smiles warmly in return.

"I have to say, I love your name. How did your parents choose it?" Lily asks inquisitively.

"Well, it's kind of a silly story." I blush, "When I was born, I had bright red hair. It made my mom think of Daphne from Scooby Doo. My name was originally going to be Jane after my great grandmother. So, instead my parents decided on Daphne Jane."

"I love that," Lily gives me a generous smile.

"I do, too," Tanner says, running his fingers through my auburn hair.

"So, what are you two kids up to this evening?" Lily asks, changing the subject.

"I was thinking we'd do a little wine tasting. Daphne loves wine."

"Oh, you'll love the vineyards here, Daphne. All of the fruit wines are so refreshing and tasty." Lily smiles widely.

"Would you like to come with us?" I ask.

Lily glances at Paul and they smile knowingly at one another before Paul responds.

"That's very sweet, but I think we'll stay in this evening. Maggie should be arriving in a few hours. We don't want her to show up to an empty condo. Plus, you two should spend some time alone before all of the wedding events tomorrow."

"Will you, at least, join us for dinner then?" Tanner asks.

Paul glances at his watch. "Alright, maybe a quick bite to

eat and then we'll send you two on your way to the vineyards."

"Do you like cherries, sweetheart?" Tanner asks as we arrive at the first vineyard.

"I adore cherries. They're my favorite. In fact, I *love* them." I smile, squeezing Tanner's hand gently as we walk into the winery. He raises a suspicious eyebrow at me. Does he already have me figured out? He says nothing else as we stroll inside, holding the door open for me. His hand is gently placed on the small of my back as we walk to the counter. A woman smiles broadly and hands us the wine menus for the tasting. Tanner and I select our six wines for tasting and pass the selections back to our host.

"Excellent choices," she says as she fills our glasses. Despite the large salad that I ate for dinner, the wine is giving me a delightful buzz by the time we have finished the tasting. I playfully hold onto Tanner's elbow as we walk back to his car. Having not been affected by the wine himself, he is enjoying my tipsy behavior. He carries our purchases to the car, places them in the trunk and opens my door.

"Wow, you're such a gentleman this evening, huh?" I tease him. "I *love* that."

"Oh you do, huh?" he laughs, giving me a satisfied grin, "You are really feeling the *love* tonight, aren't you Miss Harper?" He asks, swiftly pulling me into his arms. He has literally taken my breath away. He stares deeply into my eyes. He then glances to my lips, my cheeks, my hair as if he is searching for something to say. He strokes my cheek lightly with the pad of his thumb as he takes my chin into his hands. He kisses me deeply and I respond instantly, pulling him to me with voracity and desire. After a few moments, he pulls away, gasping for air, staring into my dumbfounded eyes.

"What is it?" Why did you stop?" I ask, leaning onto his chest for support without breaking eye contact.

"I just remembered that we're in a parking lot." He

laughs.

"So what?" I ask, running my fingers down his neck.

"We're in a parking lot and you, my dear, are tipsy. And as much as I love when you are tipsy, I think we should probably go now." I give him an exaggerated pout, but cannot sustain it when he raises his eyebrows at me.

"Alright, party pooper," I say between giggles climbing into my seat, "Let's go."

We visit two more wineries, and despite my rapid consumption of the sweet crackers at each bar, I'm still enjoying a very healthy buzz. I notice that Tanner is also showing a slight tipsiness to him. Being the responsible man that he is, however, our final winery is across the street from the condominium complex.

"You think of everything, don't you?" I ask as he carefully pulls his car into the parking lot.

"Most of the time. Isn't that something you *love* about me?" he asks, patting my leg after putting the gear shift into 'park'. I take his hand in mine and stare at him intently.

"I love *everything* about you." Tanner stares at me for a moment, then smiles deviously and grabs my face with both of his hands, pulling me toward him for another deep kiss. His tongue tastes delicious, like strawberry wine. His breath is hot on my neck as he pulls away and begins to shower me with kisses along my jaw. I shudder and cry out softly as he flicks his tongue seductively on the fleshy portion of my ear. I want him so badly. Craving the touch that only Tanner can give, I stroke his inner thigh, urging him on.

"Let's go upstairs," he murmurs.

"Will that be ok?" I hesitate, "I mean, with your family?"

"Yeah, we just need to be quiet. Can you do that?" I stare, astonished at his question.

"I'm not sure," I giggle.

"I promise it'll be worth it," Tanner smirks before kissing me roughly on the lips once again. I have no choice but to nod in surrender.

188

The next morning lying next to him, I feel elated but a touch paranoid. I remember our movements and how our bodies fit together so perfectly. I remember the smell of wine lingering as he stroked my hair and I breathed roughly into his chest. The one thing I don't remember is whether or not I was able to keep my voice restrained. Eager to speak to Tanner, I stroke his shoulders, his biceps and his forearms lightly, hoping he'll be able to reassure me. Eventually he stirs.

"Good morning, sweetheart," he says, smiling widely.

"Morning, Tanner. Last night was absolutely blissful." I say, stroking his cheek.

"I agree. I *loved* it." He smirks. Yep, he has me totally figured out. Refusing to give in, at this point, I continue to play the game.

"Well, I'm so glad you *loved* it, darling. But, I'm dreading seeing your folks."

"Why?" he seems genuinely puzzled.

"Well, I don't know if I was able to control myself. I remember so many things about last night, but I can't recall if I was quiet enough...you know, so that no one heard us."

"You were practically silent, Daphne," Tanner snickers.

"I don't believe you!" I say, shoving him playfully in the chest.

"No, I swear, I swear," he says, holding his hands up in defense. "You were perfect, sweetheart. I'm certain no one heard anything at all."

I loosen up, knowing Tanner would never lie to me. And in that realization, I realize how incredibly happy I am with this man. He is honest, he is kind, and he is outright sexy.

"Hey, what are you thinking about?"

"Hmm, I was just realizing how lucky I am."

"Hmm," he says sarcastically, "What were you really thinking?"

"Well, if you must know. I was thinking about you. How wonderful you are, how sweet you are, that kind of stuff."

"Keep going. I don't think I'll ever grow tired of this conversation," he laughs.

"I'm sure you won't," I say, raising an eyebrow.

Tanner says, pulling me closer, pushing my bangs from my eyes. "I'm glad you think you're lucky. But, I'm the lucky one. You came into my life and have brightened it ever since. You're like sunshine." He pauses and strokes the stray hair from my face. "Are you hungry? I think I smell bacon and coffee downstairs."

"Sure, let me take a quick shower and then I'll be right down." I say, suddenly feeling self-conscious.

"You know you look perfect. Everyone else will be in their pajamas and robes."

"But, I don't know that I'm ready for your father to see me in my pajamas," I admit, my cheeks turning scarlet. Tanner places a tiny kiss on the tip of my nose.

"I understand, sweetheart. I'll see you downstairs."

"Thanks," I mumble, still feeling a bit uneasy. Tanner puts on his pajamas and closes the door behind him. Taking a deep breath, I head to the washroom to freshen myself up. I can hear his parents asking him about our trip to the wineries. There is no weirdness or awkward tension and I feel so relieved.

Quickly, I shower, get dressed and pretty myself up a bit before heading downstairs to join Tanner's family for breakfast. His sister Maggie is the first to greet me, crossing the room and giving me a hug.

"Good morning, Daphne! It's so good to see you again."

I smile warmly at her, "Thanks, Maggie. I'm happy to see you, too."

"Come sit down. Mom and I made breakfast for everyone. What can I get you? Eggs? Bacon? Fresh fruit?" My stomach growls loudly.

"Oh wow." I giggle, placing a hand on my abdomen, "Yes, yes and yes, please."

Tanner grasps my hand in his under the table and gives

me a chaste kiss on the cheek. I shift towards him, thanking him for the sweet contact.

Everyone is excited for the wedding this evening. Maggie convinces me to let her style my hair. I oblige, mostly because I'm terrible at styling my own hair, but I'm also excited about the opportunity to bond with her. I haven't really spent much time with Maggie and would love her to approve of my relationship with Tanner.

Lily and Paul are attentive hosts, making sure I've had enough to eat and that I slept well. I feel so at home in their world and it's encouraging. I find myself getting excited about the upcoming wedding and reception. Now that I feel accepted and welcomed into the Finley family, I'm ready to face the relatives.

That evening, Tanner and I are sitting in a small church waiting for his cousin, Victoria, to walk down the aisle. His arm is set behind me while the other cups my hand in his. He looks so satisfied to have me on his arm. It makes me swoon again knowing that he's proud of my being here with his family. I'm his one and only and the knowledge of this brings me immeasurable amounts of joy.

The Bridal Chorus begins and Victoria strolls down the aisle. Her dark hair cascades down her back, and the lace of her dress matches the delicate veil atop her head. She's a sight to behold.

The service is beautiful and the joy of the newly married couple radiates throughout the chapel. Tanner leans in closer as the bride and groom exit the church.

"Hope that wasn't too painful," he smiles.

"Are you kidding? It was gorgeous. I'm a sucker for a beautiful church wedding." I take his hand and we follow the crowd out to the parking lot.

"Really? I pegged you as a get-married-on-the-beach type of girl."

"Nah, I guess I'm more traditional than you know, Mr.

Finley. I've always dreamed of a small chapel like this, my father walking me down the aisle, all that good stuff. What about you?" I tilt my head to the side with a small smirk on my face as Tanner opens my car door for me and holds it open, staring me deeply in the eyes.

"Honestly, I've never given the actual service much thought. I've always thought more about the woman I'd marry." He then plants a strong kiss on me before strolling around the SUV to the driver's side. I'm left stunned and realize that I'm still standing outside of the vehicle as Tanner starts the engine.

"Daphne," he laughs, "Want to get in the car, sweetheart?"

"Right," I say, shaking off my bewildered expression.

We spend the next few minutes in complete silence. I'm too afraid to speak, my emotions are too strong. I'm afraid I'll confess my love right here in the car. No, Daphne, you must wait for the right time.

"Are you alright?" Tanner asks, breaking my chain of thought.

"Did I freak you out back there?" He looks perplexed and nervous. He thinks I didn't like what he was hinting at, but he is so wrong.

I look at him confidently and say, matter-of-factly, "Absolutely not, Tanner. It's just the opposite."

"Oh, thank goodness," he sighs. I'm so eager to tell him how I feel. I want to ease his fears and my own. But, first, I must confess my hidden talents that will surely be revealed at Victoria's reception.

"So, there's something I really should share with you," I say nervously.

"Go ahead," he says, focusing on the road. He looks tense.

"I sort of have this talent. It's an odd one to have, I admit...but, well, I catch every bouquet at every wedding I attend even though I don't want to. There, I said it. It's off my chest. Phew." I exhale deeply and push my head back into the seat.

"Seriously," Tanner grins. "Every time, huh?" I nod.

"How many weddings?" he asks.

"I'm starting to lose count, to tell you the truth. Nine? Maybe ten?"

"I'm not gonna lie, that's a little odd. But, maybe the universe is speaking to you." I sit up with a start.

"That's what I've always wondered! But, honestly, it's been going on for so long now, who the heck knows anymore. I don't want you to be freaked out if I catch it tonight."

"If you catch it?"

"Ok, when I catch it." I roll my eyes playfully.

"It won't freak me out."

"Really, are you sure?" I ask, giving him my best attempt at a sexy smile.

"I am absolutely certain. I promise it won't freak me out." He is so calm and self-assured, as he speaks these words. A strong wave of calm spreads through me as he pulls his SUV into an empty parking space. He shifts the car into park and gives me a small kiss on the lips.

"Come on, I'm starving. Let's go eat!"

Several hours later, it's time for the bouquet toss. My heart begins to race. Normally, I would be thrilled to catch the bouquet. I'm in a committed relationship with a wonderful man; a man with whom I can imagine planning a future. I can picture myself walking down the aisle, walking towards Tanner, a huge smile on his face. I can envision him as my husband. However, I'm growing tired of my curse. Part of me wants nothing more than to see some other young woman catch that bundle of flowers. But, would Tanner be disappointed?

Slowly, I make my way to the dance floor. Several of Tanner's young cousins are on the dance floor, giggling and ready for the main event. My lungs expand, breathing in the warm air of the reception hall. Glancing back at Tanner, I position myself amongst the cousins.

Sure enough, the bride tosses it behind her and it lands perfectly in my hands. My breath escapes me. I've never been so happy catching the bouquet before. My cheeks, my ears, my neck all burn hot with pure elation. This time, I truly want to be the next one in line for marriage. I want a future with Tanner. And I need to tell him so.

Slowly, I saunter back to Tanner who is grinning from ear to ear. He raises his eyebrows as he shrugs.

"Well, that was a perfect catch, sweetheart." He looks as happy as I feel.

"I told ya," I grin.

"Do you think I'll be as lucky?" he asks, pulling me into his arms.

"Hmmm," I sigh, "We'll have to see if my gift has rubbed off on you."

Tanner strolls out to the dance floor. There are several men in their twenties and thirties waiting for Chris the groom to toss the garter. Tanner places both of his hands in his pockets and glances at me with a naughty expression. I gasp and do the "tsk, tsk, tsk" sign with my fingers. He laughs heartily and takes them out of his pockets, raising them above his head in surrender. He is so freaking cute.

Chris, who is a bit tipsy, saunters up to the group of men, winks and turns his back to them. He whips the garter behind his back and it is a line drive straight to the floor. The crowd erupts in laughter. The groom, after seeing where the garter has landed, doubles over in hysterics, holding onto his thighs for support. He then picks it up and flings it straight at Tanner who grabs the garter looking stunned. He then turns to me, wide eyed and holds it up in the air. I giggle uncontrollably. He walks towards me and shrugs his shoulders, his cheeks a deep crimson red.

"What are the chances?" I practically squeal with delight. Tanner pulls me onto the dance floor as a very familiar song

194

fills the room, "Till There Was You" by The Beatles, one of my absolute favorites. This man has been paying attention.

"Oh my goodness," I say, recognizing the tune immediately. "Did you request this song, Mr. Finley?"

"Maybe." He smirks, "Ever since you told me how much you loved it, I can't get it out of my head. It makes me think of you." Pulling me into his arms as he hums along to the song, he sings snippets of the lyrics as he gazes istanto my eyes. The lights of the banquet hall are reflecting on the tiny green specks of his deep brown irises and my heart is aflutter. Tanner pushes my hair out of my eyes and tucks the strays behind my ears, smoothing my hair to the tips. His hand continues down my spine and lands on my backside. An impish grin upon his face, he leans in close to me, so close I can feel his breath upon my forehead.

"Daphne, there's something I need to tell you. Something I've wanted to say for a while now," my heart thumps in my chest as I await his words.

"Yes, Tanner?"

"I feel so blessed that you came into my life and I want you to know the depths of my feelings for you." He pauses, licking his lips before biting them nervously.

"It's okay. Tell me." I reassure him. He smiles in relief.

"I love you, Daphne. I've never said that to anyone but, I've never felt this way before. It's a little scary, but in an amazing way. I love you more than I ever thought I could love another person." His eyes grow moist as he speaks.

"Oh, Tanner! I love you, too. I love you so very much." I say, throwing myself into his embrace. He sighs deeply as I clutch his chest. We sway slowly on the dance floor for the rest of the night, even through several techno dance songs. We don't even notice. We're in love and we're dancing to the music we are creating together.

Chapter 30
Glowing

"You really don't need to chaperone us, Elise. Tanner doesn't mind my hanging out with Evan." I giggle as Elise and I walk up to Evan's apartment.

"I'm not chaperoning you, silly girl. I've wanted to see this band for months now." I raise an eyebrow at her and she looks away quickly. She and Henry are awfully protective of Tanner and my relationship. Deep down, I know she is curious about my friendship with Evan. "But, I will say, it is rare for you to have casual friendships with men, so I'm a bit curious to see how you behave around this Evan character."

"I knew it. There is absolutely nothing to worry about. He and Tanner have met. It's all fine. Tanner *trusts* me."

"I trust you, too." Elise attempts to reassure me.

"I hope so," I reply. "I love Tanner, Elise. It's real. And as soon as you meet Evan, you'll realize you are worried about nothing."

"Why do you say that, is he an ugly troll?" she asks

sarcastically.

"No, of course not. He's very attractive. But, our relationship isn't like that."

"Even though you've slept together?"

"Yep." I nod. Somehow I knew that was what was driving Elise crazy.

"Wow," Elise says as I buzz Evan's apartment, "Who are you and what have you done with my best friend?" Giggling away her skepticism, I'm confident that in just a few minutes she will observe the rapport I have with Evan and no longer worry about my relationship with Tanner.

Evan comes through the door of his building. He is wearing a black leather coat and he looks very handsome. Out of the corner of my eye, I observe Elise. Her mouth is agape at the sight of him and I have to keep myself from giggling at her.

"Hey ladies, are we ready for some music?"

"Oh yes," I nod, "Evan, I'd like you to meet my best friend, Elise."

"Great to meet you," he says warmly, extending his hand to Elise. She looks away briefly in embarrassment before returning the gesture, a huge smile upon her face. Evan has charmed her already.

"I'm surprised Tanner didn't want to join us tonight." Evan observes, focusing his attention back to me.

"He's not a fan of the band," I shrug, "he's going to grab a beer with some friends from work, but he said he'll stop by later if he can."

"Okay, next time then." Evan smiles warmly, "Shall we head to the bar?"

We make our way into a Northwestern campus bar where local bands play. As Elise and I get comfortable at a table, Evan makes his way over to the bar to order our drinks. He chats easily with the bartender and I instantly wonder if they've met before. Evan has a terrible habit of dating the wrong women.

"You seem to know your way around campus, Evan." Elise says when Evan returns to the table with a round of drinks.

"Well, I should. I spent four years of my life here," Evan replies.

"Oh, I had no idea," Elise replies sheepishly, biting her upper lip in embarrassment. "Hey, I'm going to head to the ladies room, I'll be back in a minute," Elise stands up and before I can offer to go with her, she scurries off to the restroom. I can't hide my amused expression.

"Spill it, what's up with your best friend?"

"I think you make her nervous," I suggest with a laugh.

"Me?" Evan asks. I nod. He looks taken aback, "Why on earth is your friend nervous around me?"

"Well, aside from your obvious good looks and charm, she is here under false pretenses."

"How do you mean?" Evan asks, raising a curious eyebrow and tilts his head to the side slightly, looking for more information.

"She's babysitting us."

"Oh, did Tanner send her?" Evan looks a bit disappointed.

"No, he would never do that. In fact, I'm not even sure that Tanner knows she is here with us tonight since she decided to join us at the last minute." Evan's posture relaxes immediately with my reassurance. "She's just very protective of me. And he is very close with her husband, so…"

"Ahh, I get it. No worries. I'll play nice," he chuckles and I roll my eyes in return.

"She likes you already, I can tell. But, she's suspicious about my track record. Having guys for friends has never really been my thing"

"You don't have many of them?"

"Other than you?" I ask. Evan nods and I shake my head.

"Wow, I'm surprised, Daphne. You're so easy to hang out

with, I would think you'd have lots of male friends." I shrug my shoulders just as Elise slips back into her seat.

"Okay, what did I miss?" she asks, wide-eyed.

"We're just talking about the band," I smile, giving Evan a quick glance. He winks sweetly back at me.

"They're about to start their set," Evan adds. Elise takes a sip of her drink and I can tell she is ready to grill Evan in order to gauge his intentions towards me. Thank goodness I prepared him for my friend the detective.

"So, Evan, what do you do for a living?" she begins.

"I'm in marketing. I love it because I get to spend my day thinking about how to spread the word on concepts and products. And I get to spend my day talking with people."

"You seem like you would be really good at that," Elise adds.

"He is," I nod, "He tells me about the projects he's working on, and the ladies who distract him," I wink at Evan, before taking a sip of my cocktail.

"Alright, alright, yes Daphne has been clued in to my messy love life." Evan chuckles as he sips his beer.

"Why is your love life messy, if you don't mind my asking?" Elise may be great at investigation, but her manners never fail her.

"No worries, Elise. I just have a bad track record with women--"

"And he likes girls who are all wrong for him," I interrupt, nudging him in the arm.

"Yes, Daphne here is trying to help me work on that. But, sometimes I can't help myself. The heart wants what the heart wants," he shrugs, sarcasm dripping from his words. I roll my eyes at him playfully.

"Daph, isn't that Tanner?" Elise cranes her neck, looking toward the door. In a split second, I'm off my bar stool, searching the room for my boyfriend. I glance at Evan, who is observing me with a relaxed smile. After scanning the room, I find him. He is walking through the bar, searching for me as well. Our eyes meet and I grin from ear to ear, waving him over to our table as Evan grabs another stool.

"Tanner, you made it," I say, wrapping my arms around him. I slowly release him from my ecstatic grip.

"Hey, Evan, how's it going, man?" Tanner says, extending a friendly hand to Evan who squeezes his hand in return.

"I'm doing well. Here, sit. I'm glad you were able to make it. Daphne mentioned these guys aren't really your favorite. Decided to come anyway, huh?"

"Yep," a grin forms upon Tanner's face, "I thought I'd hang out with you guys."

"I'm so glad you did," I say, gazing at Tanner. He takes my hand in his and kisses my knuckles softly.

"Okay," Elise says giddily, "I really need a refill. Evan would you join me at the bar for a few minutes? I think we should allow the love birds a minute to themselves."

"Of course," Evan stands, gesturing for Elise to walk into his outstretched arm, "We'll be back in a bit."

As soon as they walk away, Tanner turns and plants a sensual kiss on my lips. I place my hands on his cheeks, so happy to have a moment alone with him.

"I didn't think you'd come out with us. You made my night, babe." I smile.

"In all honesty, I couldn't stay away. Work has been really stressful lately and today was no picnic. But, I knew seeing you would make it all better."

"Really?" I ask.

"Always, Daph. You *always* make things better," he leans in and places his forehead on mine and all of a sudden, I'm no longer interested in hearing the band. All I want to do is take Tanner back to my apartment and have my way with him. But, I can't do that to Elise or Evan. Instead I give Tanner a soft kiss on his lips and ask, "Are you staying over tonight?"

"Definitely," he smiles.

"Alright, alright, break it up," Elise smiles. "We brought reinforcements." She places four drinks on the table. We settle in and listen to the band, occasionally stopping to talk between songs. Evan and Tanner discuss their respective jobs and their similar taste in music. Elise, seeing their relaxed interaction gives me a look of approval.

The band finishes their first set, and Tanner excuses himself to the washroom. Evan gives me a knowing look and I can't tell if he's about to tease me or congratulate me.

"He's a good guy," Evan says, "You two are a really good fit."

"You think so?" I ask, genuinely wanting Evan's approval.

"I do. You're *glowing*, Daphne. I've never seen you like this before. Ever since he walked through that door, you've been a different person." I throw my head back slightly in surprise, raising one eyebrow. Evan chuckles, "I meant it as a compliment to *him*, not as an insult to you."

"I don't mean to be different," I say softly.

"No, of course not. But you're happier and more at peace when he's near you. It's really cool. I can see with my own eyes how happy he makes you and I like it."

"I see it, too," Elise adds, nodding. "Evan's right, you're a good match. But, I already knew that," she says, nudging me in the arm.

We continue the evening listening to music, while enjoying light conversation. Evan and Tanner spend a lot of time discussing guy stuff as Elise and I share knowing glances and rolled eyes.

When the bar closes, Tanner and I walk hand in hand out to our respective cars, saying a quick goodbye, for the moment. I know that I'll be seeing him after dropping off my friends at their respective homes. In the car, we continue laughing and reminiscing on the music of the evening. It feels good to share Tanner with my friends and that they can see and feel my happiness. Simply thinking about their reactions makes me smile as I pull into my parking lot and see Tanner's SUV is already here.

Tanner wraps his arms around me, kisses me on my temple and we walk up the steps to my apartment. I feel so protected, so appreciated, so loved. Life is good.

Chapter 31
Japan

My brow furrows as I hear Tanner's news. He is not happy about the recent development either, so I try my best to act as if I'm not upset, scared or hesitant so as to be supportive. "Well, it's only for four weeks. And we can Skype, right?"

Tanner lets out a sigh into the phone, "Yeah, I know, but we've spent this entire summer together. The idea of even one week apart is trying, let alone four. But, my boss says I'm the only developer that can fix the problems the client is having in Tokyo. Don't get me wrong, this is a really great opportunity for me career wise. But, I'm wishing they had sent me months ago, before I met you. We'll be in completely different time zones. I'll be awake while you're sleeping and vice versa."

"I know, Tanner, I know." My heart is aching, "But, we'll have email and we can Skype every day. I'll miss you like crazy, though." I pause, sighing, "When do you have to leave?" I ask, hoping I'll still have some time with him.

"That's the worst part. This trip is based on immediate problems and they need me to arrive this weekend, which means I have to leave tomorrow."

"Tomorrow?" I practically shriek into the phone.

"I know, it's awful." Tanner says roughly. "But, I can't say 'no'. If I could, you know I would."

"We'll be fine. We'll do whatever we need to do to stay connected. You are getting the opportunity of a lifetime. The thought of spending an entire month across the globe is fascinating, really."

"You're being a really good sport about this. Thanks, sweetheart. Listen, I had better get packing. They are putting me on an afternoon flight, so I will try to stop by your school before I leave for the airport. I can't imagine leaving without kissing you goodbye."

"Me neither," I mutter, dragging my hand through my hair, staring up at the ceiling holding in my tears. "Yes, please come by tomorrow. We need a respectable goodbye. Get started on your packing, call me if you need help deciding what to bring."

"Will do. Thank you, sweetheart. I love you."

Thankful that a new school year has arrived, I know my job will distract me while Tanner is away. We've only been together just short of five months. We're still in the honeymoon phase where we can't stand to be apart. Compound that by the fact that we just exchanged "I love you's" for the first time, and this trip is sounding less appealing with every minute that goes by.

I glance at the clock. It's eight o' clock in the evening, which means I have a few hours to stew on this before going to sleep and facing the next month without Tanner. I try calling Elise, but she's not home so I resign myself to watching television in an effort to distract myself. I'm starting to drift off to sleep when my cell phone dings from my purse. My curiosity piqued, I retrieve my phone to find a text message

204

from Tanner:

I can't wait until tomorrow. Please unlock your back door.

Ecstatic, I run to the back door of my apartment and throw it open. Tanner is standing on my deck, his back to me. He quickly turns and reveals a large bouquet of roses, lilies and gardenias. His smile is wide; his eyes are filled with hope.

"I couldn't wait, I'm sorry. I had to see you." He says, with a small shrug. I grab the flowers, smelling them briefly before placing them on the nearest surface. Dragging my boyfriend into the apartment I slam the door and jump into his arms, kissing him deeply.

"Take me to my bedroom, Mr. Finley. We need to say goodbye properly."

"Yes, ma'am," he replies with a chuckle, supporting my backside with his strong hands as he ambles confidently to my bed. I weave my hands through his silky dark hair as he lays me down across the plum colored comforter. His lips find my ears, my neck, and finally my mouth. I part my lips, welcoming him as he greedily thrusts his tongue in and out at a feverish pace before pulling away abruptly. He lifts his head and stares into my eyes, startling me to my core. He tilts his head slightly and brushes my hair from my eyes ever so gently.

"I love you, sweetheart. I love you more than I can ever express."

"I love you, too." Still startled, I stroke his hair gently, trying to relieve the obvious pain he is in. His concern is plastered across his furrowed brow, his suddenly pink cheeks, and his growing pupils.

"I can't bear the thought of being away from you."

"I know, honey. I know," I say softly, "I'm not going anywhere. I'll be right here when you get back."

"Do you have any idea how adorable you are? Do you have any idea what you do to me?"

"What do I do to you?" I purr seductively. "Tell me, Tanner." I stroke his cheek gently with my index finger in a way that makes him shudder. He closes his eyes briefly before responding.

"You make me lose control in the best possible way. You bring out the best in me, you make me feel things in a way I never imagined."

"Are you saying I'm *that* good in bed? Wow, I never knew I was so talented," I tease, raising an eyebrow.

"And that," he says, pointing his finger at my forehead, "Your sense of humor, it's maddening and yet so brilliant. You are constantly making me laugh. You always know what to say to make me laugh, to ease my tension, to make me fall deeper and deeper in love with you."

"Tanner, you make me so incredibly happy. I know that I joke around a lot, and maybe that's just me avoiding uncomfortable moments. But, never, ever mistake my humor for a lack of feeling. You're marvelous and sexy and wonderful and I'm so lucky to have found you. Now will you please, please make love to me because at this rate, you'll be walking out my door and I'll be left completely unsatisfied, if you know what I mean," I say with as straight a face as I can manage.

"Gladly, sweetheart," Tanner says as he leisurely removes my tank top and traces my ribs with his fingertips, teasing me with each movement. I'm aching for his lips and desperate for our dance that makes my skin go numb and my heart explode again and again. But, he's taking his time. He leans down and plants tiny kisses just below my belly button tickling my hot skin. A distressed groan leaves my mouth as I can hardly bear the torture of his lips grazing my torso.

"Please, Tanner, now," I pant, desperation filling my hoarse voice. Tanner quickly sheds his clothes, leans up on his elbows and enters me. All at once I am full, full of Tanner and full of desire. Our love making is slow as we savor every last movement, every last kiss and every single toe-tingling touch. It will be four weeks until we're able to make love again; to kiss and hold one another as we drift off to sleep.

The next morning, my emotions get the best of me as I watch Tanner slumber soundly in my bed. My eyes well with tears as I try to imagine the next month without him beside me, without feeling his soft kisses, without touching his silky hair. It is overwhelming; the thought of saying goodbye. My pillow is unable to contain my sobs and I feel Tanner's arm wrap around my stomach as he pulls me close to him.

"Shhhhh, sweetheart. It's going to be okay," Instead of calming down, my sobs grow louder, more intense. I'm terrified to watch him walk out that door, terrified of what the separation could do to us, terrified of losing someone else who I'm hopelessly in love with. I can't tell Tanner that I had horrible dreams last night; dreams of his plane crashing, dreams of him being hit by a crazy taxi driver in Japan, dreams of him never coming back to me.

Eventually, I'm able to compose myself and the time comes to say farewell to Tanner. "I'll text you as soon as I can so you'll know when I've arrived in Tokyo," he says, holding my hands in his as we stand next to his car. It's a thirteen-hour flight, though, so you won't see it until tomorrow. Try not to worry, alright?"

Reluctantly, I nod with a forced smile so that Tanner will not be troubled by my anxiety. He pulls me in for one last, deep, delightful kiss and I melt into his arms, clutching his shirt so tight I can feel my knuckles growing pale. Watching him drive away, I climb the steps to my apartment and hope to God that the next four weeks go by quickly.

Chapter 32
Distance

His lips press firmly against my neck. His hot tongue draws a line up to the nape of my hair. His fingers slide gracefully down my back as I clutch my pillow in anticipation of his next move. His hand cups my backside and he presses and holds my skin firmly in his hand. I squirm. His tongue flicks my shoulder blades, my spine, and finally the small of my back as he makes his way lower, lower and lower still.

Excitement builds in every square inch of my body as I ache for him. When I can't take one more moment of anticipation of his kiss, I turn to face the man in my bed. But, something is wrong. His brown hair is now a sandy blond. His speckled eyes have been replaced with emerald green. And his sweet, endearing smile, the one that makes me feel like I don't have a care in the world, has been replaced with a cocky, arched grin.

"Hey Puddin'" my companion says.

"Stop," I yell at myself. But, it is too late. I am his. I stare into his green eyes before pressing my hungry mouth to his. I have ached, yearned for his touch and I can no longer deny it, no longer deny the love, the desire, the attraction I still feel...for him.

I wake from my dream, sobbing that Mayson has left me once again and it takes me several excruciating moments before I'm able to return to reality. Mayson is gone and Tanner, although across an ocean, is the one who owns my heart.

"It was only a dream," I say to myself between sobs. Disgust fills my brain. How could I be dreaming of him once again? I thought I was over him. I thought I had moved on, I thought...I thought a lot of things.

Pulling myself together, I glance at the clock. It's 3:00 am, which means it is 6:00pm in Japan and Tanner is most certainly still awake. He has been in Tokyo for two weeks now and it has been close to unbearable. Cell service will not work, so text messages are impossible. E-mail has been our main form of communication as our hopes of daily Skyping were dashed when he began working twelve-hour days. But, this was my chance; this was my opportunity to reach him. I could only hope he was in his hotel room.

Quickly, I splash some cold water on my face, doing my best to hide the redness in my blotched cheeks. Turning on my laptop, I quickly open the Skype application and dial his email address. After several minutes of empty ringing, I give up. Instead, I will send an email. Defeated, I finish my message to Tanner and crawl back into bed. I need him right now and he isn't here. He isn't able to ease my fears. He isn't able to chase Mayson from my subconscious or from my dreams. After an hour of tossing and turning, I'm somehow able to fall into a troubled sleep.

Several days later, I arrive home after a grueling day with my students. I was not my normal patient self with them and I feel terrible about it. My mood has been quite sour since the night I dreamed of Mayson. Each spare moment I have, I find my mind drifting to him and to the dream. I am angry with myself for allowing him back into my mind and into my heart.

The phone is ringing as I enter my apartment. Quickly, I grab the phone without glancing at the caller ID.

"Hello?" I ask, out of breath.

"Daphne, honey, it's Cece." Nerves throughout my body flare as I'm not sure she is the person I can handle speaking to today.

"Hey, Cece. How are you?" I rally myself enough; she does not seem to notice my hesitancy in speaking with her.

"I'm doing pretty well, Daphne. I was thinking of you this afternoon. You popped into my head and I wanted to say hello. How is work?"

"Well, today wasn't the best. My students were a bit squirrelly and I'm afraid I didn't handle it as I should have. I haven't been sleeping well."

"Oh no, I'm sorry to hear that, dear. Is anything the matter?" I can't. I can't tell Cece that I'm dreaming of her son. And I certainly can't tell her why it has me so upset. She knows nothing of Tanner. I'm too cowardly to share for fear of hurting her and threatening our friendship.

"No. I think it's just beginning of the school year stuff, nothing major."

"Well, that's good. I started taking pottery classes. It's been a really good stress reliever for me, so therapeutic. You might need an outlet like that, honey. Teaching is a really stressful profession. You deserve to unwind, take it easy."

"I'm thinking of treating myself to a massage," I sigh.

"Great idea, dear. I think it would do you good."

"Enough about me, Cece. How are things with you? How is your husband doing?" Cece groans a bit into the phone.

"Ah, well, Jack is still struggling, Daphne. Mayson was his world. Getting him to talk to me has been a challenge, especially about his son."

"He's trying to be strong for you."

"I know, but it is maddening at times. I know everyone grieves differently, but I wish he would still talk about Mayson. He acts as if he never existed. And when I want to talk about him, to remember the good stuff, he shuts down. And then I feel guilty. It's a vicious circle." She pauses, taking a deep breath and sighing into the phone, "I shouldn't be putting this on your shoulders, Daphne. I'm sorry. You lost him, as well."

"No, it's really alright. I still miss him, of course. We understand one another in a way that others do not."

"I guess that's true, dear." She replies before a long silence lingers in the air. I bravely ask the question I've been wondering for months.

"Do you ever hear from Brynn?" I ask.

"No, I'm afraid she cut off contact with us shortly after the funeral. I think she needed to move on and I remind her of the pain my son caused."

"And the pain that I caused, as well," I suggest. "Do you think she is angry with you for embracing me, for being open and welcoming towards me? I can only imagine how that must've felt for her."

"I know. I suppose I hurt her deeply when I reached out to you. But, the truth is, in situations like these, I must let emotion rule my actions. I felt a bond with you and I pursued it. And now, we've built a friendship. Yes, it is based on pain, but it is precious to me. I wouldn't trade it. My Mayson is gone, but you, you've brought a light back into my life and I am so grateful. That is a role that Brynn was never able to fill. And I think she knew that."

"I treasure our friendship, too." This is it; this is the moment to tell her all about Tanner, to tell her about my love for him and my conflict regarding her son. She will know I am not trying to hurt her. Do it, Daphne. Say something, anything. I open my mouth to speak when Cece beats me to it.

"Oh, Daphne, honey, I need to run. My husband just got home and he seems chipper. I need to seize the moment. Maybe he'll actually take his Missus out for dinner tonight," she laughs. My heart sinks, but hearing the levity in her voice causes me to retreat. I can't say anything, not yet.

"Thanks for calling, Cece. I hope you have a nice evening with Mr. Holt."

"I'll speak with you soon, dear. I love our chats."

"Me too," I smile. It's the truth.

The breeze is refreshing and light up here, so high in the sky. Down on the street below, buses are zooming by and dozens of people are enjoying their picnics on the grassy knoll. His arm is wrapped around me as we gaze at the streets of Paris. I breathe in a happy, refreshing breath of air as I glance at my hand. The sparkling diamond ring is so new to me, yet so familiar. It sparkles and shines on my left hand, a wedding band sits beneath it. My brow arches as I struggle to remember my wedding. I search my brain to remember how I came to be perched atop the Eiffel Tower, wrapped in my husband's arms. He speaks, his husky voice is unmistakable.

"I always knew I wanted to bring you here, Daphne. Ever since the day I arrived here all those years ago. Do you love it as much as I do?" His voice is robust and deep, yet so light and full of hope.

"Of course I do, Mayson. It's everything I dreamed it would be," the words come out as if someone else is speaking them. My brain continues to panic and I yell at myself to wake up, to come out of my Mayson induced euphoria. But my subconscious fights me with all its might, and before I know it, I am turning to my husband and kissing him deeply, stroking his pale skin with my fingers and loving every second.

The panic is gone and I am completely wrapped up in my dream, in my fantasy of being Mrs. Mayson Holt as we stroll through the streets of Paris. Mayson points out the distinct French architecture as he wraps his arm around my waist, never letting go. It is blissful and romantic and I never want to wake up.

Suddenly, a taxi is speeding towards us. We attempt to make it across the street as the driver furiously honks his car horn. Beep! Beep! Beep!

I wake up with a start, realizing the beeping is not from a horn. I am not in Paris and there are no rings on my fingers. I'm in my bed, alone, after dreaming, yet again, of Mayson. I quickly switch off the alarm and stare at the ceiling in agony. The tears begin to flow at full force as I wrestle with my dream. Why does my subconscious continue to torture me?

Guilt fills my heart as I realize that my boyfriend is halfway across the globe as I continue to dream about another man. This would kill Tanner. But, the dreams are becoming more frequent and more comfortable. I am being pulled towards Mayson once again. I am powerless to stop the magnetic tow of the love that I still feel for him. I cannot purge him from my heart, from my soul.

That morning, Tanner calls. I can't pick up the phone. His message brings tears to my eyes.

"Daphne, Daph? Are you there? Please pick up. I miss you so much, sweetheart. We haven't spoken in days. Where are you?" He sighs heavily into the phone, "I hope you're alright. I wish I could see you, feel you and hold you in my arms. Daphne, I love you. Please call me."

Tears wet my cheeks as I listen to his message over and over again. But, I don't call him back. I fear he will hear the hesitation in my voice and sense the betrayal in my heart. Instead, I walk to my dresser drawer and slowly pull out the box that has been hidden away since Mayson's funeral. The feel of the velvet box in my hand sends shivers down my spine. Without another thought, I open it and place the ring on my left hand. The band feels so foreign on my finger, but I cling to it as I walk through my apartment, wondering if it was meant for me. I spend the day in my bed thinking about Mayson and what we could've been.

"How long has he been gone?" Morgan asks over Saturday morning breakfast at our favorite Mom and Pop diner. The cool fall weather is perfect for dining outside on the patio, although I don't feel so chipper this morning.

"Three weeks now." My voice is sullen as I push my scrambled eggs around the large white plate.

"You must miss him."

"Yeah," I shrug.

"What do you mean, 'yeah', Daphne? What the hell is going on with you?" Morgan slams her fork down. Her gorgeous engagement ring sparkles in the morning sun. After breakfast, we are headed to Morgan's wedding venue to meet with the caterer.

"I don't know, I've had a lot on my mind, I guess."

"Care to elaborate, dear cousin?" I stare off into space, knowing Morgan will be livid if she hears the truth.

"I've been having these dreams. They are getting more and more intense. They are romantic and sensual and altogether wonderful."

"So, what's the problem?" Morgan looks legitimately confused.

"They're not about Tanner," I whisper.

"Mayson?" I nod. "Seriously, Daphne, we're back to Mayson again? He's gone, sweetie. Why are you torturing yourself?"

"I wish I knew, Morgan. It's awful. I feel myself pulling away from Tanner. We've hardly spoken in over a week and I know it's because of me. He emails me every day and I don't always respond. I guess I'm getting used to being apart from him."

"That's bullshit!" Morgan snaps, smacking her hand on the table. I gasp in shock, startled by the harsh tone of her normally chipper voice. "I'm sorry, Daphne, but it is. It's complete and utter bullshit. I'm not going to let you screw up the best thing that has ever happened to you!"

Morgan pauses, staring at me with inquisitive eyes.

"You've been talking to her again, haven't you?" I know exactly who she is talking about.

"Yes." My head hangs in shame, staring at my toes. Morgan reaches across the table and takes my hands in hers.

"This isn't right. You need to end this relationship. Do not allow your friendship with this woman to destroy what you have with Tanner. You will hate yourself forever if you do."

"I can't do that, Morgan. She means too much to me. She's the only one who I can to talk about him. If she is gone from my life, it's almost as if he never existed."

"Why can't you live in a world where Mayson was a part of your *past*? Why do you have to destroy your future by clinging to what might have been? Daph, this isn't healthy. And I'm afraid that you are self-sabotaging a loving and respectful relationship for the memories of really hot sex."

"That's not all it was, Morgan."

"Well, it wasn't much else, other than frustration and heartache. Is Tanner not doing it for you?" Morgan is not trying to offend me. She is searching for an answer, digging like a detective into the twisted brain of Daphne Harper.

"No! Sex with Tanner is like nothing I've ever experienced…even with Mayson. It's…amazing."

"So, then, is it his personality? You guys are always in sync; you're always joking around with your little quips. Is that all for show?"

"No, absolutely not. I love how we tease one another relentlessly. It's part of his charm. He makes me feel sexy and funny. I love it."

"You weren't funny with Mayson, Daphne."

"You're right. I wasn't."

"Then, seriously, what the hell is it?"

"It's the 'what if', Morgan? It's haunting me to my very

soul. I wish I had never accepted that engagement ring. It keeps popping up in my dreams. It's a reminder of what could've been."

Morgan's eyes grow harsh as she glares at me, "You did what?"

Panic spreads throughout my brain. I've revealed my secret to Morgan. I hadn't planned for her to ever know about the ring. But, my conflicted heart has gotten the best of me.

"Cece gave it to me," I whisper.

"And you kept it? What on earth were you thinking? Need I remind you that we don't even know if that ring was for you?"

"I know! I couldn't part with it," I say, pleading with her to understand.

"Ugh, I could kill that woman. She is ruining your chances at happiness, you know that, right?" She shrieks at me.

"No, it's my fault. I made the decision to keep it and hide it from everyone in my life. I could've mailed it back to her; I *should've* done that. But, I didn't. I held onto it."

"I know this may seem harsh, but it's time for you to let it go. He wasn't the one. It's that easy. I've said this before to you, but I'll say it again now, don't be afraid of the real thing. It's here. He's here for you and if you let Tanner slip through your fingers, you'll have more regrets than you'll know how to handle and no piece of jewelry is going to make you feel any better about that." I nod as tears stream down my swollen cheeks. I know Morgan's right. I need to snap out of this. I need to be with Tanner, body and soul. I need to summon the strength to send the ring back to Cece. But, I'm not sure that I am ready.

Chapter 33
Secrets

"Your parents are so much fun," Tanner says as we enter my apartment. We've just returned from a Sunday night barbecue at my Mom and Dad's place. He arrived home from Japan a few days ago and I've done everything in my power to hide my inner turmoil from my boyfriend. But, Tanner has been quiet ever since we left my childhood home. I'm relieved that he is finally speaking.

"I'm so glad you get along so well." I reply, running my hands over his shoulder, trying to assess if he is alright. "You spent quite a bit of time chatting with my mom earlier. She seems to really like you." I smile.

"Yep," Tanner tenses up immediately.

"Babe, what's the matter?" I ask, running my fingers through his hair.

"Nothing, just still a little jetlagged, that's all," he offers a weak smile.

"Hmm, maybe we should get ready for bed. You're

staying over, right?"

"Yeah, but I don't have anything to sleep in. Aside from my birthday suit," he raises his eyebrows playfully.

"Well, you won't hear any complaints from me, but I do have a couple of your t-shirts in my dresser if you want something to wear." I say, walking towards the bathroom.

Tanner peeks in and I glance at him through the mirror, "Thanks, sweetheart," he smiles warmly.

I run the water and pull my hair back into a pony-tail. Splashing my face with the warm water, I lather up my face wash and scrub my skin gently. As I am rinsing the suds from my face, I hear Tanner calling my name. I quickly grab my washcloth, dabbing my cheeks gently as I walk out of the washroom.

"What is it, babe?" I ask, "Do you need help finding a t-shirt?" I stop dead in my tracks. The top drawer of my dresser is wide open and Tanner is holding a small velvet box in his hand. His expression is unclear. He looks baffled, confused, lost.

"Daph?" he laughs uncomfortably, "What is this?"

My pulse quickens and my face falls. I cannot speak. I turn and walk towards the kitchen, escaping the questions that follow me.

"Daphne, what *is* this?"

Still, I do not answer. I turn and my tears give me away.

"Is this from *him*?" Tanner has never been able to say Mayson's name. He just can't do it. He looks down at the ring as if it is poison.

"I don't know," I choke out the words, responding as honestly as I can.

"What do you mean, you *don't know*?" I've never seen Tanner like this. He is angry, defensive and demanding answers.

"It may have been for me. Cece gave it to me after the funeral. She felt it belonged to me."

"Who the hell is Cece? You said she was your *aunt*."

Tanner snaps. My lies are unfolding. Oh God, I am going to lose him. "She isn't, is she?"

"Please don't be mad," I whisper.

"Who is she, Daphne? Your mom and I were talking tonight and she mentioned her sister's name was Jennifer. And I already know your Dad doesn't have any sisters. I was going to let it go, bring it up another time. But, now I know she is tied to this ring, which means somehow she is connected to him…"

"She's Mayson's mother."

"And she gave you an engagement ring? Why?" I stare into his eyes, pleading for him to stop his demands. But, he presses on. "Why, goddamnit? Why do you have an engagement ring hidden in your drawer?" His cheeks are growing red with anger and frustration.

"I don't know. She gave it to me and I couldn't get rid of it."

"He was going to propose to you? I thought he had a girlfriend. None of this makes sense, Daphne, none of it. I thought you were past all of this, I thought you were ready to move on…with me."

"I am, Tanner, I am!"

"No, you're not! That's clear now. If you were ready for a future with me, you wouldn't have *this*. Here, take it, I can't stand touching it," He presses the ring into its slot and snaps the box shut. I extend my hand and grasp the box.

"Tanner, please listen to me."

"Tell me about Cece. Tell me about why you have a relationship with her. Why does she call you so often? Why is she texting you? I don't understand."

"We connected when Mayson had his accident. We formed an instant bond. It's hard to explain, Tanner."

"Okay, so why did you feel the need to hide this bond? Why couldn't you just tell me about her?"

"I was afraid it would scare you away. You were so afraid of being my rebound. I didn't want to tell you for fear that it would break us apart."

"And so, instead, you lied to me?" His voice drips with disdain.

"Yes, and I'm so very sorry."

"Does she know about me?" Tanner persists. My pulse races and panic sets in. My mouth feels dry and parched. I don't know what to say. I glance away for just a moment, but that's all it takes. He knows me too well.

"She doesn't, does she?" he asks incredulously.

"I didn't want to hurt her, Tanner!"

"And I mean so *little* to you that you were willing to lie *to* me and *about* me for months? How can I possibly trust you now? You've been hiding this for our entire relationship! I've been giving you my heart, giving you my *soul* and you've been lying to me. And the worst part is, I've told everyone how crazy I am about you, everyone! And you've been keeping me a secret, like you're ashamed of what we have."

"You know that's not true, Tanner. I love you."

"I'm finding that hard to believe. But, at least some other things are making sense now. All of those text messages that you get when we're together. My god, the woman calls and texts you all the time!"

"She's my friend. We talk."

"About what? What do you talk about? I'm obviously not important enough to come up in discussion," he hisses. Feeling trapped, I lash out at him.

"Speaking of friends, who is Tracey?" I ask defensively.

"Tracey's a co-worker. Why?"

"Earlier today, your phone buzzed. I picked it up in order to hand it to you, but I saw your text history with her. You didn't tell me she went to Japan with you. You must have hundreds of messages from her on your phone. Obviously, I'm not the only one who's been keeping secrets."

"I'm not cheating on you, Daphne." Tanner replies matter-of-factly, his eyes rolling slightly. He knows what I'm doing.

"Well, I'm not sure I believe you." I attempt to stand

strong. But, he knows me too well.

"I would never do that to you. You're making assumptions. I'm not *him*, Daphne."

"How dare you say that? How dare you bring him up just to distract me from what is obviously going on behind my back!"

"And what is so obvious? A co-worker sent me text messages? I hate to tell you this, but in the world of technology, co-workers send messages to communicate with one another every damn day. Tracey and I were working cooperatively in Japan. That's it!"

"But, she wanted to see you after work. And you agreed. I read the messages, Tanner. There was no mention of a project. More importantly, I can read you. You've been so different ever since you got back from Tokyo. How do I know you two didn't hook up while you were there?"

"We didn't know anyone else in the country, Daphne. She's happily married with two children. I've met her husband several times. He's a great guy. And me? I've been the same person I've always been. You're jumping to conclusions because you've been down this road before, only you didn't find out until it was too late. I know you're afraid to feel that way again. But, I'm not *him*, Daphne."

"You need to stop talking about Mayson as if you know what happened, as if you know how he felt about me. Because, you don't! And you have no right to insinuate that, that---"

"That he cheated on you? That he cheated on his girlfriend of several years with you? I don't need to insinuate anything, Daphne. It's all pretty transparent."

"You didn't know him, Tanner. He cared about me. He loved me." Tanner's eyes widen. He throws his hands up in the air, exasperated.

"God, would you listen to yourself? Do you honestly think that man treated you the way he did and actually loved you? And do you really think that I would be standing here, fighting for you as I always have, if I didn't love you?"

"Stop it! Just go, please." I regret the words as soon as they spill from my jaw. It will kill me if he walks out that door.

Tanner walks to me, places his fingers on the bottom of my chin, lifting it up so that our eyes meet. He looks forlorn, beaten and tired. "I hate him for doing this to you, Daphne. I hate that you defend him all the time and that you allowed yourself to keep that ring. How could you *do* that, Daphne? I hate that you're unable to move on from him and that you've attached yourself to his mother in order to keep him in your life, even in a minute way. I hate that you keep comparing me to him...I hate that you compare me to...to... "

"To a dead man?" I shriek in horror.

"No, damnit! To a person who didn't deserve you. A person who made you feel as if you weren't entitled to all of the happiness in the world. A person who couldn't, or wouldn't, give you all of himself. And now, because of him, I fear you can never give me all of you. And I need all of you, Daphne. I won't settle for less."

Sobbing, I collapse into a heap on the floor, hanging my head in shame. I would do anything to escape this confrontation, escape what Tanner is forcing me to deal with.

"I wish I could go back...just go back" I sob uncontrollably, choking on the words as they exit my mouth. Tanner is silent for what feels like hours. Then, he kneels before me, placing his hands gently on my thighs. He speaks in a low whisper.

"I wish he had never shown up to Elise's wedding. I wish you had joined me for that drink after your speech. Maybe then you could've gotten to know me before your world fell apart. I wish a lot of things, Daphne. But, it feels like your regrets are different than mine. I should go."

"No, no, wait. I didn't mean...." I've pushed too far. Tanner has misread me. I want to go back and reject that ring.

I want to tell Cece all about him. I want to tell her that I've fallen in love. I want to let her go, let the ring go, finally let Mayson go. But, he is done listening to me. It's too late for redemption.

"It's alright," he says as he climbs to his feet, "Maybe I pushed too hard. Maybe this isn't right." Tears are forming in his eyes, but he won't look away from me.

"You said you would fight for me. Please, don't go."

"I can't fight anymore, Daphne. As much as I love you, this is killing me."

"But, I love you, too, Tanner. You know I do," I whimper.

"But, you still love him, too. It's obvious to me now." He says, looking down sadly at the velvet box nestled in my hand. "I can't compete with a memory. I thought I could, but I can't. I don't think anyone can. You will always remember Mayson the way you *want* to remember him. Over time, you'll forget all of the bad stuff and focus only on the good. You'll focus on that ring in your hands and the future you could've had with him if things had been different. How can you and I possibly have any sort of future together if you are clinging to the past? You need to sort through your feelings. I can't do it for you."

"Tanner, I—"

"I'm not leaving to hurt you. But, I must protect my own heart. And right now, it's breaking. I can't take any more, no more rings, no more comparisons. *No more*, Daphne." He leaves my apartment and I am completely alone. My heart is broken.

Chapter 34

Coffee

It's been almost a week since Tanner left my apartment. He hasn't called, hasn't emailed or sent a text. It's like he was never here. As if he was never in my life, never in my heart. I've been unable to leave my apartment, torn between the man I lost and the man who I don't think I ever really had. My phone, my link to the outside world at the moment, interrupts my wallowing thoughts. At first, I'm tempted to ignore the phone, until I hear a familiar voice talking into my answering machine.

"Hey Daphne, it's Evan. Are you home? Pick up, Daphne. Morgan told me you haven't been leaving your apartment. I know you're there." Slowly, I make my way to the telephone, placing the receiver to my ear.

"Evan?"

"Ah, she's alive," his voice is dripping with sarcasm. "Hey, what are you doing in, say, thirty minutes?"

"I don't know, sleeping?"

"Want to meet me for a cup of coffee? It's my treat."

"Hmm, that's a tempting offer." My voice is laced with mockery, but the sadness that lurks behind my attempt at derision is terribly obvious.

"Come on, Daphne. We haven't hung out in a while. I'd like to catch up."

"I don't think I'd be very good company, Evan," I say softly, "Tanner broke up with me."

"Yeah, I'm sorry. Morgan told me."

"So, you and Morgan are buddies now?" What the hell?

"Look, Daphne, she filled me in. Thirty minutes, at the Starbucks on Lake Street." He is not taking 'no' for an answer.

"Alright, I'll be there in an hour. I haven't showered yet."

"Yeah, definitely take care of that. Bathing is essential. I don't want to feel like I'm hanging out with Pigpen from the Peanuts cartoons." A slight chuckle escapes my lips and it shocks me. I haven't laughed all week.

Walking into the Starbucks, I see Evan. He is as handsome as ever, seated in a leather armchair near the fireplace. His short brown hair has been recently trimmed. His olive skin looks beautiful against the dark black t-shirt that clings to his muscular arms. He gives me a sensitive and knowing smile as he stands to greet me with a warm hug. As we pull apart, he glances at his watch.

"I thought we said we'd meet in an hour. You're a bit late, my dear." He teases.

"Yeah, I forgot to mention I needed to wash my hair multiple times." He raises an eyebrow, "It's been a while." I shrug.

"Things are that bad, huh?" he winces.

I nod, holding back tears. "Come on, let's get something to drink and you can tell me all about it." He takes my hand and leads me to the register. Evan orders my favorite pumpkin spice latte, handing it to me with a gentle smile as if I am too weak to do it myself. Perhaps I am. Moments later, we find ourselves seated back by the armchairs. It is a secluded area of the small café and I am grateful that Evan has chosen this spot for that reason. The thought of having strangers see my tears makes me sick to my stomach.

"So, spill it, Daphne. Why did Tanner break up with you?"

"Well, you've been talking to Morgan, so I have a feeling you already have this information, Evan."

"Guilty as charged." He admits, shrugging his shoulders and blowing softly on his mocha latte. "But, why don't you tell me anyway?"

"It's about Mayson," I pause, reluctant to continue, "Tanner thinks I'm still in love with him."

"Well, *are* you?" Evan's voice is stern and direct. I find it hard to make eye contact with him.

"No," I snap.

"Daphne? Come on, it's me. I know how much Mayson meant to you; how much he hurt you. You can tell me the truth." His no-nonsense approach is wearing me down. I feel my resolve slipping away. My heart is getting ready to spill.

"I still feel connected to him, yes. But, I'm not in love with him anymore. I love Tanner."

"Well, I think he's great, and I saw how you were with him at the bar. You seemed so happy. Morgan is certain that he's the one for you."

"I'm guessing that's why she sent you?" Disdain fills my voice once again.

"She didn't *send* me, Daphne. I was concerned. I wanted to make sure you were all right. And I wanted to help if I could."

"And how can you help me, Evan?"

"Well, you've heard my sob story. You know what Kate did to me. She ripped me to shreds. And from what I gather about Mayson, he did the same thing to you. I hate to think that his ghost is haunting you and keeping you from being happy with someone who's actually worth your time."

226

"Well, it's not all about Mayson. It's about his mother, too."

"His mother?" A large crease forms between his eyes. He looks genuinely perplexed.

"Morgan didn't fill you in on that part of the story, huh?"

"Nope, I honestly have no idea how Mayson's mother could possibly fit into your break-up with Tanner."

"I know; it's bizarre. She and I formed a friendship after Mayson's accident and I neglected to tell Tanner about her. In fact, I lied about it. Tanner is someone who has no tolerance for dishonesty."

"Isn't that a good thing? I would think you'd be so thankful to be with a man like that after all of the lies Mayson told you over the years."

"It is, but I didn't want to hurt him. And I didn't want to hurt her."

"So, let me guess---she didn't know either?" Nodding, I hang my head.

"That's messed up, Daphne. I'm sorry, but it is. He had every right to walk away. I think I'd have done the same thing." As the words pour from Evan's mouth, I suddenly realize how ridiculous all of this sounds.

"Well, there's more."

"Tell me," he says, sitting back, taking a sip of his coffee. I take in a big breath.

"There was a ring."

"You need to be more specific," Evan raises an eyebrow as he speaks.

"An engagement ring," I say softly.

"From Tanner? Did he propose to you?" Evan presses. I shake my head as I stare at the floor.

"Cece gave me a diamond ring that she found in Mayson's apartment. She felt it was mine."

"But, that doesn't make much sense." He looks skeptical, "You told me months ago, that he had a very serious girlfriend." I nod again. He groans, shaking his head in obvious disbelief at the tangled web I've weaved. "So, you kept the ring and Tanner somehow discovered it?"

"Yes, and all my lies began to catch up with me."

"Listen, here's the deal, Daphne. I really do think this relationship is salvageable. He didn't walk away because he stopped loving you or because he wanted to see someone else. He broke up with you because you *hurt* him. We may act tough, but men's egos are easily bruised. We don't like competing for a woman. And if we genuinely care for her, we don't want to be hidden from her friends or family." Evan takes a deep breath, assessing my eyes for tears before he continues, "Listen, this is like a storm. You must decide if you want to weather it. Do you want to weather the storm with Tanner or not?"

"I do." I've never been so sure of anything in my life.

"Then, you must let go of Mayson's ghost. That's all he is now, a ghost who is haunting your every decision. He's your "coulda-woulda-shoulda." You need to let that go. It's not going to get you anywhere. You have some big decisions to make, Daphne. And once you make them, that's it. You can't go back. The question is, is Tanner worth it?"

"Yes, he is *so* worth it."

"Good. You're lucky. I still haven't found someone who has been enough. No one has been enough for me to let go of Kate, even though I know I should. But, learn from my mistakes. There have been so many women who I couldn't let in. They're quickly becoming my 'coulda-woulda-shouldas.' Don't live your life like that.

I've been involved with wonderful women who wanted to pursue something real with me. But, I couldn't do it. I couldn't commit because I couldn't let go of her. It sucks. So, have a glass of wine, sort through your emotions, tell Tanner how you feel. Fight against the storm and let go of the ghost. And for the love of God, get rid of that ring. It has no place in your life. You will never be happy if you keep holding on to the past. And that ring is part of your past. It's not your future."

Evan's right. I'm not ready to let go of Tanner. I want nothing more than to weather this storm together, to be with him fully and completely. I need to let go of the mirages, let go of my vision of happily ever after with a man who was never faithful to me. I must let go of Mayson's ghost and convince Tanner that I love him. I need to fight for him as he has always fought for me. He is worth it. His love, his devotion, has been a gift. I can only hope he will be willing to weather the storm with me after all I've done to push him into the rain, covering myself with my fantasies, with my mirage, with my ghost.

But, first, I must go to Charleston. I need to return the ring to Cece.

Chapter 35

Charleston

"Daphne, dear, I'm so happy to see you," Cece hugs me tight then grasps me by the shoulders. "It was such a pleasant surprise to hear you would be in town." We are standing outside of Blossom Restaurant in downtown Charleston. Cece insisted it was the very best seafood in town.

"Well, my aunt has a place in Charleston. I've been meaning to check it out. I thought it would be great for us to catch up in person." My nerves are flaring. I'm terrified to hurt this kind, gentle woman who has welcomed me with open arms into her family, into her life.

"This is a lovely restaurant. The smells are incredible," I muster, trying to sound casual.

"Let's go in, dear. I'm sure our table is ready."

After ordering lunch and chatting briefly over garlic rolls and iced tea, I know it is time to admit why I am really here. It is time to end my friendship with Cece in order to reclaim my relationship with Tanner. Taking a deep breath, I begin the conversation I've been dreading for weeks.

"Cece, I have a confession to make. Yes, my aunt really does live in Charleston. But, I'm really here to see you."

"Oh? Well, I'm flattered. That's so nice, Daphne," Cece replies, not sensing the regret in my tone.

"Well, this is going to be hard to say."

"Go ahead, dear. You know you can talk to me."

"Yes, I know and I love that about you. You see, I've been hiding something from you, something really big. I've met someone."

Cece breathes in deeply, leaning back ever so slightly in her chair. "Oh. Well, Daphne, of course you must know that I didn't expect you to stay single forever. I didn't expect you to never date again. Besides, you told me your date with that strange movie snob."

"That was different."

"Why is it so different? You didn't make me uncomfortable telling me about your date. You're a young woman. I knew, on some level, that eventually you would start seeing other men besides Mayson. Life goes on." She shrugs, her eyes growing moist as she speaks. She lifts her spoon and stirs her tea, avoiding my prying eyes.

"It was different because I didn't have any feelings for Abram. I'm in love, Cece. And I'm terrified that I'm going to lose him."

"Why would you lose him?" She pauses, looking deep into my eyes. She sighs before continuing, "Does this have something to do with Mayson? Are you still in love with Mayson, honey?" Her expression is pained and ridden with guilt.

"I think a part of me will always love your son. Part of me will always wonder what could've been. But, the thing is, I've met someone incredible. Someone who makes me feel alive for the first time in so long. He makes me feel things that even--" I hesitate, not wanting to make her hurt even more. I feel like a terrible person.

"It's ok, Daphne. I can handle it. How does he make you feel?"

"He makes me feel things that even Mayson did not. He knows me; the real me. I don't think Mayson ever did. And that wasn't necessarily his fault. I never let Mayson see me for who I really was. The thought of losing him scared me so much that I wanted to be perfect all the time. It was exhausting. And I'm finally realizing that with Mayson, I was always on edge, always afraid of it coming to an end."

"And you don't feel that way now?" Cece asks. I shake my head in response, happy tears forming in my eyes.

"No, I don't. He understands me. He loves me for who I am. He knows the deepest voice in my heart and he cherishes me for it. It has got to be the best feeling in the world." I smile from ear to ear, a lone tear gliding down my face. I am feeling elated and guilty all at the same time.

"Well, that is fantastic. Truly, it is. I don't really understand why you felt you had to hide this from me. How long have you been dating this young man?"

"We were together for about six months, until a few weeks ago."

"Oh, no! What happened, darling?" She seems genuinely concerned. I love that she is pressing me for more information and not walking out of the restaurant. She is truly the beautiful person I've always believed her to be. Her response helps me to open up and I am comfortable sharing more with her. I remove the ring box from my purse and place it gently in front of her. She gasps softly.

"He was tired of competing with a memory; tired of competing with Mayson." I say, looking down at the box, "I denied it, I fought him every step of the way, but he was right. It took losing him for me to realize how ridiculous I was behaving. I can't keep the ring. And so, I am giving it back to you. I realized it doesn't belong to me; and it never really did."

"Oh no, did I cause this?" her skin turns ashen, "Did you

lose him because I gave you this ring?" her voice is shaky. She is terrified.

"It's not just the ring, Cece. But, it was wrong of me to keep it. And worst of all, I hid it from him. He came upon it innocently."

"But somehow, I must be connected to all of this in some other way," she pauses, searching my eyes, "You've never mentioned him to me in all this time. Did you fail to fill him in on our friendship, as well?" For the first time in our conversation, Cece looks disappointed in me.

"Yes. He had no idea."

"I see." Cece stares at the table. "Look, I'm not going to pretend that this conversation is easy for me. But, Mayson is gone and so you *must* move on. You can't spend your life thinking about what could've been. I know that I didn't help matters by showing you that ring, but I want you to know that I really do support you in moving on. I want you to be happy, dear. Truly, I do. Selfishly, I don't want to lose our friendship, but if that is what you need to do in order to move on with this young man, then I will support that, too."

"Oh, Cece, I don't know what to do."

"I do. You need to go back to Chicago and regain his love and trust. You need to do whatever it takes. You had too many regrets with my son. I don't want that for you this time. No regrets, Daphne."

"No regrets?" I swallow hard, forcing back the tears that are threatening to spill from my eyes at a feverish pace.

"That's right. Proclaim your love, make a gigantic gesture, do what it takes for you to be happy with this young man." She pauses briefly and then laughs, "I just realized you never told me his name. He means so much to you and I don't even know what to call him."

"Tanner. His name is Tanner and he is *the love of my life*."

Chapter 36
Boombox

Morgan's clunky old boombox bangs into the passenger door as I pull it out of my car. His SUV is parked in front of his garage. The lights in his condo are on and I can only hope he is inside alone. If not, I am about to be one embarrassed redhead. But, it will work. It has to work.

Approaching the light of his living room, I notice that Tanner is seated in his armchair, his reading glasses placed gently on his perfectly shaped nose. Concern is spread across his face and I know instantly that he is devouring another dystopian novel. Grateful for his concentration, I position myself in front of his front door, ready to make a complete ass out of myself. It is worth it if only to show him how I truly feel.

Deep breaths, Daphne, you can do this. It's show time! Pressing 'Play' on the tape player, I am grateful to my library for having this song in their ancient music selection. Cranking the knob as far to the right as it will go, the notes of the song pour out into the open air. The guitar riffs are enough to grab my love's attention. He quickly jumps from his chair and walks cautiously towards his front door. I place the boombox above my head, just like Lloyd Dobbler in "Say Anything."

Shock is plastered across Tanner's face as he stares at me. I hold the boombox above my head, mouthing the words to "Till There was You" right along with Paul McCartney. Tanner chuckles to himself, placing his hand over his mouth to mask his laughter. I sway and shimmy my bottom as I keep the boom-box above my head.

Neighbors begin to file out into their yards, all coming to inspect the source of the noise that is invading their normally peaceful neighborhood. Tanner looks around, crosses his arms and grins at me, as if challenging me to go on. And so, I stop lip-synching and begin to sing at the top of my lungs, along with the song. I sing my little heart out, even though an extensive crowd has gathered around Tanner's front porch. A few of his neighbors have taken it upon themselves to raise their lighters and sway with the music. Giggling from embarrassment, I continue until the very last note of the song.

The crowd erupts into laughter and applause. Neighbors shout out to Tanner, "Keep her around, Dude!" "That was awesome!" "Lucky guy!" "Get a room!" and all the while he stands there, grinning with pride. But, as much as he smiles at me, the hurt in his eyes is the same as the day we last spoke. He needs to hear me out. There is so much to explain.

"Well, that was quite the performance," Tanner says hesitantly as the crowd thins. We are left alone and the tension is now high. No longer is the mood light and airy. Instead it is filled with misconceptions, untruths and hurt.

"I practiced a lot. I wanted to get it just right. Do you remember that song?" My question is full of hope.

"I do. It makes me think of you, of us."

"I know." An uncomfortable pause fills the air. Goosebumps rise on my arms.

"Why are you here?" Tanner asks, arms still crossed over

his chest in defiance.

"You must know why, Tanner. I miss you, terribly. And I need to explain myself."

"Well," he responds, "come in before it's dark and someone calls the cops for random street performers without a permit." A tiny glimpse of my witty Tanner comes through. Perhaps he hasn't given up hope just yet

Walking into his condo, I notice immediately that the framed picture I had given him of us in Door County is no longer on his bookshelf. In its place is a simple candy dish, with no candy in it. My heart sinks.

"You haven't called." My voice is soft and, all of a sudden, I can no longer bear to look him in the eye. My picture is down and I am terrified that he is ready to be done with me.

"Neither have you."

"Well, I've been busy. You know, planning my stellar performance." My attempt at a joke falls hideously flat. Tanner does not laugh; he does not chuckle. He simply nods.

"Look, I know I screwed up. I know I've done so many things that I shouldn't have done. I know hiding things from you and from Cece was wrong. But, there's something you need to know. My regrets, they're not so different from yours. In my apartment, you walked away thinking that I wanted to go back to Mayson. It isn't true, Tanner. You need to know that."

Tanner blinks again and again as he listens to my plea.

"When I said I wanted to go back, I meant that I wish I'd been honest with you. I wish I'd been honest with Cece. She knows everything now. I flew to South Carolina to tell her."

"You did?" I hear a tinge of hope in his inquiry.

"Yes, I did. Would you like to know what I told her?" Tanner nods hesitantly. "I told her all about you, about your warmth and your love for me. I told her about how you bring out the best in me. But, most importantly, I told her that you're the love of my life. Because you are, Tanner, you are, without a doubt, the absolute love of my life."

236

"And him? What about him?"

"I'm not going to lie about that. There was a time when I felt that way about Mayson. But, it wasn't real, Tanner. It was a mirage, a fantasy that I invented in my head so many years ago. He was never the man for me. It's as simple, and as complex, as that. I returned the ring to Cece. It doesn't belong to me…and I don't belong to it. I belong to you, Tanner. I am *yours*, completely yours. If you'll still have me."

Taking a few steps closer to Tanner who is visibly more relaxed than he was when I first entered his condo, I smile cautiously, hoping he will allow me to move even closer to him. He laughs, reading me like a book. Raising an eyebrow, I take another cautious step until I'm just inches away from him. Placing his hand over my heart, I press him towards me.

"Do you feel that? Do you feel how fast my heart is racing? This is me, terrified that you will walk away again. Being apart from you is killing me. Please, please, Tanner. Can you please find it in your heart to forgive me, to give me another chance?"

"Of course I want to be with you, sweetheart. I just wanted you to fight for me." A tear runs down his cheek as he wipes the many that have rolled down my face. "And now you have. That's all I ever wanted."

Unable to contain my happiness and excitement, I wrap my hands around his neck and hurtle myself into his arms.

"Just promise me something, Daphne."

"Anything, my love, anything." I sigh into his neck.

"Please don't ever sing again. That was really rough." Laughter consumes me and I howl with amusement as Tanner pulls me in for a long, deep hug.

"But, the prop was good, right? You've got to give me props for my prop," I giggle, "That boombox is ancient," I pull back and give him a playful smirk.

"You know, Daph. I always thought I was the dork in this relationship. I'm starting to think otherwise," Tanner teases, before yanking me off the floor and carrying me towards his bedroom.

"We have some making up to do." His voice has turned raspy and I know the time for jokes has passed. I've told him how I feel. Now it's time to show him.

Later, as we lay tangled in Tanner's bed, he strokes my hair gingerly.

"I can't believe you did that, Daph. I can't believe you did the John Cusack thing."

"You love that scene. It's your favorite," I reply matter-of-factly.

"I know, I just….I can't believe you did that for me. And when my neighbors gathered around you, you didn't shy away, you actually started to sing!"

"Anything for you, my love," I grin.

"You amaze me, you know that?" Tanner says, stroking my back. Quickly, I glance at the clock. Sitting up, I place my hand gently on Tanner's cheek.

"Are you ready for Part Two of my plan to win you back?"

"There's more? You've *already* won me back, sweetheart."

"I know, but I'm not finished yet. You kind of interrupted me with the sex."

"Oh, my deepest apologies, sweetheart," Tanner smirks.

"Get dressed and meet me in your backyard in ten minutes," Swiftly, I jump out of bed and pull my clothes back on. Giving him a chaste peck on the lips, I smile craftily and run out of the room, closing his door behind me.

When Tanner emerges through his sliding glass door, his mouth is agape. Spread out on the grass is a large checkered blanket. Sitting atop the blanket is a picnic basket, citronella candles and a bottle of Moscato di Asti. Chunks of cheese, grapes and crusty French bread sit on plates awaiting the two of us.

"Wow," Tanner exclaims, still a bit in shock. "Daphne, I

don't know what to say."

"Well, I do," I say, taking his hands in mine and leading him to the blanket. "Have a seat so that I can elaborate." Tanner sits on the blanket, still looking a bit stunned.

"Do you remember our first date?"

"Of course I do, sweetheart." He smiles affectionately at me.

"Well, I do too. You went so out of your way to make that night special with my favorite wine and the candles to keep the bugs away. It was perfect; you were perfect. But, we were interrupted that night, in a way that we've been interrupted for months. There will be no cell phone calls this evening. There will be no baggage, or ghosts or mirages. I want us to have that night again. But, this time there will be no interruptions."

"Just you and me?" Tanner asks, pushing my bangs from my face.

"Just you and me."

Chapter 37
Bachelorette

Morgan and Matt's wedding is only a few weeks away. Tonight is her much anticipated Bachelorette Party. Morgan has always wanted to visit a strip club, yet has never gone. Well, tonight that is about to change. Her other bridesmaids and I have her blindfolded, sitting in the car as we drive to Lake Geneva. She is a little tipsy after our delicious meal at a local restaurant on the lake. After several margaritas and one Long Island Iced Tea, Morgan is feeling no pain and will not stop giggling.

"Can I please take this thing off?" she asks, giggling yet again.

"Nope," answers her friend Susannah, our designated driver, "We'll be there in a few minutes. Relax and enjoy your buzz!"

The girls giggle and chat in the SUV as we approach our destination. Slowly, we guide Morgan out of the passenger seat and position her so that she is facing the sign of our destination. When we take her blindfold off, she busts out into laughter.

"The Sugar Shack?" she yells, jumping up and down. "Daphne, you knew I wanted to come here! You are so awesome!"

Morgan's laughter is contagious and we all do our best to keep calm as we enter the large white building out in the middle of nowhere.

"We're here for the male dancers," Morgan says, giggling as we enter the building. The young woman behind the counter is friendly, but does not seem amused by Morgan's excitement and laughter. I'm sure she has seen it all...bachelorettes, birthday girls, horny college girls with fake ids. I give her a meek smile and shrug my shoulders as she checks each of our IDs and points us in the direction of the performance.

"This is so friggin' exciting! So, do they take it off? I mean, do they take it *all* off?"

"You betcha," says Julie, Morgan's old college roommate and the only one in our group who has already seen the show.

"Really?" a few of us gasp, looking at one another before bursting into fits of giggles.

"Well, not the whole time, ladies. They come out to the stage in costumes. And then, they take their time stripping down. Morgan, do you have your singles?"

"Yep!" Morgan says holding up her wallet filled with $1 bills given to her by her lovely bridal party. We've thought of everything. Morgan has plenty of money to give the dancers. She also has a "hottie whistle" to beckon them with, handcuffs in case they wish to restrain her during her inevitable lap dance and a crown so that the dancers will know who the bride is in our group.

After climbing the set of stairs to the performance area, we quickly find our seats. There is a small, elevated square stage in the center of the room. Above the stage is a tray ceiling to accommodate the height of the male dancers as they perform.

Seating surrounds the stage and a bar sits off to the side. The walls are black, as are the tables, the chairs, the stage, everything. There are three other brides with their friends here tonight, as well as a few birthday girls. Our bartender quickly takes our orders and before we know it, the lights are flashing and an announcer in a black tuxedo takes the stage.

"Ladies, welcome to the Sugar Shack! We have a fantastic show prepared for you tonight. Now, if you were planning on taking pictures tonight, listen up!" We each look at each other, and I slowly place my camera in my lap, feeling busted.

"Take as many pictures as you want! That's right, ladies, our guys aren't shy! This is a party and we want you to live it up!" Everyone goes wild, and the cameras start flashing like crazy. The announcer looks pleased, "Yeah, that's more like it! Now, are we ready to get this party started?" Again, the ladies in the room go crazy, many jumping up and down, clapping and screaming, ready to see our first dancer.

"Please welcome our first performer to the stage. He's Latin, he's sexy and he's waiting for you, ladies! It's Diego our Latin Lover!" The ladies scream as a beautiful man strolls onto the stage wearing a Zorro type costume with black faux leather pants, a cape and a mask over his eyes.

"Holy crap!" Morgan yells as she stares up at the stage. The music pounds and our Latin Lover makes his way to our section of the stage. He slowly takes off his shirt as he gestures for Morgan to approach him. She looks at me with a huge grin.

"What do I do?" she yells over the thumping music. At this point, he is working on his belt and is swaying his hips back and forth. The women across the room are out of their seats and screaming. Julie grabs Morgan's wallet, takes out a dollar and hands it to her.

"Get over there, put this in your bra and smile. That's it. He'll take care of the rest!" I slap Morgan's ass, urging her to walk over to the sexy man who looks ready to peel off his chap-like pants.

Morgan hops off of her barstool and strolls in her sexiest walk towards the stage. Diego smiles, nodding as Morgan approaches the stage. She quickly places the dollar bill in her bra so that one end is sticking out, she looks back at us so that we can see the proper placement of the money, then turns back towards Diego. In the blink of an eye, Diego drops down to his knees and moves seductively towards Morgan, grabbing the dollar bill with his teeth as he rubs one hand down her back.

"Oh my God!" she yells as she strokes his shoulders and abs. He turns away from her, still supporting himself on his knees, and places her hands on his ass. Morgan giggles, but moves her hands playfully, even placing her fingers inside the back pockets of the pants. As she does, Diego pulls the pants apart with his fingers and Morgan jumps back to see the dancer wearing absolutely nothing but a g-string.

He smiles again at her, mouthing, "Thanks, baby" and walks to another area of the stage where another group of women are waiting in anticipation for the Latin lover to dance for them. More dollar bills are stuck into bras, laughter and screaming fill the stage as Diego is eventually wearing nothing at all. He moves to each corner of the stage, swaying and thrusting for his adoring patrons. When the song ends, he quickly collects his money and exits the stage, blowing kisses to all of his new fans.

The night continues in this manner. After Diego, we are graced by Tommy the Surfer followed by Rick the Policeman. Finally, we meet Dylan the Fireman (my personal favorite) who is tall and lean with short, jet black hair and rock hard abs. He is introduced and climbs with all of his heavy gear onto the stage. He wastes no time at all stripping down to his skivvies. Drawn to this dancer, I decide to approach the stage, dollar bills poking out from each bra strap. He looks down at me and smiles, wearing nothing but his g-string, he slides down onto his belly and retrieves the money with his teeth while placing my hands on his abs. Alcohol is coursing through my veins and I can't stop smiling at the adorable dancer. He turns me around and wraps his arms around me as Morgan takes our picture with my camera.

"You're a very sexy fireman," I yell into his ear, "You're definitely my favorite!"

"Aw, thanks, darling," he smiles as he continues to shake his hips and sway next to me, stroking my hands up and down his back. He smells of body spray and soap. "You know, I'm very good at lap dances."

"Oh really?" I ask, raising an eyebrow at the scantily clad young man before me.

"Yep, they're my specialty. I highly recommend you get one."

"I'll have to think about that," I smile, knowing full well I have no intention of receiving a lap dance. "Our bride will be receiving one later. We'll have to see who she chooses. Maybe it'll be you, Mr. Fireman," I flirt.

"I sure hope so," he replies and in an instant, he is on his feet, swaying towards another group of ladies who are waving money and dancing to the techno music blaring through the speakers.

"So, who's it going to be, Morgan?" I ask the now incredibly drunk Bride-to-Be. But, she has no idea what I'm talking about.

"What do you mean? Do I get to keep one?" she asks, cracking herself up.

"No, silly, who is going to give you a lap dance? I'm fully prepared to pay your favorite dancer his required fee."

"Daphne, are you serious? I can't do that, Matt will flip out!"

"No, he will not. I already received his blessing. He knows I am here watching out for you. He said no private lap dances, but if it is out in the open, he is fine with it. Come on, who's it going to be? Are you in the mood for a little Latin love? Or have you been a bad, bad girl and need to be punished by the law? Or is there a fire in your pants?"

244

Susannah, Julie and the other bridesmaids are laughing hysterically as I do my best to entice Morgan with the performers.

"Hmm, I definitely choose the fireman. Oh, I love a good fireman," Morgan nods. Secretly I am thrilled that she has chosen my favorite. I can live vicariously through the sexy dance she is about to receive. Dylan is standing near the stage chatting with another bride, but smiles seductively and tilts his head back slightly to acknowledge my presence as I walk to him.

"Well, hello there, Red," he says referring to my hair.

"Hello, Mr. Fireman. We need your help. It appears my friend, Morgan, has a fire in her pants. She is badly in need of some assistance."

"Oh, I think I can help. Lead me to her, please," he says playing along.

Dylan follows me to our table, wearing nothing but a g-string, but holding his fake ax in his hand and wearing his protective headgear.

"Morgan?" Dylan asks after I lead him to the exuberant (and quite drunk) bride-to-be. "I'm going to need you to take a seat over here, Miss. It's time we took care of that fire."

"Yes, sir." Morgan replies, looking sheepish yet terribly excited. She is blushing from ear to ear as she quickly takes a seat in a chair. All of her friends and I gather around. Dylan gives her one hell of a show as he slides up and down, bending over to show his backside, grinding on her lap and bouncing up and down. The rest of us can't tear our eyes away as we are enjoying the show almost as much as Morgan. She stares wide-eyed at the dancer, her eyes never leaving him as he dances, shakes and swivels his hips on her body. When Dylan finishes his dance, Morgan looks a bit like a deer in headlights. She thanks him for the performance, and I guide her towards the door as she giggles continuously.

"I can't thank you enough for tonight, Daphne. Seriously,

that was an absolute blast." Morgan says, sipping her strawberry martini. Everyone else has gone home, but Morgan has asked me to join her for one last cocktail at a martini bar near our neighborhood.

"You're so welcome. Do you think your friends all enjoyed themselves?"

"Are you kidding me? They had a blast. It was the best bachelorette party ever. And you know I'm going to repay you someday," she raises an eyebrow, tilting her head towards me. I know exactly what she's hinting at.

"Let's not get ahead of ourselves. Don't get me wrong. I would like nothing more than to plan a future with Tanner, but I don't know if he's there just yet. It has taken a lot of time for us to move past all of the Mayson baggage. And even though he says it is alright if I continue my friendship with Cece, I worry that it may bring us trouble in the future."

"He is absolutely crazy about you. Anyone who spends a bit of time with the two of you can see that."

"Thanks, I know he loves me, and I love him. We'll wait and see on the marriage stuff."

Morgan shrugs, "I see you together. I see it happening. That's all I'm saying. And from what I know about Tanner, if he tells you that he has made peace with your relationship with Cece, then it's the truth. He's really one of the most honest people I've ever met. Hold on to that one," she says, taking another sip of her drink, a silly grin spread across her tipsy face. She's so adorable.

"And how about you? Your big day is just a few weeks away. Are you getting nervous?" I ask, trying to move the attention of the evening back to where I feel it should be, on the bride.

"Oh yeah. It's been a lot of work, almost like a second job. But, I'm excited to be Mrs. Matthew Renbeck. For all of my feminist talk and all of my independent woman behavior, I'm a softy at heart. I'm ready to settle down and be his wife."

"That's the way it should be, Morgan. Matt is so in love

with you. You two have a very bright future ahead."

"Thanks, Cuz. It will feel weird when I have to move away from you. I've loved living so close to you these last couple of years."

"That will be strange, I know. But, Matt's place is probably best. You don't even have room in your current place for all of your shower gifts."

"You're right. Matt's condo is much bigger and there is a spare bedroom and an actual basement for storage. But, it's not the same." She places her head on my shoulder as I lean my elbows on the bar.

"I know, Cuz. I'll miss you, too."

Chapter 38
Bride

Morgan looks positively stunning as the last buttons are fastened on her gorgeous lace wedding gown. She presses the fabric down with her palms as my Aunt checks the bodice and skirt for any imperfections. It's almost time for the ceremony and Morgan's anticipation shows in her slightly pink cheeks and serious expression.

The clock reminds us that it's time to head to the back of the church so that the bridesmaids can lead the way down the aisle. Morgan and I walk hand in hand and stand together as the organ begins to play. The bridesmaids slowly take their turns walking down towards the nervous groom, who wipes his brow continuously with his handkerchief. It's now my turn, I squeeze Morgan's hand and whisper, "knock 'em dead" before heading down the velvet carpet. Looking straight ahead, I receive smiles from Matt, Evan and another groomsman, my Tanner. I feel beautiful in my gorgeous plum cocktail length dress as I stroll confidently down the aisle.

Sneaking in one last glance at Tanner, he blows a tiny kiss and I give him a satisfied smile.

Hours later, Mr. and Mrs. Renbeck are swaying in one another's arms on the dance floor. Leaning against my boyfriend, I watch them in awe. Their happiness, their contentment is everywhere in this banquet hall. My aunt hasn't stopped crying exuberant tears since the ceremony when her daughter was pronounced Mrs. Matthew Renbeck. The bridesmaids and groomsmen are happily chatting along the sides of the dance floor. The bride gazes at her husband with such happiness, such admiration, it's downright contagious to anyone who catches a glimpse of her.

Tanner wraps his strong arms around me and squeezes each of my shoulders. A gentle peck is placed atop my head and he breathes a large sigh into my loose up-do. I feel his body straightening and I lean back into him, so content in this joyous moment. My cousin is now a happily married woman, and for the very first time, I'm positively certain that I'd like to be next.

Two hours later, my heart beats rapidly in my chest as the DJ announces it's time for the bouquet toss. For the first time in my life, I feel like this tradition means something to me, something real and true and wonderfully scary. So desperately, I want this moment to be the very first in my future with Tanner Finley. So nervous, so anxious, I walk as calmly as possible out onto the dance floor, positioning myself in the spot that has always been lucky for me, about eight feet behind the bride with just a couple of steps to her left. I'm not taking any chances.

The music plays and Morgan grins from ear to ear before tossing her bouquet of lilies out into the sea of single ladies. But, my lucky spot has proven to be so very unlucky. The bouquet goes nowhere near me as she tosses it to her right. It lands in the hands of my second cousin, Charlotte who jumps, screams and hollers, "Finally! Finally!" as she runs back to her family.

Stunned, I turn and walk off of the dance floor with empty hands. Tanner is waiting for me at the edge of the dance floor, a cautious look upon his face. Like a zombie, I walk right past him and he follows close behind. Choosing a random chair from the plethora of tables before me, I plop myself down, searching the table for alcohol.

"Sweetheart," Tanner says cautiously. Doing my best not to make eye contact for fear I will cry and not be able to stop, I stare at my hands.

"Daphne, what's the matter? It's about the bouquet, isn't it?" My eyes betray me and tears erupt within milliseconds of his questions. I muster a nod.

"It's just a tradition, my love. Sooner or later your curse or your gift—whatever you want to call it, had to come to an end. Did you expect to be seventy years old and still catching that thing?" he teases gently.

"No. But, I *finally* found you. I finally found the man who I envision an actual future with. I know I'm probably scaring the crap out of you by saying these things, so please feel free to walk away, get a drink, hang out with Evan and the other groomsmen. I'll be alright." Tanner hands me a napkin from the table. Dabbing at my eyes, I finally look at him. His smile is warm and I know he isn't going anywhere.

"Hmmm," he says, sliding into the chair next to mine, "maybe we need to think of this differently then, Miss Harper."

"What do you mean?"

"Well, do you ever remember 'Opposite Day' as a kid? The little girls in my class always drove the boys nuts with that. 'It's Opposite Day, so I don't like you today', they'd always say to us. This little girl Mandy broke my heart on Opposite Day," he shakes his head, staring at his feet dramatically and I'm finally able to laugh, enjoying the levity that only Tanner can bring to my heart.

"Okay, so you're saying today is *my* Opposite Day?"

"That's exactly what I'm saying. Most women never catch the bouquet, so when they finally do...."

"But, I always catch it..." the light bulb forms figuratively above my head. But, it's not enough. My heart is still sinking.

"What is it? You still look upset. Your brow is still furrowed up so very tight," he says, leaning in to kiss the deep creases above my nose.

"You're a guy, you wouldn't understand."

"Try me," he says confidently.

"I really thought it would be nice to catch Morgan's bouquet. I had hoped that if things worked out with us, I'd have it, you know, as a memento." My head hangs in shame, again avoiding eye contact with Tanner for fear of scaring him away. Instead, he chuckles softly to himself as he stands.

"Come take a walk with me. I think you could use some fresh air to take your mind off of all this bouquet stuff." Rising out of my chair, I gladly accept Tanner's extended hand. Placing my fingers in his warm palm, I feel at peace once again as he wraps his hand around mine.

We walk slowly to the patio, the brisk March air pierces my skin, but before I can even react to the weather, I feel Tanner's tuxedo coat wrap around my shoulders.

"Thank you."

"Daphne, sometimes things aren't as they seem. Remember that, alright?"

"What do you mean? You're sounding cryptic."

"I was attempting to be, but I guess you see right through me, don't you?" he laughs, pulling me towards his chest. "What I'm trying to say is that there is a reason you did not catch the bouquet tonight. I wanted tonight to be different. I had no idea you would take it the way you did. I thought you would understand..." his voice trails off. My heart begins to race for I still have no idea what he's trying to tell me.

"I asked Morgan to aim the bouquet as far away from you as possible. I didn't realize you'd be so heartbroken. She tried to warn me, but I didn't really listen. I was too busy with other things."

"Wait, I'm confused. You asked Morgan to *not* throw the bouquet my way? Why would you do that?"

"Like I said inside, I wanted this to be your Opposite Day. I wanted you to see that you didn't catch it for a reason. You didn't need to catch it, my sweet. And I hope that when I give you *this*, it will be all you ever need as a memento from this night." He reaches into his pocket as he kneels on the patio below. My heart leaps from my chest as the man I love pulls a small velvet box from his pants pocket.

"Daphne Jane Harper, I've been in love with you from the moment we first started our witty banter at Henry and Elise's dinner party. You've set up a place in my heart and I can't imagine, nor do I ever want to imagine, you not being there. I want you forever in my life."

Choking on my tears as he speaks, my heart continues to expand with every word.

"And so I kneel before you, asking you to be my wife. Would you please, *please* marry me Daphne Jane and make me the happiest man on the planet?" Tanner's eyes are glistening as he holds the ring between his fingers. It is exquisite, just like Tanner.

"Yes! Yes, of course I will marry you, Tanner. Of course!" He places the ring upon my finger, stands and pulls me into his arms. I am his, completely his. No more baggage, no more ghosts, no more lies. I want Tanner and no one else.

We stroll, arm in arm, back into the reception in order to tell my parents our big news. They pretend to be surprised, but judging by their terrible poker faces, Tanner has already asked for their permission and blessing. As I'm finishing a long hug with my elated mom, the bride pounces on me.

"Is it official? Did he ask you?" Morgan practically screeches.

"Yes, he did. Did you know about this, Mrs. Renbeck?" I pretend to chastise her for her involvement.

"Guilty, I know. I almost lost it the night of my

bachelorette party. I was still coming down from my drunken haze at the martini bar and I was terrified that I would somehow tip you off! Your fiancé had just asked me to help him find the perfect ring." God, I love that word, fiancé, especially when it is in reference to Tanner.

"So, you knew then? I had no idea!" I laugh, loving all of these revelations, first my parents and now Morgan. Within an instant, I recall Morgan's confidence that Tanner was as emotionally invested as I was and that she would someday return the favor of a bachelorette party.

"Yes, I did. And, I have something for you. I'll be right back." She scurries off, dragging her gorgeous lace skirt behind her. Matt approaches to congratulate Tanner and me. It is clear that he is in on the secret, as well. Perhaps I am the only one who did not know, I think to myself, as I watch Evan smile and pat my fiancé on the back. I seem to be the only one who is, at all, surprised that this proposal has taken place.

"Here you go, sweet cousin of mine," Morgan says, tossing a large bouquet gently into my hands, as she continues to stroll towards me. Luckily, my reflexes act quickly and I'm able to catch it before it hits the floor. It's different than the bouquet that she tossed earlier this evening. It's larger, fuller and much more elegant; orchids and calla lillies gathered together and tied with a satin ribbon at the base.

"I tried to warn that man of yours that you would need this. You've gotten very used to catching these things. It felt cruel to send it in the opposite direction. So, I asked the florist to make this for you. It's the last bouquet you will ever 'catch.' Now you can look forward to *your* bouquet. The one you will hold as you walk down the aisle."

"Oh Morgan," I practically sob as I pull her towards me, "I can't thank you enough. I'm so lucky to have you. You know me so well, don't you?"

"Yep, I do." She says, satisfied with her crafty little self.

"Thanks for not giving up on me," I whisper into her ear.

"Never." She smiles.

Epilogue

"I now pronounce you husband and wife. You may kiss your bride."

My husband smiles appreciatively at the man of the cloth. He then grins playfully before lifting the ivory veil over my head. His kiss is gentle and loving, yet satisfying in a way that no other kiss has been in my life thus far. After our kiss is forcibly ended, knowing we have a chapel full of people in the audience, my husband reluctantly pulls away but holds each of my hands tightly in his own.

"Ladies and gentleman, it is my pleasure to introduce Mr. and Mrs. Tanner Finley," the pastor announces. Rousing applause fills the chapel as I lift my bouquet up in the air in celebration. Smiling at Tanner, I say, "We did it!"

Tanner lifts my hand to his mouth and kisses it ever so gently before placing it over his heart. His eyes moisten and he smiles. "Yes, we did." His simple words send a chill of delight down my spine and I do my best to hold back the tears, but one slips by and drifts down the side of my nose. Tanner wipes the tear gracefully with his handkerchief.

Our road to the altar was not all sunshine and roses. We

had obstacles to overcome, misunderstandings to resolve and ghosts to evict. But, we did it. And I am overwhelmed at the amount of happiness this man brings to my life. I don't ever want to know what it feels like to be without Tanner Finley.

As we turn to face our friends and family, my eyes search for the one invited guest who did not send in a reply card. I'm not sure if she will be here, but I am hoping to see her, to feel her support as I embark on the next chapter of my life with Tanner. As we continue to walk towards the doors of the church, my heart sinks just a bit knowing she was unable to be here to see this moment. But, I understand. Some things are just too hard.

As we're nearing the end of the chapel, however, I see her. She is seated at the far end of the pew and she is smiling, tears streaming down her face. Taking both of her hands, she forms a 'V' and blows me a kiss. And I know, in this moment I have her blessing.

I place my hand over my heart and I mouth, "Thank you, Cece." She nods in solidarity. Deep down, I know she will not be staying for the reception. This is her goodbye to me.

Tanner rubs the side of my arm and waves to Cece. So proud of the man I have just married, of the man who has accepted me with all of my faults, all of my baggage, all of my links to the past. I glide my hand across his cheek when we reach the foyer of the church.

"You are truly incredible, Mr. Finley. I'm so proud to be your wife."

"I can't wait to start our lives together, Daphne."

"Ahem." I tilt my head accusingly at Tanner. He knows what to say next.

"I'm so sorry....*Mrs*. Finley."

"That's much better," I tease. "Now, let's get to that party of ours."

Four hours later, the cake has been cut, the open bar is about to close, and it is time for the bouquet toss. Standing on the dance floor, holding my gorgeous bundle of red roses, each adorned with a pearl in its center, I smile to myself. My life has changed considerably since I caught my first bridal bouquet. I never dreamed that I'd be standing here today, the happiest I've ever been, with an incredible man, an incredible partner with whom I am prepared to share my life. The young women gather on the other side of the dance floor and I look at each of their faces, remembering my own emotions at each of the weddings I attended in my early adulthood.

Tanner's cousin, Mindy, looks nervous. She is here with her boyfriend of several years and I know she would be thrilled to catch these roses. My eyes wander and find my co-worker, Samantha, rolling her eyes. She was pushed onto the dance floor by the rest of the women at her table. All at once, I understand both of these women as I've experienced every emotion there is to have in regards to this silly tradition.

While planning the wedding, I suggested that we cut this from the reception's activities convinced that somehow, it would bounce off of the ceiling and land back in my own hands. But, Morgan, Elise and my mother were having none of that. "It's a right of passage," my mother said.

"And after everything, you need to toss the shit out of that thing," Morgan added. And so I agreed.

The crowd erupts as I toss the bouquet. Mindy scoops that sucker up with an enormous grin. She does a small victory dance before presenting it to her boyfriend, Troy. Troy rolls his eyes, but puts his arm around her as he turns back to me. He winks in my direction as he pats the pocket of his suit. I gasp with happiness, knowing Mindy is about to become engaged.

Next up is the garter toss. The groomsmen seat me in a chair and Tanner kneels before me, a naughty grin in his eye. He gently raises my dress up over my knees and pushes it further to reveal my powder blue garter. He removes it seductively with his teeth. I hear my Dad yell, "Hey, that's my daughter out there!" and the crowd laughs. Tanner turns to my dad and gives an innocent shrug. I move off the dance floor and watch as Tanner tosses my bit of lingerie. Evan catches the garter, looking shocked as it lands square in his hands. I point to him as I jump up and down, so happy for my friend.

"Looks like the curse continues here," I tease as he gives me a big hug. He shakes hands with Tanner and pats him warmly on the back. Tanner grins at his new friend, *our friend*, Evan.

"You know, my friend Samantha is single." I gesture discreetly towards the young woman with flowing blond hair and deep sapphire eyes.

"And cute," Evan says, wide-eyed, staring at my co-worker.

"Go for it, buddy," Tanner laughs, patting him on the shoulder, giving him a bit of a nudge towards Samantha. Evan lets out a hearty laugh and saunters up to Samantha. She looks pleasantly surprised by his approach and nods her head as he gestures towards the bar. I smile at Tanner, wondering if we've made a love connection.

Before I can say anything about our two friends at the bar, Tanner pulls me onto the dance floor. We sway together to song after song. My shoes are now off and I am starting to yawn. It has been a long, yet perfect day.

"So, was it everything you had hoped for, Daphne?" Tanner asks, pushing a few stray hairs away from my face. Even this small touch makes my heart soar.

"*You* are everything I had hoped for, Tanner. I thought you'd never arrive...and even when you did, I almost couldn't see it. I—"

"Daph, sweetheart, don't do this to yourself. I'm here now and I am yours...always. We're past all of that. It took some time, but it was worth it," Tanner smiles.

Where have I heard those words before? Lost in thought, I search my memory for the moment when I first heard that sentiment: "*He brings you peace and a tremendous amount of happiness, although you may not realize it when the relationship begins. It will take some time, but it will be worth it for you, for him, for both of you. He is the one I see."*

"Oh my god, Tanner! How could I have not realized this sooner? The psychic; you're the one the psychic told me about!" I practically yell, jumping into his arms.

"Daph, sweetheart, what are you talking about? When did you visit a psychic? I'm a little lost here."

"I'm sorry, let me explain. Morgan dragged me to a psychic when I first started seeing Mayson. Her name was Kim and she didn't see me with Mayson, not in the future. She saw a tall man with brown hair and brown eyes. She said he would bring me immense happiness and peace." My cheeks warm at this realization.

"She was right, Tanner. She was so, so right." Once again, my eyes fill with tears. I look into Tanner's gorgeous speckled eyes and he is gazing at me in wonder and appreciation.

"So, you mean to tell me that in all the time we were dating, you never mentioned that you believe in psychics?" Tanner teases.

"Well, I do now, that's for sure!" I say, wrapping my arms around his neck.

"So, don't tell me, you're now wondering if you should visit her with more questions like where will we live, how many children will we have, where will they go to school...."

"Nope," I shake my head with absolute certainty. "No need for that. Whatever the future has in store for us, we'll take it as it comes. That's all I need to know, Tanner. Besides, our children will be attending the University of Illinois. That's obvious."

"Oh really?" Tanner raises an eyebrow, knowing I'm only teasing. "Well, I don't know....I think my sons will want to follow me to U of M..."

"Sons, as in plural?" I ask, playfully acting as if I am horrified.

Tanner laughs, "Well, maybe we can have a girl or two as

well." He pulls me close, stroking my hair.

"So, are you planning for me to be barefoot and pregnant immediately or will I have a grace period?" I joke.

"We will be leaving for our honeymoon tomorrow. Should we get right to work?" Tanner raises his eyebrows with a sexy grin.

"Or we could just practice," I say, raising my eyebrow.

"Well, you know what they say about practicing..."

"What do they say, Mr. Finley?"

"It's a hell of a lot of fun." He twirls me around the dance floor as I throw my head back in laughter. Once again, my husband makes me laugh in a way no one else ever has.

"Will it always be this way? Will you always make me laugh like this?"

Suddenly serious, Tanner gazes into my eyes. "I don't know, Daphne. But, I do know that I will always be devoted to you. I will always do everything in my power to make you happy, to make you look back on this day knowing that this was the best decision you ever made. Because I know, deep within my soul, there is no one else for me."

My eyes moisten as I gaze into my husband's deep irises, knowing it has been a difficult road to get to this point, but a road worth traveling. Through the heartache, the confusion, everything that I went through with Mayson and Cece, it somehow brought me here, to this moment with Tanner. We are about to begin our lives together and I wouldn't change a thing.

Tanner pulls me close, and peace envelops my soul. Kim's words echo through me, *"He is the one I see."*

Acknowledgments

Writing Bouquet Toss has been one of the greatest learning experiences of my life. And thanks to so many people who have come into my life, it's now in print and available online. Sometimes I still can't believe it.

Thank you to my friends and family who took the time to read: Beth, Calia, Maggi, Kim, Lisa, Jules, Julie, Sara Z., Fred, Colleen, Lex, Sarah, Kelly, the hubs, and my wonderful Mom, Deb. You each helped to build my confidence and many gave great suggestions to help make the story better.

Sarah Hansen of "Okay Creations" made the beautiful book cover for Bouquet Toss. It is elegant and timeless and I feel so lucky every time I look at it, that I was able to work with such a talent. Thank you, Sarah, for all of the time and energy that you put into making the outside of my book so gorgeous. www.okaycreations.net

Colleen Hoover, you helped me to learn one of the greatest lessons in this entire experience...that I have to tell the story that makes me happy. I will always be grateful to you for putting things in perspective for me and for teaching me to follow my gut.

Kim August, thank you so much for all of your wonderful ideas regarding the story and also for your unbridled enthusiasm for my 'career' as a writer, including planning a book release party for me in order to celebrate. You are an incredible cheerleader! I will also never erase the voicemail you left me....it's just too special.

Melissa Perea, wow....just wow. You are an unbelievably talented beta reader, writer, and you can see the tiniest plot change making a huge difference. Our brainstorming sessions were so much fun. After talking with you, I always felt ready to dive into the story and make it just a little bit better. You inspire me.

Jennifer Hall, my editor, thank you for editing Bouquet Toss. Your faith in me as well as your enthusiasm for the story were both so special! Not to mention how truly gifted you are at editing---I see a bright and successful future for you in the world of books!

Kyla Linde, thank you so much for all of the wonderful advice about marketing a book, formatting it properly, etc. And I cannot thank you enough for sharing Bouquet Toss with your many fans.

Janna Mashburn, you are such a gift, such a blessing in my life. You encouraged me, cheered me on, fell in love with the characters and helped me to do right by them. You, my sweet Book Twin, helped to create the story that is Bouquet Toss, and I will be forever grateful to you. I will also always be thankful for those two broken Nooks...our kindles brought us together and it is because of our taste in reading that we now have decades of friendship to look forward to!!

Chris Brown, the love of my life (and the inspiration for Tanner). I am so lucky to have you in my corner. Thank you for your flexibility and support, as well as your amazing proofreading skills and ideas. I love you so.

I had the idea for this book almost ten years ago. I began writing, but then stopped…life got in the way, and I lost faith in myself. And then, I read a book called "The Opportunist" by Tarryn Fisher and it changed me. The passion I felt for the characters and the story was like nothing I had ever experienced. Tarryn, I cannot thank you enough for renewing my love of reading and writing. It is because of your unique gifts as an author that I was inspired to find the story I had abandoned years ago and do my best to make it something worth reading. You also introduced me to an incredible online community of readers and writers. And it is because of you that I know many of the people who are mentioned above. You have changed my life and I will forever be grateful for the impact you have had on me and my future as a writer. *Thank you.*

About the Author:

Melissa Brown is a hopeless romantic living in the Chicago suburbs with her husband Chris and their two children. Aside from writing, she enjoys reading and baking. She also has a slight obsession with actor Henry Cavill.

Connect with Melissa Brown online:

Melissa's Blog:
http://melissabrownauthor.blogspot.com/

Facebook page:
https://www.facebook.com/MelissaBrownAuthor

Goodreads Author Profile:
http://www.goodreads.com/melissabrown

Twitter:
LissaLou77

Bouquet Toss:
Copyright © 2012 Melissa Brown
ISBN-13: 978-1479218684